PARALLEL LIVES - THE PATHS NOT TAKEN

KRIS MAZE

MAZE

Parallel Lives—

THE PATHS NOT TAKEN

Kris Maze

ISBN (Paperback): 978-1-957944-09-8

ISBN (eBook): 978-1-957944-08-1

Cover design by Anze Ban Virant - ABV Atelier design

Interior design created with Vellum

Editing Services by Bublish

Published by Maze Publications

BISAC Subject Headings:

- FIC028090 Fiction / Science Fiction / Time Travel

- FIC028100 Fiction / Science Fiction / Action & Adventure

- FIC027040 Fiction / Romance / Science Fiction

- FIC043000 Fiction / Women

Keywords:

time travel science fiction novel; speculative fiction about alternate lives; mind bending sci fi book for adults; character driven time travel story; dark romantic science fiction novel; women's fiction with speculative twist; psychological science fiction about identity

To Smiles

PART I
Parallel Lines

Chapter One

The name tag scratched at Harriet's neck.

Her blazer, slightly snug in the shoulders, shifted each time she adjusted her bag or flipped through the color-coded event brochure. There had been a coffee spill earlier. Not her fault, but somehow, she'd still stepped in it. She'd dabbed at the hem of her slacks with hotel napkins, now crumpled in her coat pocket like small, soggy regrets.

A buzz of voices surrounded her, professionals talking coverage tiers and policy loopholes, the occasional chuckle of someone who actually found this interesting. The overhead lights gave everything a grayish tint. Standard convention hall sconces shed dim light against the inlaid wainscoting. She pressed her conference badge flat against her chest and tried to act like she belonged there.

Half a hall away, someone from the Kansas City table shouted, "There she is!" The sound of light applause followed. Harriet glanced over. No one she knew. Wrong "she."

The printed program in her hands felt too thick, like it was trying too hard to convince her of the value of its contents. She skimmed it anyway. Her assigned breakout session was titled *Client Retention Through Leveled Incentives*. Room 204B. Two floors up.

Great. She had ten minutes to kill.

To her left, the vendor booths began in earnest. Banners promised upgraded claims software, next-gen security platforms, and agentic AI bots. Pens, mugs, and stress balls spilled over folding tables covered in navy polyester. More landfill candy. She dodged a man handing out light-up pens as she scanned for her boss. Just as she stepped past a booth offering posture assessments, she caught sight of something different.

A small, squarish structure sat at the end of the aisle. It was an odd-looking booth, more like a free-standing capsule. It pulsed faintly with light. The sign above it read: THE EXPERIENCE.

There were no pamphlets. No prize wheel. No garishly out-of-place pop music. But it was out of place for this convention.

No one stood in line.

She stepped closer, thinking she'd misread the sign. The thing didn't look like anything else in the hall. It wasn't giving away wrapped striped mints or showing slides of retirement plans. She looked for all the tell-tale signs of getting stuck in a sales pitch, but it was the simplicity that made her curious. Curious enough to waste the next ten minutes chatting about the Experience. Whatever that was.

"Would you like to see a better version of your life?"

Harriet froze. Then she said, "Excuse me?" and turned toward the voice.

"You look like you could use a vacation."

"I look like I need a vacation?" Harriet raised an eyebrow, the sudden urge to throat-punch the too-chipper salesman temporarily suppressed. She had moved into the farthest aisle of the insurance convention's vendor hall, looking for a corner to hide in before her mandatory positivity seminar. Of course, she had ended up in front of this tech display.

The man, in his mid-forties with a graying beard and suspiciously calm expression, smiled with robotic patience. His red polo shirt screamed midlevel Big Tech, but he looked like someone who had not quite gotten used to being customer-facing.

"Don't we all need a vacation sometimes?" he asked, pulling a glossy flyer from the rack tucked onto the side of the matte-black monolith beside him.

"I'm already late to something," she said, adjusting the tote on her shoulder. She wasn't very good at giving convincing lies.

His smile didn't shift. "This will only take a moment. A preview, really. No cost. You don't even have to sign up for a subscription." He chuckled at that last one.

Harriet hesitated, then glanced around. No one was near enough to pay any attention to them. The pod thing didn't even look connected to anything. Without cables or obvious screens, she had doubts about its true capabilities. There wasn't a sales team behind him, lying in wait.

Her feet were tired. Harriet let out a sigh and squinted at the box. It looked like something between a tanning bed and a vertical coffin with an accordion-style door. A small banner drooped above it that read, FEEL YOUR BEST. TRY THE EXPERIENCE.

She took the flyer reluctantly. "What is this thing, exactly?"

"This thing," he said, gesturing like a game-show host, "can improve your whole life."

The man introduced himself as Ted. His shoulders slumped slightly, and he kept one hand in his front pocket as if he were still adjusting to this new sales gig or maybe was just uncomfortable in his own skin. Harriet was used to that type. She lived among that type.

She scanned the glossy page in her hand. "You're telling me this thing will give me a better life?"

Ted's smile twitched. Harriet narrowed her eyes. Of all the booths she could have chosen, she had ended up at this one. "It's like a mini-vacation, except immersive. The Experience App shows you up to three optimum versions of your life. You step in, sync up, and let it take you through personalized memory simulations to unlock what's been missing."

"Personalized memories?" Harriet looked around. The main hall traffic was lightening as people made their way to sessions. Her boss had to be lurking nearby, looking for her. "Right. Sounds perfectly safe."

"It's in beta," he admitted. "There might be a few glitches. But most users say it's enlightening."

She turned back to the black pod. "Looks like a prop from a nineties sci-fi show."

Ted chuckled. "That's the paint job. We're still refining the design."

"Still refining the science too, I hope." Harriet did a little snort laugh and tapped the flyer against her leg. "Okay, fine. What's the catch?"

"No catch. You try it, you give feedback, and you're entered in a vacation giveaway."

"How generous."

"You seem like someone who's looking for a life change."

That made her pause. It was not what he had said. It was how he had said it, like he knew. Like he had read her file.

She crossed her arms. "Do I really look that desperate?"

"No, no, not desperate. More like ready to make an impact," Ted said. "Just ready."

Ready. That word echoed around her mind, settling in. Harriet had been holding herself together with duct tape and to-do lists for months. But she was not looking for a solution, not right now. Just a quiet place to disappear. And the box and its promise of some movie nonsense looked like an ideal hideaway for a few minutes.

Time to pull herself together. "I'm not signing my soul away, right?" she asked with a light but wary chuckle, lifting her phone.

"Terms and conditions apply," he said with hesitation, and he turned to pick up a tablet.

She snapped a quick selfie with Ted in the background just in case she ended up in a true-crime podcast. Then she texted it to Lilli with the message: *If I vanish, check the weird box marked the Experience.*

The tablet's screen blinked to life, and Ted showed her a QR code. "This will take you to the download page. It's part of the Experience."

She scanned it quickly, typed in her first name, and check-boxed the terms and conditions. Then she waited, watching as the Experience App began downloading onto her phone. A progress bar filled with jittery green light, followed by a launch screen that displayed a pixelated frog in mid-hop. A bubble popped above its head that read, *Welcome, Harriet. Ready to begin?*

"Seriously?" Harriet muttered. "All this for an early-model video-game frog?"

Ted swiped to a new page on the tablet, one with the digital waiver. She noticed him glancing at her phone screen, checking the progress bar beneath the frog. "I don't know. I think he's cute. And you know, he started out as a tadpole," he said with a silly grin.

"Hmm. This is like a quick vacay?" She skimmed the page. No mention of organ harvesting.

"You bet. Each Experience is tailored to the individual. That's why we need this." He tapped the tablet.

She signed with her off-hand. "Alright. Let's see what's so life-changing about this thing."

Ted swiped again. "Just one more page . . . this just confirms you're allowing the program to access your memory stream," he said. "It won't store anything. Just mirror your biocognitive patterns."

Harriet gave him a sharp look. "How many waivers are there?"

"Local only," he added quickly. "Nothing goes to the cloud. No ads, no data trail."

Still, she scrolled through the first few lines as if she could decode legal tech-speak on the fly. Then she tapped *Agree* and handed the tablet back.

"Okay," she said. "Do your demo. But if this launches into a sponsored wellness seminar, I'm out."

Ted smiled politely. "Understood."

She crossed her arms but didn't move away.

Ted gestured toward the door. "You'll be guided once you're inside. If you need anything, I'll be monitoring."

"How reassuring." Suddenly, over Ted's shoulder she spotted her boss, walking through the exhibits. She held up the flyer to her face. Then she stepped toward the pod. "So I just pop on in there?" Harriet asked with hurried skepticism and peeked inside the space, no bigger than a changing room at Target. "It looks tight."

"It's bigger on the inside than it appears," he assured her as she stepped in with a rush.

The door slid closed behind her with a whisper, and it activated some kind of soundproofing, blocking all evidence of the convention outside. Tight as a drum. And maybe it was soundproofed on the inside too, she worried, as her true-crime habit snuck more ideas into her suspicions that this could also suppress her own ability to yell.

Darkness surrounded her. A darkness she welcomed, when it came down to it. This darkness involved a moment to herself. A moment to forget the maddening monotony outside this pod. A moment of peace. No positivity session. No work drama. No boss.

Then a breath of cool air and the faint hum of something spinning up. Harriet's phone glowed softly in her hand. The frog blinked.

Then the world around her shifted.

BEHIND HER, outside of the pod, Ted's smile faded. He watched the flicker of green from his tablet while monitoring the screen.

He had told himself it would feel differently this time. Cleaner. Less invasive. But as the chamber sealed with a soft magnetic click, he felt it again: that pull in his gut. Memories, once resurfaced, never stayed in the past. He of all people understood this. No matter how carefully you tried to accurately reconstruct them.

No matter whose memories were intertwined.

The algorithms had showed him this clearly.

But not with Harriet.

Chapter Two

Inside the machine, the lighting was soft and oddly neutral. Neither warm nor cold. The surfaces around her were curved and smooth, like standing inside the hushed interior of a museum exhibit. There was no obvious interface. No controls to press. No headset to wear. A faint hum tickled at her ears, the kind of sound you didn't notice until it stopped.

A soft ripple of light shimmered across the interior wall ahead. Then it stilled.

The brightness intensified and the hum deepened around her. Not loud but insistent. A wash of color drifted across her vision, folding into gradients that moved like mist. It felt, strangely, like the machine was syncing with her breath.

Her eyelids fluttered. The last thing she heard before the world shifted was her own voice, just a whisper.

"What the hell is this?" she asked in awe, taken in.

The conference coffee line. She stood behind her coworker, trying not to emotionally combust.

The mist of muted colors dissipated, and the floor of the Experience pod snapped into the patterned carpet of the convention center. Her reality shifted in full, and the activity of a coffee shop stalled around her. Harriet realized with disgust that she was reliving her most humiliating episode from her vantage point in the Experience chamber.

The conference coffee line snaked slowly forward. She instantly was overcome with a sense of déjà vu, but a kind that was vivid and permanent. She felt transported back to this morning when her coffee run had gone completely sour. Harriet shifted from one foot to the other inside the simulated memory, trying to ignore the ache in her lower back and the unmistakable stickiness of her blouse under her blazer.

Lilli adjusted her scarf for the third time in two minutes. Harriet could practically feel the judgment radiating off her. She stood to Harriet's left, inspecting the pastry case like it held the keys to happiness. She turned with a knowing smile. "Isn't that Sal from mortgage?"

Harriet craned her neck and spotted him at the pickup counter. Tall, confident, ordering two drinks with practiced ease. Her heart sank.

"You know you're avoiding him," Lilli said, her voice low but stern.

Harriet kept her eyes on the lineup of branded travel mugs at the far end of the kiosk. "I'm avoiding coffee that tastes like burned mulch. There's a difference."

"He's buying two," Lilli whispered, listening to his order. "One's got extra foam. You know what that means?"

"That he's a foam guy?"

"That he's bringing someone a chai with love in his heart. Maybe even a cinnamon swirl."

"Please stop. I have no idea who it's for. And I don't want to."

Lilli grinned. "You're the one who said he smiled at you in the elevator. Twice. And then lingered at your cubicle. That's not nothing."

Harriet bit the inside of her cheek.

"Mmm." Lilli's brow arched as she leaned closer. "You think I didn't see that quick escape earlier? The moment Sal walked into the networking hall, you vanished."

Harriet reached for a napkin even though she didn't need one. "Maybe I had to use the restroom."

"For twenty-five minutes?" Lilli made a show of checking her watch. "Girl, please."

Harriet sighed, shifting her weight again. The line was still crawling, and the smell of over-roasted beans wasn't helping her headache.

Lilli didn't let up. "He's just a person, you know, maybe he's rethinking that breakup. You dated for what, three months?"

"Two," Harriet said. "If you count the part where he ghosted me before the last dinner we were supposed to have. He's not a person. He's a mild trauma."

Before Lilli could respond, the man walked in their direction, and a panic ball whirred under Harriet's rib cage. Lilli could hardly contain her excitement. But Sal stopped a few feet in front of them and started a conversation with two women in line. Harriet focused on the top of his head. Same too-perfect part in his hair, same dark-rimmed glasses. Her spine went rigid.

Lilli noticed too. "Oh," she breathed. "And he's right in front of us."

"Don't look," Harriet hissed.

"Too late. He saw me see him," Lilli said, smiling a little too widely. "And now he's pretending he didn't."

Harriet took slow, calming breaths and stepped forward in line. "What do I do?"

"Oh hi, Sal!" Lilli said as lightly as the whipped cream she liked on her drink.

"Don't call him over here." Harriet said in a low, strained voice.

Sal gave a slight wave, more of a flick of the hand, and continued talking with the two women. They were up next, and he was apparently joining their little group. It took forever for each of them to order. Harriet slouched and pretended to scroll on her phone.

Lilli pointed to a plain-looking egg sandwich. "Want to split one of these?"

"Nope. I'm good for now." Her stomach was in knots, and she wasn't sure even a chai wouldn't come back up.

Sal laughed and slapped one of the coworkers lightly on the back, his hand staying perhaps a bit too long and lingering down her spine. They waited off to the side for their order.

"Come on, it's your turn," Lilli said with a gentle redirect toward the register.

A line had formed behind Harriet. Her eyes scanned the extensive menu. She stepped forward to order, still undecided, rolling her fingers across the counter. The barista's perma-grin melted away, and, full of dull distaste, he asked, "How can I help you?"

"Spicy chai latte, please. Extra spice." Harriet wanted to show the world she could actually handle the extra flavor in her life.

"One crunchy granola! Extra dirty!" the barista yelled to the silent coworker making drinks behind the bar. He swatted at the man with a towel, but the man making drinks didn't flinch. He poured together the coffee and foam, and the barista whined, "You're no fun." He turned back to Harriet and said, "That's six fifty-six, please."

She paid and waited with a multitude of others caught in coffee limbo. While Lilli made small talk, she pretended to not be within an arm's distance of the man who had stood her up. She weighed whether sneaking off to a different bathroom would be subtler than that barista yelling her name after she left. Right then, he called her order, and she hurried to the counter to nab her drink without eye contact with Sal.

The barista handed her a chai with her name scribbled on the cup. She barely had time to thank him when she felt the jolt of impact. Warm liquid splashed across her blouse.

"God . . . sorry!"

Sal's voice. Familiar and horrible. He'd bumped her elbow as he'd turned with his own coffee in hand.

Harriet froze, her cup dripping. The wet patch on her chest was already seeping through her blouse. It dribbled down the front of her pants, forming a puddle on the top of her shoe.

Sal reached for a stack of napkins. "Harriet. Wow. I didn't think you were attending this year."

"I am." She accepted a napkin from him, brushing at the stain.

"You look . . . great."

Lilli leaned in, voice sugary-sweet. "She does, doesn't she?"

Sal nodded, clearly unsure of what to say next. Harriet beat him to it. "Well. This has been charming." She tossed the ruined napkins into the trash and turned sharply, Lilli trailing behind. As they exited the coffee kiosk area, Harriet let out a breath she hadn't realized she'd been holding.

Lilli gave her a sidelong glance. "You handled that better than I expected."

Harriet wiped the last of the chai from her fingers. "The goal was no eye contact and minimal homicide."

Scalding chai cascaded down her sleeve where the cap had come loose.

"Hot! Hot!"

Lilli lunged, offering yet more napkins. Harriet held her dripping arm out. "I'm fine," she muttered even as her skin prickled and burned. Injury to insult. She tried to dab at her sleeve. Then Harriet took her chai back from Lilli and sighed. "I'm officially cursed."

"You're officially dramatic. Come on. Let's find a seat where you can spill the rest of that one in peace."

Harriet followed her toward the seating area, trying to ignore the sticky sleeve clinging to her arm and the sting of not-missed connections.

HARRIET STOOD there covered in chai, blinking. She was still holding the semi-filled coffee cup. The front of her blouse, damp. Her shoe, soggy. But when she looked around, the coffee kiosk was empty. The line was gone. Lilli was gone. Sal, thanks to absolutely everything that was holy, was also gone.

The world around her shimmered slightly, like heat rising off pavement. For half a second, she thought she could hear the faint beep of a microwave or the hiss of milk being steamed, but it was more like the idea of those sounds. Echoes without source.

She took a breath. The chai scent was still there, sharp and spiced, but everything else felt . . . thinner. Not quite right.

The coffee line hadn't moved. Because it didn't exist anymore.

Harriet looked down at her hand again. The cup was gone. So were the napkins. Her shoes were dry.

Her breath caught.

That wasn't a random memory. That was today.

That was this morning: the barista's attitude. The spill Sal could have avoided. The awkwardness of meeting her ex while he chatted up his next set of victims. Lilli's smug but helpful insistence that Harriet expect better for herself.

She hadn't remembered it. She had just been there. Again.

"What the hell is this?" she repeated, slowly turning in place.

The light shifted around her, subtle and fluid, like the walls were made of fog and glass. The low vibration thrummed once again beneath her feet, faint but steady, like the machine was thinking. She felt her body go lax and smooth, as if she were entering light anesthesia, not fully in control of her movements, not fully in touch with her senses.

She wrapped her arms around herself, not quite shivering. She noticed the inside of her wrist—a small map of mountains on her skin, her only tattoo.

This wasn't just a demo.

Chapter Three

The chai memory snapped off like a poorly edited dream, yanking her back into the dark void. She stumbled, catching herself before face-planting.

"Welcome, Harriet," said the disembodied voice, smooth, but slightly robotic . She stewed about this computerized overly cheerful greeting, as if it were welcoming her back from a massage and not her most recent embarrassing moment. "I am your digital guide, in charge of making sure you have the best Experience. Let me know if you have any questions. I will do my best to answer them."

"This Experience thing feels real," Harriet said, still processing, mind still spinning. "Is this a time machine?" She touched the front of her pants, noting that the wet spot had almost completely dried from the real spill that morning.

"No, it's just your memories. The simplified explanation is that it is somewhat like VR without goggles. That initial loop was for calibration. According to your baseline emotional set data, you're adapting well."

"Calibration? That was me bombing my last attempt at small talk and taking a chai tea bath. Not exactly inspiring."

"Many participants gain insight through recent stressors."

"Many participants have lower standards."

Silence.

She watched the green frog get stuck in mid-bounce and replied with caution, "This Experience is free, and a trial. I could experience some glitches. I bet *that* was what the fine print said."

"We assure your satisfaction. Guaranteed. Are you satisfied so far, Harriet?"

"I don't think I can answer that just yet. And I can't see anything at all in here right now. It's disorienting." She groped into the darkness, not ready to take a step. "It's like I was living that moment again. Hey, Guide, can you assure me that this is okay for my brain?"

"Sorry about the disorientation, Harriet. I can assure you that from what studies we have done so far that there is zero impact on one's daily cognition. But a disclaimer: Long-term effects have not been studied yet. The technology is still in its infancy stages."

"In beta . . ." Harriet took a deep breath, this was far more interesting than the positivity session she was supposed to attend. "So it's going to be one of *those* days. The type of day when you think you've won the lottery and then lose the ticket."

"Cheer up, Harriet. Your report just came in. We have great news. You are a perfect candidate for the Experience."

"Wonderful," Harriet said, eyeing the frozen app screen on her phone that was glitching like a skipping record. "I'm also sure my friends are waiting for me. Maybe we could speed this up to something more current?"

"Time has a different feel inside the Experience. What seems like a day could only be a minute on the outside. I'd hate for you to miss the important shifts in your life by not being thorough. Please trust the process."

"Oh, trust the process?"

"Sorry for the delay. There is a little lag in the beta version. We would like to set a good foundation for your Experiences and have a quick question to ask."

"Ask away," she replied dismissively, but with hope that the hyper-realistic Experience could be a little bit of fun in a tropical location. "Especially if it will get me to the good parts. Like the vacation part."

"First, you have to identify your true desires. Without thinking, what three things would improve your life the most?"

She looked to the source of the voice, not seeing a ceiling. "Three things I'd like to improve. Like three wishes from a genie in a bottle? Are you kidding?"

"A starting point for us to explore. Three general changes you want in your life. I recommend that you answer off the top of your head. It's best if you don't think about your answer too much."

"Okay, bossy pants, that's enough explaining. Off the top of my head, what I would change is pretty easy: better relationships, better job, better cat."

The voice paused in a way-too-long moment of silence, memorializing how terribly optimistic her requests had been as she listened to a shuffling beep-boop while the machine processed them. She glanced to her phone, where the frog on her screen twitched and finally gave a wide froggy smile. A speech bubble appeared above its pixelated head: *Please prepare for Phase One: Foundational Memory Alignment.*

"Foundational. I thought we already made the baseline or whatever. What does foundational mean, Guide?"

"To continue our optimal calibration, the machine needs to know your growth stages, emotional sets, and developmental history. We can check which of your formative memories resonated with you the most in order to build you your best futures."

"That means childhood, doesn't it?"

"Correct. Initiating memory track."

"I don't really think it's necessary to relive my childhood, Guide. I didn't sign up for therapy time travel."

"You signed the Beta User Agreement, Harriet. It is only a brief tangential Experience that is necessary for the process. Other users have found this part of the Experience endearing and tender as they see themselves as little children once again."

"Endearing and tender? Whatever. I'm sure this isn't that necessary. Hey, I'm willing to skip this part and accept whatever crazy futures come from it. Call it research. Guide? Do you hear me?"

The void rippled. The floor dulled into a blurry mess that slowly turned into a lush lawn.

"Hello? That last transition was like getting hit by a truck. Give me some sort of heads-up, maybe? Oh, we're going again. Is that grass? What the heck?"

Then came a woozy, stomach-drop sensation as the darkness swirled into light colors, finding their stasis in some latent memory from her past. The scent of fresh-cut grass overwhelmed her and heightened the feeling she had been to this outdoor space many times before. The warped tones of carnival music filled her ears, and she could see hands through the eyes of a younger version of herself. Harriet's body had shifted—her limbs were chubby, her balance uneven. Sunlight filtered through leaves above her head.

She looked down at her legs. Dimpled knees. Sticky fingers resting above them on her red and white dress. Sandals with tiny daisies on the straps.

"Oh no," she groaned, a sound that was high-pitched and small. "This just got weird."

TED LEANED back against the partition, the soft glow from the tablet casting shadows on his face. On-screen, the simulation was progressing—visually seamless, emotionally chaotic.

He hadn't meant for her to see that chai memory first. The machine had scanned for recent stress, and, well, that coffee disaster had clearly left a mark. Still, she was reacting better than most. Her personality was coming through and staying intact. Some people couldn't handle hearing their voices recorded and played back to them. This was a fully immersive, living experience. She was acting bristly, defensive, and was quick with sarcasm. But she was not frozen. And that was something.

He tapped the side of the display, watching her vitals spike as the toddler overlay engaged. The biometric graph jittered, then stabilized. A good sign. At least for the machine. He wasn't sure if it was good for her.

"She's not going to like this part," he murmured, mostly to himself.

He glanced around the thinning convention hall, then squinted at the screen, pulling the tablet closer to his chest.

The voice modulator had kicked in late. She'd noticed the tone shift. That bothered him. The illusion had to hold, at least for now. He could call in the expert in London anytime now, but only once Harriet progressed a little further along. Long enough for her to see what he had seen. Long enough to understand why she mattered.

Ted rested his hand over the manual override. Just in case. The truth could wait. But not forever.

And Harriet's Experience continued.

Chapter Four

The shift was not gradual. One moment, Harriet stood in darkness with her phone in hand, the frog blinking its wide-eyed approval. The next, she was a stumbling, bumbling, a novice walking, talking, tiny version of herself.

Harriet heard the music morph into singing birds. She felt fuzzy, like from standing up too fast. When the sandy, sleeping-foot feeling left her body, she found herself in a digitalized version of a city park. Sunlight dotted her chubby arms through the swaying leaves above. Grown Harriet watched through the eyes of Little Harriet, who wobbled to a table, admiring glittered jewelry and metal toy race cars.

"How far back did you take me?" she asked, her demands subsiding into curiosity. "Everything around me is huge." Her voice echoed and ebbed as the image formed around her like old reel-to-reel movie footage. She could almost hear the tick-tick-tick of the film against the metal reel.

Her vision sharpened into a community event, and she was drawn in with cautious interest. Rarely was one given a chance to relive a time from their past, and it was practically impossible to feel, see, hear, touch, and—Little Harriet made a beeline toward the snack table—taste the world in which she had once lived. She looked around the park while making her way to the snacks, noting its grainy texture and the bright seventies clothing popping through the sepia tone.

Carnival games lined the park's perimeter to her right. A kid stood on a stool and dropped clothespins into an empty milk carton from above. Some children pulled floating plastic ducks from a pool and turned them over for a mystery prize. Blindfolded kids stumbled toward an obligatory donkey poster, trying to attach its missing tail.

Once she reached the table, a standing popcorn machine reflected her toddler face. She was wearing the cherry-patterned dress Nana had sewn, the one in the photo on the piano. She wandered to the Dixie cups and took one filled with red liquid. It burst into her mouth as an ocean of sweetness and stickiness that spilled down her chin.

She moved on to an open cooler of treats and took one with her tiny hand, fumbling open the waxy package of the popsicle. Her hair fell into her face and tickled her nose while she ate. Little Harriet swiped at it, tangling the sticky hair around the wooden popsicle holder.

"I can't believe I'm stuck in the body of a toddler." Harriet watched the scene unfold, soaking in her personal history. Too mesmerized to exert her own movements up to this point, she noticed the tickle on her cheek also made her itch. Her little body, however, did not respond to her movements within the Experience chamber. She was at the complete will of the replay, fishing for a reason why she was watching this seemingly insignificant moment in her preschool life, a captive audience.

Little Harriet wandered, exploring games and snacks, until her popsicle became fully tangled in her ponytail. Stuck and dripping, its sugared juice covered her cheeks. From the nearby grass, a young boy abandoned the Matchbox car he revved along a rather large anthill to eye up her treat. He rose from the grass, pushing himself up into an inverted *V* before standing and toddled toward her.

She had the uneasy feeling he wanted the popsicle, and she tried harder to yank it from its hairy bind, walking backward and away from him. He came closer at a toddling-turtle speed and stopped inches from her face. They looked at each other, about the same height, the same unsteadiness on their little toddler feet. Suddenly, he ripped the popsicle from her hair, pulling it toward the ground when it didn't give. Pain stung her scalp as tears welled up in her toddler eyes when he didn't let go.

Grown Harriet winced, just as surprised as her younger version and just as unable to defend herself. "Damn. That hurts more than I remembered."

As Little Harriet started to cry, a man crouched beside them. "Now, buddy, let that go and get your car over there."

The boy pouted, sticking out his pinched lips, but immediately returned his attention to the toy car and to overtaking the anthill.

The man gently placed a hand on her shoulder. "What's wrong, little girl?" He pulled the remaining pieces of the treat from her hair. "Did you lose your popsicle?"

Grown Harriet panicked. "Stranger danger! Where are my parents?" She scanned the crowd of adults, not knowing if she would recognize her parents in this scenario. "Hey, Guide, is this one of those life's-most-cringe moments you're forcing me to relive? Like am I really on some hidden-camera show?" But there was no response from the machine, only more of the scene that drew her in in the most immersive way.

Then, at the snack table, a woman with long thin hair wearing a ring of daisies on her head reached into the cooler and pulled out another treat. "Here you go, Mr. Hopper," the woman said, unwrapping and handing a fresh Bomb Pop to the man. "I saw her parents over by the music stage a few minutes ago."

He nodded to the woman and turned to Harriet. "There you go," he said, handing her the new treat. Little Harriet clutched it.

The man ruffled her hair and said, "Let's go find your family."

She looked up. He wore wire-rimmed glasses and a mischievous smile. Harriet didn't quite know where to place him, although the community park a couple of blocks from her first childhood home was clearly a part of this memory. He walked her to another part of the park with a stage.

"This picnic has nothing to do with my alternate lives, does it? Where and when exactly did this happen?" Harriet asked, wondering how the guide would hear her and whether it would respond during these movie-like sessions.

The guide finally answered during the quiet walk to find her parents. "The Experience is confusing at this young an age, but test clients found that experiencing earlier versions of themselves helped clarify their goals. There must be something here for you to notice."

They passed the boy, who grabbed his car and, catching up to her and Mr. Hopper, tried again to grab her popsicle. Little Harriet shrieked.

Mr. Hopper separated them each at an arm's distance. "No, buddy. That's hers. You had yours already," he scolded. "Where is your mom?" The child reached forward to try again.

Little Harriet's arm shot out like she was holding a shield. "Don't eat mine!" she grumbled, glaring. Her sticky fingers spread wide as she blocked the boy's grubby hand from her treat. She stuck out her tongue. He did too.

The boy wiggled out from under Mr. Hopper's grip and tried to grab her Bomb Pop again. This time, she was ready to defend her right to eat her snack in peace. Her brows knit together in fierce determination as she blocked his third attempt and made contact with his shoulder.

With a wobble, the boy lost his balance and toppled backward onto the soft grass. Then his palm scraped the sidewalk. "Ow!" he cried softy at first, then ran to Mr. Hopper. Little Harriet stood back, wondering how he could have fallen to the ground. Then the boy hollered louder: "Ow!" And, seeing no response from Mr. Hopper, louder still: "Ow! OW!" Each cry echoed like a siren as he grabbed hold of the man's leg, tugging urgently. Harriet tucked herself behind Mr. Hopper, the boy's cries cutting through her each time he yelled.

On the sidewalk, she saw who she believed were her parents approaching from across the park. The tall man wore her father's bushy mustache that twitched as he laughed at the scene between her and the boy. "Well, thanks, Don," her father said, clapping him on the shoulder. "This one's always getting into something."

Harriet felt herself being scooped up, her father's big hands lifting her like she was weightless. "There you are, Peanut!" he said, settling her on his shoulders. Her sticky fingers tangled in his curls.

"She's filthy," her mother said, dabbing at her own jeans. "Harriet, you can't go around pushing other kids."

"He pushed me!" she cried, pouting. "He took my popsicle!"

"Oh Harriet. You're a mess."

The adults continued making small talk about politics and the price of milk. The kids hung out, bored while they chatted. Harriet reached up, plucked a leaf, and let it fall. The boy below laughed and spun in a circle. Another leaf. Another laugh.

His mother approached the group and took the boy by the hand. "Sorry, Don, I got to talking with the new neighbor down the street. She has a boy the same age as this guy. I had to get her phone number."

The parents would talk all day. "I'm tired," Harriet complained and pulled another leaf from the tree. She heard her mother say something about cookies for the next field trip and her father mention something about motorcycles to Mr. Hopper, and she wondered if she would ever get to walk on her own two feet again.

The memory blurred. Her toddler self dropped another leaf. He caught it in midair. Their laughter mixed in the crisp afternoon air.

"Miles, let's try the duck game," his mother said, taking his hand and leading him down the path toward a tiny wading pool filled with plastic ducks.

Grown Harriet blinked. "Miles?" she whispered. "What's going on?"

And just before the world pixelated again, Miles turned, grinning ear to ear, and waved his little red car.

Harriet stood in the Experience as her family and the fading park disappeared. Curious and suspicious, she said, "Something odd is happening."

Chapter Five

A round Harriet, the trees had dissolved, the leaves that once sparkled in the sun now dulling into a silvery mist. The circus mayhem faded, replaced by the soft strains of classical music. Just as she opened her mouth to question the guide about the significance of the young boy in the park, the walls of a new memory took shape.

A grandfather clock ticked solemnly in the corner, commanding order and precision. Lace doilies adorned the arms of a striped couch, their edges curling like frozen petals. In the center of the room sat a baby grand piano, polished to a dull shine, its lid half-raised like a sleepy eye. Her own eyes dipped as she sat on the couch, her mind tired after a long day of school, her stomach underfilled after rejecting an olive-loaf sandwich for lunch, and her lesson a forever time away. Through the frosted window, pale afternoon light filtered in, casting long shadows across the worn carpet.

The music—if it could be called that—was choppy and uneven, each note trailing the last like a child reluctant to leave recess from the playground. Harriet sat hunched near the hallway, fingers clasped in her lap. She already knew this place. Remembered the faint smell of lemon Pledge and rosin, the sound of a muffled metronome ticking from the top of the baby grand. She was back in the squat brick house of her piano teacher, Mr. Brooks.

On her left, a coffee table held framed pictures of Mr. Brooks and a stern-looking elderly woman, probably his mother. Otis, the gray poodle, lay curled at her feet, a bundle of shaggy warmth against the cold tile. She scratched behind his ears, her fingers sinking into his curls. Her sneakers, striped and well-worn, pressed against the linoleum. Mittens still threaded together dangled from her sleeves like sleepy puppets. Outside, snow drifted past the window, barely sticking.

The piano in the next room gave a stubborn clunk. The boy playing it stumbled through the same measure of "Over the River" she had practiced the week before. Harriet winced as a sour note rang out, and Otis lifted his head.

Inside the living room, Miles stopped mid-phrase, then resumed from the same painful spot. Mr. Brooks sighed heavily and turned toward the couch. "Harriet, you're next."

Her stomach knotted, a mixture of hunger and anxiety. Miles hadn't finished, not really. She sure didn't want to go yet. She was supposed to get parent signatures for practicing five times that week, which had not happened.

The front door creaked open. A gust of wind carried in a swirl of snowflakes, crisp and glinting in the light. Otis sprang up with surprising energy and scampered to the door. Harriet reached instinctively to grab his collar but missed. Mr. Brooks signaled for Miles to continue as he stood to greet the visitor.

A man in a heavy coat stepped into the entryway, shaking snow from his shoulders. He clipped a leash onto Otis's collar as Mr. Brooks reached into the doorway. The two men exchanged murmured words, something about "helping out" and "being too much," but Harriet's focus stayed on Otis. The dog looked back at her as if she were being left behind.

A low rumble came from her belly. Otis turned his head, judging her with one brown eye. She giggled, then quickly covered her mouth. From here, the piano keys looked like a tray of Oreos lined up in rows.

Otis took the time while the men talked to break free, and he trotted back to Harriet. "I like Otis," she whispered to the neighbor, who had crouched beside her to rub the dog's neck and reattach the leash.

"Keep practicing," he said softly, straightening the collar so the tags hung in front. "You'll be glad you did someday."

Harriet gave Otis one last stroke. The poodle leaned into her palm, then sped to the door, tail wagging, the man close behind.

Mr. Brooks called again from next to the piano, "Harriet, did you practice the duet part from last week?"

She straightened herself on the couch. "A little," she lied. Miles was still at it, still tangled in the same section. His back was stiff, posture straight, jaw clenched in frustration. Harriet's eyes wandered from the piano to a ceramic horse on the mantel. She tried to will herself invisible.

"Come take this half of the bench," he said. "Let's see how you two play together."

She stood, slowly opened the piano book to the duet part. As she approached the piano bench, the grandfather clock struck five. The sound of the gonging felt too loud for the small room, mimicking the thumping of her own panicked heart. There was no way this duet was going to sound any good, and it was definitely going to show that she hadn't practiced one bit.

She stepped to the side of the bench and set her music on the built-in stand above the keys. The gonging hit the last of its five notes, signaling for the next lesson to start. Miles suddenly rushed through the final bars of the piece, skipping several notes, and leaped from the bench as if it had caught fire.

"See you later," he said, grabbing his backpack without looking at her. His sneakers squeaked on the hallway floor. Then he was out the door. She heard the slap of his tennis shoes on the pavement as he ran, followed by the hoots of the boys waiting for him outside.

Mr. Brooks clapped and rubbed his hands softly as he watched his pupil dash across the street. He gestured toward the piano bench. "Your turn."

Harriet took a deep breath and sat, her legs stiff under the keyboard. Her fingers hovered over the keys. She had practiced the song she liked a couple of times. Really, she had. But not enough to count for a parent signature. But the notes had never felt natural under her hands. Now they looked foreign and cruel.

Behind her, the teacher set the metronome. Click. Click. Click.

She began to play, hands trembling. Distant noises of kids playing outside loudly filtered into her mind, distracting her. The notes she played came out thin and hesitant. Each wrong note rang louder than the last. Mr. Brooks said nothing, just tapped his foot in time, the metronome echoing him like a threat.

Through the front window, Harriet caught sight of Miles riding his skateboard in a lazy arc down the street, the other boys chasing him and laughing. They had freedom, momentum, ease. All she had was a pair of aching fingers and the weight of expectation from Mr. Brooks's wary glances.

One note at a time, the piece unraveled. Her face burned as she worked her way to the end of the song. She didn't look up. She didn't stop. She played the entire song, the metronome still clicking, still waiting, Mr. Brooks silent and deep in thought.

Grown Harriet watched her younger self with a twist of pity and pride. She'd forgotten how hard she had tried to impress people who had never really seen her.

"Let's try that again," he said, taking out a red pen to mark the problem notes in the piece.

When the lesson ended, Little Harriet grabbed her coat and scarf with haste, rubbing her fingers where the teacher had corrected her too firmly. She cast one last glance at the piano with equal parts longing and resentment before slipping out the door.

Outside, she ran down the sidewalk, past quiet homes with puffing chimneys. The icy wind nipped her cheeks, but she didn't slow down.

Across the street, the boys zipped up and down the sidewalk on skateboards, aiming for some kind of a ramp with a plywood board balanced on bricks. The laughter rang loudly through their neighborhood, their breath puffing in winter-is-coming-type clouds. They didn't seem to notice the cold.

Harriet paused while waiting to cross the street and watched the smooth movements of the slim boards on plastic wheels coasting across the sidewalk. It looked fun, much more fun than the lesson she had just endured. She didn't wave. Didn't shout. Boys still had cooties, after all.

But her eyes lingered on the wobbly ramp, as one would with a morbid curiosity usually reserved for gawking at car accidents or trying to identify a roadkill. The boys stacked and fortified the thing.

A breeze slipped through the back of her coat. She shivered and crossed the street.

MILES DROPPED his piano book on his front porch, letting it fall open to the wrinkled pages Mr. Brooks had written notes over in the margins. He ran down the steps two at a time, scarf flapping like a tail behind him. The air smelled like snow, though none had stuck yet. Next door, the neighborhood kids were huddled around a makeshift ramp of plywood and bricks.

"Look what we made, Miles!" Davy shouted, breath puffing white in the winter air. "Bet you can't beat it."

Leon grinned, already winding up their handshake routine. "Up top!"

They slapped hands.

"Down low!"

He yanked his hand away. "Too slow!"

Juan Pablo was bouncing on the edge of the plywood ramp like a ferret on a trampoline, testing the give. "It's got just enough flex. We braced the bottom with milk crates from Matt's garage."

Miles crouched down to inspect it, brushing stray leaves off the warped surface. He knocked twice on the plywood. "Well, no doy. That's some great brickwork there."

"That'll be strong enough for anything," Matt said, smirking. "It's the Ramp of Doom."

A clatter echoed down the sidewalk. Quintin arrived at full speed, a yellow, oblong plastic skateboard under his feet. "Let's goooooooo!"

Miles was already pulling his own roller derby board complete with red urethane wheels from under the porch. Holding the scuffed deck that was lined with duct tape to make it look even more cool, he rushed to the ramp. His sneakers crunching over the frozen grass, he nabbed the center spot. "I'll go first."

"Wait!" Juan Pablo started, voice high with warning. "I didn't finish reinforcing . . ."

Too late. Miles ignored him, egged on by the cheering from Matt and Davy. He kicked off hard. The board rolled straight, then wobbled at the base of the ramp. It caught the edge.

The plywood dipped. One brick shifted.

He flew. And the board stayed, gentling rolling backward in defiance.

There was a collective gasp as each boy waited for him to land as he flew several feet from the pebbled sidewalk. A thump, as his belly made contact with a neighbor's garden gnome. A roll, just missing the trimmed-back, winterized shrubs of her decorative hedge. Then nothing, as Miles lay sprawled on the frosty lawn, arms flung wide.

"Oh man, he's dead," Davy moaned dramatically. "Listen!"

Miles sucked in and grimaced. He tried hard to get a tiny breath, but his face pinched with panic. Sounds like a grunting seal came from his throat as he patted his chest.

"He's not dead," Leon said, crouching beside him. "He just got the wind knocked out."

Miles wheezed again, blinking at the sky.

"Lay on your side!" Matt shouted.

"Drink water backward!" Quintin suggested with an authoritative nod.

"That's for hiccups, genius," Leon corrected.

"How does that even work?" Quintin asked. "Like, how do you drink backward?"

"Like this." Matt pretended to hold a cup tilted away from himself and made slurping noises.

"No way," Leon said. Not missing a chance to entertain a crowd, he jumped to face away from the boys and threw back an imaginary glass of water as he tilted his head way back. "Get it? I'm drinking *backward*. Get it?"

Juan Pablo moved closer to where Miles lay gasping on the ground like a fish out of water and hovered with his hands out, nervous. "Just breathe in sips. Like soup."

Miles sucked in air, a tiny breath. "I . . . hate . . . soup."

The boys erupted in chaotic laughter as Leon shook his booty and drank his backward water. The next-door neighbor's curtain shifted in the full-glass storm-door window.

"Mrs. Hendershot's watching," Matt hissed. "Miles, you better get better quick. Or you're going to die for real!"

Leon paled. "She's got that dog. The Beast."

"It's fine, it's fine. She's not going to do nothing." Quintin stepped up and nudged the ramp with his toe, sizing it up as if it were a quarter pipe. "The ramp is fine. Just needs more bricks." He set his board at the top, preparing for the neighborhood sidewalk version of a drop-in.

"Let me fix it . . ." Juan Pablo tried. "Didn't you see what just happened? Quintin, man, stop!"

Too late again. Quintin was aiming his board down the ramp, step-ping up to put his full weight on the top side of the ramp to sail on down. He bounced. "See? Fine!" he announced as, at that very moment, the ramp buckled. Quintin launched backward, nearly knocking his head flat on the cement. His board veered left. He flipped over to his right side, landing in Mrs. Hendershot's dormant flower bed. His skateboard shot into the street.

The front door exploded open. Curlers. Robe. Wrath.

"Mrs. Hendershot!" the boys said and scrambled to remove parts of their ramp.

"You little hellions!" she bellowed. "Get off my lawn!" Her Yorkie, a snarling blur of bark and fury, bolted past her furry slippers.

"Run!" Davy shrieked.

"Hide the ramp!" Leon grabbed one end.

"Under Miles's porch!" Matt yelled, already dragging a corner.

Miles, now upright and brushing grass from his jacket, pointed. "Hurry!"

They grabbed what they could. Bricks clattered across the walkway, only a few feet from the garden where they had intended to return them. The plywood screeched like thunder as they jammed it under the porch.

Mrs. Hendershot charged forward, broom raised like a saber. The dog nipped at Matt's shoelace as he vaulted over a shrub with theatrical flair.

"Quintin, you good?" Miles called out, sitting up, breathless.

Quintin limped over, triumphant. "Totally worth it." He pulled Miles to his feet.

Miles caught sight of a neighbor two houses down raising a beer in lazy salute. "Hey, Milt!" he tried to shout, but it came out more like a mew of a soaking-wet kitten.

The man returned the nod, then, setting the beer on a picket fence, resumed cutting back his hydrangea bush like nothing had happened. They hobbled off Mrs. Hendershot's property and headed toward Miles's covered porch.

Miles paused, hand on the porch rail, Quintin had retrieved his board from the street and waved before nearly getting hit by a motor-cyclist. "Watch it, you meathead!" he heard the motorcyclist shout at Quintin. Quintin flipped him a live-long-and-prosper *V* with his fingers and jumped on his board taking his chances from the edge of the street.

"See you at school, Miles! I've got to get home for dinner!" Quintin flashed the Spock Vulcan greeting and took off. Miles lifted his hand from his chest, breathing easier now, and waved back.

Across the street, a girl sat on the stoop of a pale-green house. She had her knees pulled up, a piano book beside her. Harriet. She looked small bundled in her coat, curls falling over her cheeks. Harriet didn't glance up. She hugged her legs tighter and stared at the sidewalk.

Juan Pablo nudged him. "Do you mind if I hang out here awhile? My mom works until six tonight."

"Nope."

He stepped inside, leaving clumps of dirt on the mat, and they took off their shoes next to the door. Through the window, Miles watched Harriet from across the street. She stood slowly, brushed off her coat, and walked inside the house. She never looked up.

The street fell quiet again. His curtain settled back into place.

GROWN Harriet lingered in the memory, the edges of the scene softening but not yet dissolving. She looked at her younger self through the lens of distance and fatigue, wishing she could wrap that stoop-sitting girl in a blanket of reassurance. That kid had learned early how to keep still, to stay quiet, to make herself small when things got loud. And across the street, Miles was already collecting bruises with a grin, surrounded by chaos and laughter and loving it.

They had lived on opposite sides of the same street. She wondered, not for the first time, what might have happened if either of them had waved.

Chapter Six

Snow dusted the schoolyard like powdered sugar, patchy and lightly covering the already grimy asphalt filled with slushy boot tracks. Third-grade classrooms glowed from tall windows, amber and distant, as Grown Harriet studied the faces of the kids in this simulation and it drew her in. She seemed to float within the space, entering and watching the busy classroom work through presentations until her Experience settled her into her grade-school body.

Her classroom. Her presentation. Her pit of the stomachache that made her want to take a nap and throw up all at once.

Oh gawd.

Inside, the buzz of post-lunch chatter faded to Miss Proust's sharp but cheerful tone: "Harriet, it's your turn."

The scrape of her chair was too loud. Her project crinkled in her grip on her yellow construction paper, drawn on what she had found at home and not crisp white drawing paper like the others. Her crayon-colored drawing flopped forward as she stood. *Perry the Platypus*, it read on the top, and the crudely drawn animal wore a green triangle hat and held a suitcase next to a plane labeled *Australian Air*.

She scratched at the back of her hand, the itch from healing chicken pox scabs driving her crazy. Harriet had been the fourth in her family to catch it, and even if she hadn't been sick herself, she hadn't been allowed to go to school and spread the germs. Explaining why she had missed nearly a full month of classes.

At first, staying home had been great. She could watch cartoons, eat chicken soup with funny rectangle noodles, and binge on endless hours of *Captain Kangaroo* and *Schoolhouse Rock!* But weeks turned into boredom. By the time she had finally gotten sick herself, she'd played every game in the house, drawn on every scrap of paper, and even made multiple pine-cone bird feeders just to have something to do.

When Miss Proust called their house, Harriet's mother looked worried. "Nineteen days?" she repeated into the receiver. Harriet remembered peeking around the corner, watching her mother sigh and promise she'd get Harriet caught up. Miss Proust even dropped off a stack of homework on the front stoop, waving through the window before driving off. That stack haunted Harriet for days.

She cleared her throat. "'Perry the Platypus' . . . by Harriet Last. Perry was a platypus who lived in Australia. He wanted to go to the zoo and visit his family. He met his twenty cousins, and they had a great time."

She glanced up. Blank stares. A snort from somewhere in the back.

"The end."

"That's it?" a boy called out. "Why didn't she do facts?"

"Where's the habitat part?" Annabelle's hand shot into the air before she hopped up. "Miss Proust, she didn't follow the directions."

"Annabelle, sit." Miss Proust's clipboard tapped against her knee. "Thank you, Harriet. Would you like to tell us why you picked a platypus?"

Harriet's voice came out quieter now. "Because they're weird. They lay eggs but they're mammals. And they look like a duck mixed with a beaver."

A spitball hit her sleeve. Someone hissed, "Platypus girl."

Miss Proust shushed the class as they giggled. "You may take your seat, Harriet."

She sat quickly. Her chair legs squeaked, and she tucked her drawing under the desk.

A desk over, Miles slouched with one sneaker kicked out, desk lid open enough to stir crayon bits into glue. He had shaped one into a sticky claw and flexed it toward Harriet.

"Gross," she whispered. "Don't touch me."

"Miles!" Miss Proust called him next. "Please come up and give us your presentation."

Miles strutted to the front, flexing his arms like a cartoon wrestler. "'The Incredible Bulk at Bikini Beach: A Hermit Crab Report,'" he said proudly. "Herbie the Hermit Crab lived in a rad shell and got ripped lifting driftwood weights."

Laughter rippled through the room. Even Miss Proust cracked a smile.

Harriet dropped her head to her arms. The room felt too warm, her wool sweater too itchy, tickling at the remaining chicken pox scabs. The glue claw sat on her desk where Miles had tossed it at her. She didn't swat it away. She just closed her eyes and it disappeared.

Outside, snow swirled as recess began. The kids burst from the building in winter coat-padded chaos, their breath small poofs floating above them like smoke signals. Harriet walked alone along the blacktop's edge, her footprints marking a solo path. Her head hurt and she had been excused to go home.

Across the yard, Miles balanced his skateboard on a low step. Juan Pablo shouted something about testing the ramp again after school.

Harriet pulled her coat tighter. Her fingers tucked into her sleeves, pressed against her backpack with her presentation poking out of the top. There was a faint crayon smudge on her drawing.

She didn't wave.

But she saw him.

THE IMAGE THINNED like stretched film, the blacktop blurring into streaks of shadow. Snowflakes slowed, froze, then reversed in motion as if rewinding.

Harriet's head buzzed with static. Her hands itched from phantom wool sleeves. She opened her eyes to the familiar hush of the chamber, her adult breath fogging in the coolness of simulated air.

The Guide's voice reappeared above her, oddly gentler than before. "Thank you, Harriet. That concludes the early-childhood tier. Your calibration is going very well. We hope you have enjoyed this formative part of your Experience so far."

"Felt more like a leg day in CrossFit," she muttered.

"We're moving forward in time. Please remain still as the Experience recalibrates for the next series."

The platform beneath her gave a faint shudder. "What series are we talking about now?"

The guide added in his chipper monotone, "Puberty zone approaching."

"Oh no," Harriet groaned. "Not middle school."

But it was already happening, and the guide's voice muted as the next simulation started.

The air thickened. The color palette shifted to a blend of more neon hues, less forgiving on her eyes as she adjusted to their blaze. Fluorescent lighting buzzed overhead. The hum of hallway lockers, the clatter of hard plastic-soled sneakers, the smell of drugstore perfume and dusty chalk trays.

And she was back into her own memories.

Middle school.

Chapter Seven

Harriet pressed her forehead to the car window as the brown Rambler slowed to a stop. In the driveway ahead, her father parked the borrowed work truck behind a patch of lawn that hadn't seen a mower in weeks. The cedar shake house looked smaller than she remembered, with sagging shutters hanging slightly off-hinge beside its chipped white trim and lopsided porch rail. Another fixer-upper. At least this time it would fit the family. And the dog.

Benji's leash pulled tightly across Harriet's lap as the dog scrambled to get a better look out the back window. His nails scraped across Eugene's legs and then hers.

"Ow! He's scratching me." Harriet shoved the dog's scruffy back end off her shin.

Eugene yanked the leash, half-heartedly as usual. "He just wants out."

"Make him sit down," she said, rubbing the red marks where he had pushed off with his clawed paw. Benji's head popped out the half-cracked window, and he started barking at nothing in particular.

The twins sat in the middle seat, sucking their fingers and squinting out at the new place like it had personally offended them.

Between them and the towers of boxes, there was no room to think. Moving was stressful for everyone.

Their mother stood on the porch, flapping her arms like a traffic cop. The glass storm door had been propped open, and a backup of furniture had formed on the walkway entering the house. "The piano goes on that wall. Not that one. The other one . . . the wall facing the front windows. The sofa goes over here."

Eugene had opened the gate of the station wagon, and the dog had spilled out after him. The twins pinned themselves to the window, watching the madness from a safe, uninvolved distance. What ensued on the front lawn of their new home was a comical attempt to corral Benji after he pulled the leash from Eugene's hand. It ended with a chase, Benji weaving in and out between movers and their heavy boxes, the leash flopping wildly behind.

One of the movers opened the back of the truck and grunted at the load of boxes labeled *Books: Harriet*. Harriet jumped out before one guy could grab her zipped bag tucked away in the side of the truck. No one touched her journals. The strap bit into her shoulder, but she didn't care.

Inside, the house smelled like old cologne and dusty fake roses, both things the previous owners must have loved. The heavy curtains filtered the light into strange shadows that danced over the thick shag carpet, also a favorite of the former residents. A matted-down pathway in the carpet clearly showed the old layout of this room; a dingy path from between a sofa and coffee table led to the entrance to the kitchen. A small rectangle of carpet showed where the TV console had sat squished next to the boarded-up fireplace. Her mother disagreed, over-riding the existing patterns, one hand on her hip as she pointed out directions to the movers.

"The fireplace is the focal point in this room. No TV for us in here," she said with pride. "The couch goes there." She pointed to a spot perpendicular to the mashed carpet path in the center of the room. The new walkway was just one of the plans she had in mind.

"Are ya sure?" the mover asked.

Her father came in the front door and set a toolbox on the steps leading to the second floor, catching the end of the conversation. "Ya.

It's good for now," he replied with a shrug. "You can't argue with the boss."

Her mother had moved on to another room and was nearing the back rooms. The head mover was taking mental notes and nodding frequently. Harriet followed closely. She had some negotiating of her own to do with the boss.

"Curtains'll have to go. Mildewed and ugly. Maybe I'll sew new ones," her mother said to herself as Harriet tagged along.

Harriet responded with a repeated "Uh-huh," placing her hand at her chin thoughtfully, waiting for her mother to stop long enough to take a breath. Long enough for Harriet to make her case. The bag shifted against her hip as she walked behind, its weight a small comfort in the strangeness of the house.

Her mother stopped suddenly as they reached the bedrooms section of the house and spun to face her. "Okay, Harriet. I'm glad you're here. You can make sure the girls start getting their stuff into their room, okay?"

"Sure!" Harriet agreed with enthusiasm. "I wanted to talk to you about that."

Her mother continued, moving through the hall like a tsunami of ideas to reset this dated home in the modern 1980s. "I believe we can use some wallpaper here in the hallway," she said as Harriet tried to get her attention again. This was important.

"Mom, I need to talk to you about the bedrooms."

"Yes. Good, I agree. The twins in the back room. You are in there too. Eugene will be in the pink one."

Appearing out of nowhere, she heard her brother shout, "Sweet!" His heavy footsteps bounced down to the small room at the end of the hall.

"What?" Harriet spoke up, the eager energy from the previous moment completely gone. "But Mom," she said in full whine, "I thought I got the small room with the bookshelves. The pink room."

"The pink bedroom is for Eugene," she repeated. "You're their older sister. They look up to you. You can handle it."

"But I'm the oldest," Harriet said, louder. "I should get a room to myself."

"They're twins. They share. They don't take up much space." Her mother opened the door to a hallway closet, sniffed the stale air and ran her finger along the dust-covered shelf. "Why are you making this such a big deal?"

"It *is* a big deal." Harriet heard her voice cracking, disappointment bubbling up from her belly. "They share? Well, so do I. With them. All the time." She pointed behind her at the tiny culprits, even though they were still hiding back in the car, instinctively waiting it out. "They draw on my stuff. They break things."

"Don't be so dramatic," her mother said, already moving on and shutting the closet door. "Keep your stuff on the top shelf, then."

"I do that," Harriet huffed and stiffened her arms in resistance. "They don't listen. They're just kids."

"As are you. And we all make sacrifices."

The phrase made Harriet clench her teeth. "We always make sacrifices! I hate this dumb house!" she shouted and stomped off to the small room that was rightfully hers, in her opinion.

"Maybe I can sew something out of those old yellow sheets. Make a new bedspread. That would help." Her mother looked at a laundry basket of bedding a mover had set down in the master bedroom.

Harriet left her mother deep in her planning, the bag of books swinging hard against her hip. Eugene ran past her to the other end of the house and out the back door. She pushed open the white-painted door of his supposed bedroom, not ready to give up just yet. Even to her, it was an explosion of aggressive pink. Wall-to-wall carpet in white-and-rose-colored shag. Wallpaper with tiny roses in looping, dizzying patterns. Even the light bulb gave the room a rosy glow.

She didn't go in right away. She stood at the threshold, taking in the mess of someone else's taste, someone else's dreams. She had dreams too, though, and this room was not for Eugene.

"It's not fair," she said, loudly enough to echo. She glanced into the larger room across from this one. It ran the span of the front of the house. Three dormer windows. Room enough for bunk beds and two dressers. One small closet.

From down the hall, her mother replied, hearing her thoughts from afar, "It's a room. It is the biggest of all the bedrooms. Make it yours."

Harriet gripped the strap of her book bag harder. She didn't want the big room to be hers. Hers with the twins. She wanted to go back to before. At least in the other tiny house, her father had turned the attic into two bedrooms. She hadn't minded the slanted walls. At least there, she didn't have two roommates who got into her journals.

In a defiant move, she tucked her bag of books into the built-in wall shelves. She staked her claim, determining that actually putting her stuff in there would somehow change the floor plan her mother had tucked away in her mind. "We'll see who gets this room . . ."

TED LEANED FORWARD, elbows against a small shelf on the Experience machine where he had placed the tablet. He squinted intently, watching the data stream in from Harriet's session. A live waveform of her brain activity danced across the left screen. Heart rate, respiration, micro-muscle tension. Every marker humming with the tension he'd expected . . . but not this much. Not like this. It was supposed to be fun. What had he been thinking?

He zoomed in on one section of her Experience: the school report. The glue claws. The spitball. That awful look she had given just before she had shut down entirely.

"Are you seeing this?" He had patched in Adriana from London for support when he had gotten a visual of Harriet wandering around the convention hall. He could hardly believe that she had appeared just as the algorithm had predicted. Harriet's Experience was the true test of the software they had been waiting for. They had just gotten lucky.

Adriana had been more skeptical and dismissed the idea of wasting company time on this chance meeting. When he had persisted and bought the booth slot at the convention, she had stopped talking to him for a week based on her disagreement over the ethics of it all.

He rubbed the side of his face, jaw tight. "Damn it," he muttered. "That one should've been filtered."

From the other side of the world, Adriana's voice crackled over the video call. "She's still inside the childhood loop?"

"She is." He tapped a slow rhythm against the console. "The

memory density is higher than projected. I underestimated how much her brain retained from that era."

"You didn't think she'd remember the platypus?"

"I didn't think it would hurt her."

He leaned back and closed his eyes for a second. This machine was supposed to offer insight. Alternate routes. A chance to reflect, not reinjure. Especially the person he had thought needed to experience it the most.

"Maybe we push her to the next tier," Adriana offered. "Skip forward. College, maybe. Something with momentum."

"No." Ted opened his eyes. "Not yet. We're too close to the inflection point."

He stared at the footage again: Harriet sitting in a new bedroom with nothing unpacked. A blanket over her head as she scribbled across her newest notebook. The voices from the vent bickered about where the dining room table needed to go. She hadn't cried once through her chaos. She had fought back with words.

And still, she hadn't forgotten. Her arm moved rapidly as she pulled out a fruity-smelly marker and started to write in the journal, barely peeking out from beneath her makeshift shelter.

Ted reached over and manually adjusted the sensory load parameters, narrowing the input band. "If she breaks in there, it's my fault."

"Your name's not even on the patent. The company is protected. Legally." Adriana moved closer to the camera, her broad-rimmed glasses filling the frame. "Trust the machine. Right? That's what we've been saying. The revelations are worth it. Right?"

"I hope so."

"Don't flake out on me now, buddy."

"Doesn't matter." He dropped his hand and whispered, "This machine opened my eyes. My situation. My repeated problems. It doesn't have to be the same for her. She shouldn't have to go through this. She was the one who kept coming up in all my searches. Here all along the way. I had to show her this. She had to know what I found out."

He watched as Grown Harriet's memory of that day, a failed coup of establishing her own domain within the pink room, disappeared around her. Her arm must have ached from the rampant pressing of markers onto the page. He saw her rub her bicep as the scene disappeared.

Ted snapped to attention as her voice popped over the video feed. "Guide? Are we going to keep doing this? When are we getting to the good parts?" she asked.

Before he could reply, he watched the next memory in her Experience cue up. Inside the machine, Harriet turned her head in curiosity, sniffing as she began to experience the memories of a family breakfast.

Chapter Eight

Grown Harriet's memory of that day fizzled into the darkness around her. Her arm ached from the rampant pressing of markers onto pages. Markers that smelled of processed foods and rubbing alcohol. A scent that lingered as her latest memory melted away.

"Hey? Are you up there?" she asked, woozy.

Instead of hearing a reply, a smell of toaster waffles entered her memories. In the kitchen of her family home, her family came into focus around her. The combination was overwhelming, and she pushed down the need to retch.

The kitchen smelled like coffee, fried food, and burned toast. Her mother took long draws of coffee from the heavy ceramic cup between tasks. She checked bagged lunches and scanned her daily planner while her father cooked bacon and eggs, but Harriet didn't have time for any of those foods. The twins ate in uniformed bites, lifting forks of scrambled eggs in unison.

Harriet took out the overcooked toast and plopped a new slice in, pressing down the level with a click. She pulled out cinnamon from the cupboard, sugar from a bowl on the counter, and butter from a tray near the stove. She grabbed a lunch bag while she waited and peeked inside: exactly one peanut butter sandwich, one day-old doughnut, and an apple from the counter.

Eugene finished his bowl of cereal and tossed it into the sink, splashing droplets onto their mother's planner. He stuck out his tongue at Harriet while she leaned over the toaster to see if she could pop the toast up early.

"Harriet's going to miss the bus again," he sang as he nabbed a bag lunch and bolted out the front door, leaving it open.

"Harriet, get your backpack and lunch. I'm not taking you to school today," her mother said as she flicked water off her planner.

Her father set down the spatula in the sink. "I have an interview. I can't take her."

Her mother slurped her coffee and set it down with a splash. "I took her yesterday."

"She'll have to figure it out." He tipped the remaining eggs from the fry pan onto his plate and returned the pan to the stove to cool. "A sixth grader should be able to catch a bus."

"Like, don't get so upset. I'm not going to miss the bus." The toast popped up, and Harriet slathered a chunk of butter on top of it and sprinkled a layer of sugar, followed by cinnamon. She took a bite and rolled her eyes in an exaggerated display of decadence. "So good."

"Do not miss the bus, Harriet," her father warned.

"Fine. Everyone just chill out."

Harriet grabbed her lunch, her jean jacket, and her prepubescent angst and rushed out the front door. But she didn't run for the bus. She let it drive off without her, its mechanical groan disappearing around the corner as if it were part of someone else's morning. Eugene and his friends made funny faces from the back seats as the bus drove off. "How mature," she said aloud. "Like, gag me." She adjusted her book bag and walked in the opposite direction.

The sidewalk cracked beneath her shoes. Most of the fall foliage had already given up for the year, and piles of leaves sat in corners of yards that she passed. Up ahead, a squirrel darted across the street, tail flicking. She imagined herself on a mission, avoiding booby traps in the leaf piles, dodging enemy lines in a spy movie.

The map in her head rerouted past the post office and behind the gas station where a shortcut through the fence led into the back end of the school grounds. Her mother wouldn't approve—there were warnings about kids loitering and causing trouble there, but Harriet wasn't loitering: she was surviving. She was saving the world.

She ducked beneath a sagging branch and stepped into the thicket of trees that edged the last stretch of road. The pine needles crunched underfoot, and in her mind, the trail transformed into a secret agent's path. One marked with codes only she could read. She practiced the way she'd tell it later: how she had escaped capture, how she had outwitted surveillance. She imagined people cheering.

The school building loomed into view behind the chain-link fence, snapping her back to reality. The bell was ringing. There was no one left on the playground. Not a good sign.

She sprinted to the edge of the four-square slab and headed to the entrance of the school. She hoped to sneak in and blend into the last class entering the building for homeroom. She really didn't want another lunch detention, and today was the day she was helping in the library. It was Harriet's favorite part of the whole week.

Inside, the hallway buzzed with voices and the scuff of shoes. She was greeted by the playground aide, Gladys, who blocked the entrance, and Harriet was forced to stop at the office to sign in. Officially. Late. Again.

The secretary wrote something on a notepad and tore the top page off. She placed it in a box for the principal. She pushed the handwritten pass into a time-stamp machine, and it slammed down the incriminating data with a thunk! The secretary slid it across the counter to Harriet. "Take this to your homeroom teacher and show it to her but keep it. It's also your pass to lunch detention."

"Okay." Harriet took the pass and shied from Gladys, who had entered the office. Gladys signaled for her to stop and nodded to the secretary. "Just a minute, young lady." The secretary returned her look from over her readers that slid down her nose and reacted with a sigh.

"Harriet, you know that area in the back of the field is fenced off for a reason, right?" Gladys crouched to eye level and gave Harriet a stern look.

"We're going to have to call your parents," the secretary said.

"Can I go to class?" Harriet held up the slip of paper. She had heard this all before.

"Yes. And go to Room 327 during lunch."

Harriet let out a stretched-out groan and reached down for her backpack. Two students stood at the microphone behind the counter, preparing for the flag pledge. When she left the office, she took her time reaching the older kids' wing, walking at a turtle's pace through the open-concept school, a newer building without classroom doors. It was like switching TV channels as she walked past each room starting off their day. Her homeroom was the last on the left, and the students in her hall didn't seem hurried to get there either.

Harriet passed lockers that still smelled like fresh paint and turned toward the locker bay near the science wing. Students shoved their coats and bags into the lockers and filtered into their first classes.

Carli was already there by Harriet's locker, slouched dramatically against the wall in her new monogrammed sweater. "You missed the bus," she said, raising an eyebrow.

"Yeah," Harriet said. "Took the scenic route."

Carli smirked. "Figures."

Trixie appeared next, sliding in from the other direction with her lunch bag swinging like a purse. "Did you hear about Darla and Trevor? They're officially going together now."

Carli rolled her eyes. "That'll last a week. Tops."

Harriet opened her locker and shoved in her bag. "She was just crying about Tyler last month."

Trixie nodded. "Well, Trevor actually walks her to class now, so it must be serious."

Harriet didn't comment. She wasn't sure why, but the idea of Trevor being anyone's anything made her stomach curl a little. Wasn't he just asking her and Carli to go hang out in the mall last week?

The bell rang, and as the hallway emptied, a teacher's voice rose above the shuffle of feet as Harriet eyeballed her desk next to Carli. "Harriet, can I speak with you a moment?"

It was Mr. Carlson from the math department. He wore the same tan slacks every day and had a way of smiling that made Harriet nervous. Almost every teacher made her nervous. Unlike some of her classmates, she never wanted to stand out for any reason.

"You've been moved to Mrs. Yamada's class," he said, handing her a slip of paper. "Accelerated math. Starts today."

Harriet took the slip without looking at it. "Why?" Her life was run by slips of paper.

"You've tested into it. Congratulations."

She didn't feel congratulated. She felt like someone had rearranged her day without asking. Again.

Harriet nodded, folded the paper into a smaller square, and slipped it into her pocket. Then she walked to her new class without speaking, but first glanced at her empty desk next to Carli, who had so many questions crossing her face and pouty lips. Her feet moved while her mind stayed behind, still halfway through the woods, still rewriting the story where she got to make the choices.

MRS. YAMADA DIDN'T SMILE MUCH. She greeted Harriet with a nod and pointed toward a seat near the front. The desks in the room were pushed into neat rows, the boards at the front already covered in equations. Harriet took her seat quickly, sliding into the desk like it could swallow her whole.

The other kids in the class had already paired off, whispering to one another or comparing Trapper Keeper contents and spiral notebooks covered with neatly written notes. One boy glanced at her with a twitch of a grin before returning to his worksheet. She didn't know his name, but she'd seen him in the library once, or maybe while helping the science teacher set up microscopes.

The announcements ended and Ms. Yamada faced the class. "Whoever can answer this question gets extra credit today. Put your solution beneath your last homework answer."

Harriet looked at the two arrows on the board, equidistant and pointing in both directions. Beneath them, a question: when will these two lines intersect?

She was puzzling over this idea when Mrs. Yamada handed her a thick workbook. "We're on chapter four. Catch up as best you can. You can use the back table for tutoring during independent work time."

Harriet nodded and opened the book to chapter four. The numbers stared back at her like strangers, familiar in shape but not in meaning.

At her old desk, Carli had passed her folded notes and scribbled jokes in the margins of her planner. In this room, no one passed notes. No one talked during the lesson. The only sound was the scratch of pencils, soft talking of constructive conversations, and the occasional cough.

Mrs. Yamada wrote something on the board—graphs, slopes, maybe a formula about rates—and Harriet tried to copy it down, but her mind kept drifting. Her hand moved, but the words came out wobbly and disconnected.

At the back of her mind, a story tried to form. Not math. Something else. A girl who decoded secret messages using algebra to unlock doors in a lost city. Harriet liked that idea better than what was actually happening.

She looked around. The other students were focused, their faces bent toward their notebooks, confident and calm. Harriet felt like she had wandered into the wrong building and someone had handed her a script for a play she hadn't auditioned for.

The bell rang suddenly, too loudly. She jumped.

As the students filed out, Mrs. Yamada called, "Harriet, a moment!"

She stayed behind, fingers clenched around her workbook, and approached the teacher's desk. "Yes? You want to see me, Mrs. Yamada?"

"You're bright," Mrs. Yamada said. "But you'll need to push yourself to get caught up. These students have been tracking at this level for a while."

Harriet nodded, unsure what part of her that comment was meant to encourage her. She walked out, workbook clutched to her chest like a shield.

In the hallway, Carli and Trixie stood near the bubbler. They glanced at Harriet's new book, then at her.

"Smart girl now?" Carli said, her tone only half-teasing. "What is that? Advanced mathematics?" She asked it with a flair.

"I guess."

"Well, don't forget us regular folks," Trixie added, elbowing her lightly.

Harriet forced a smile. "Only if you save me a spot in line at Skate Town."

Carli perked up, remembering, reveling in the best news to hit in days. "That's this Saturday. I've got my outfit picked out already."

"Oh, we need to coordinate!" Trixie opened her lunch tote and pulled out a sticker-covered notebook. "We need to wear the same colors. If we're matching, we'll look like a clique."

"Is that the goal?" Harriet asked, tucking the workbook under her arm and leaning over the bubbler for a drink.

"Obviously," Carli said. "No one wants to be the one skating alone to the Bee Gees."

"I wonder what Trevor would think of this outfit." Trixie pulled out a page from a magazine ad, one that featured shiny jackets, runner shorts, and striped tube socks in the same hue of each of the primary colors.

"Who cares what Trevor would think?" Harriet replied, nodding at Carli, who then looked closer at the outfit on the page. "It's not like you two were going out."

Carli groaned. "Yeah. Trevor is so last week. Especially after Darla's announcement."

Trixie jumped in, pointing to the ad. "The colors look cool, though."

They all laughed, the tension breaking like a snapped rubber band. The math class, the expectations, the feeling of being out of place: Harriet folded those feelings up and slipped them into the back pocket of her brain. Right now, she was back where she belonged.

Chapter Nine

By Saturday night, every middle-school kid had gotten a ticket to the Skate Town citywide dance. The students waited for their friends, lined up to go in together, as cars rolled up to the low concrete-block building. Once inside, the air punched at their nostrils, the music loud enough to feel the vibrations when they entered. To Grown Harriet, Skate Town smelled like day-old popcorn, perfumed hair spray, and sweat.

Teens swarmed the entry in tube socks and neon, clutching crumpled dollar bills and waiting for wristbands. Harriet shifted from one foot to the other, holding her entry ticket and trying not to wrinkle her carefully chosen matching outfit: dark jeans, a tucked-in rainbow-striped T-shirt, and a wide cloth belt that had once belonged to her mother. Trixie was also wearing a striped tee, but in hot pink. Carli had matching yellow tube socks and a neon-yellow shirt that she had combined with a pair of jean shorts. Unable to find the right matching clothing components in their closets, the girls had compromised to make their girl-power display at Skate Town a success by wearing the same barrettes. All three had decided they were still a matching hair clique as they clipped back the sides of their hair and stiffed up their bangs into a crunchy, puffy curl.

Carli and Trixie stood on either side of her. "This is the year," Carli said with the false deep voice of a wrestling tournament announcer. "Tonight, someone from our school is gonna win limbo." She lifted her fisted arms for effect.

"Not Darla," Trixie added, pointing her nose to the nearest car drop-off. "She cheats. Everyone knows she's double-jointed."

"No. Not Darla, Trixie. Me. I'm going to win."

Harriet and Trixie rolled their eyes in perfect unison. They handed over their tickets and rushed to beat the line to the skate rentals. Trixie pointed to their bands. "Look! The bands match our beaded barrettes. Maybe it's a sign."

They linked arms and pushed into the building. Harriet looked to the right as another contender walked past and held out her wrist for her band.

"Uh-oh," Trixie said. "I thought she moved to like Texas or something."

"No. Just changed schools," Carli said, her face tightening before looking away. "She doesn't have a chance at the limbo contest."

Janet. Janet with her clique of besties all wearing a lacy headband and matching skirts over cropped leggings. The truth was that Janet did have a shot at the limbo contest. Trixie had had a sleepover with her once, a birthday party years before Janet had moved away. There had been gymnastics trophies and medals all over her room. Janet was a real threat to Carli's dream of winning the skating contest.

The Madonna Crew, led by Janet, snapped their gum collectively and handed over their tickets for skate rentals. Carli threw them a dismissive side glance. They were also into making conga lines and taking up all the lanes too.

"Don't worry, Carli. You're going to do great," Harriet encouraged her.

Carli sniffed and said, "Hey, I'm going to get a licorice rope. Want anything?"

Harriet shook her head.

"Save my spot. Promise?"

"Mine too?" Trixie added, counting her quarters to buy herself a 7UP.

"Pinky promise."

Harriet stayed and got her skates long before Carli was able to join her in line. She went to the bank of lockers and she tucked inside one of them her sneakers and sweatshirt her mother had insisted she bring, leaving room for her friends' shoes. She found a spot to put on her skates and plopped down on the bench.

Skate Town pulsed with neon light and disco beats, making it hard to hear any one person as swarms of kids flooded the skate rental booth. Harriet laced her skates beside a group of girls from another school, their matching satin jackets glittering with sequins that spelled out *Ridgeview Rockets*. She tried not to stare.

Across the rink, a knot of boys hooted and leaned against the wall. She recognized several of the guys who used to live in her old neighborhood. There was that kid Miles, taller than before, with an uneven haircut he'd probably given himself and acted proud of as he bragged to the guys, patting it down. Some kid named Davy elbowed him and pointed toward a girl twirling near the DJ booth. Still loud. Still annoying. And there was a high probability that they still had the middle-school equivalent of cooties.

The pack of boys skated around the loop and stopped for some popcorn. Harriet finished lacing up her skates and stood. She turned in time to see Davy fall near the halfway wall in front of her. Slumped over the wall, he howled in laughter as Miles tossed popcorn pieces into the back-pants crack of an older girl reading a *Tiger Beat* magazine. The girl silently flipped him the finger from the bench where she sat, not once looking up from her pages as she dug the pieces out.

"Grody," Harriet said under her breath and scanned the rink for her friends. Instead, she saw Janet, already skating backward, her ponytail flipping like she was in a commercial. She flew by as Harriet stood at the crowded entrance. Janet passed by closely, nearly bumping into her, not seeing her. Or pretending not to. The intentional ignoring was as apparent as her intentional negative attention—was Janet locking on to her as her target? Some girls just needed competition, but Harriet was not the competitive type.

"Are we going?" Carli appeared from the bank of lockers and nudged Harriet. "Before all the good floor space is gone?"

"Did you find the locker?" Harriet nodded and pushed forward, the floor vibrating under her wheels. "I picked the same number as my school locker."

"Of course! You can be so predictable. Besides, it wasn't hard to open all the doors until I found the one with the sweatshirt your mom made you wear." Carli turned and shouted at Trixie behind her on the benches, "Come on, slowpoke!"

Trixie finished lacing her skate and joined them on the roller rink. The music shifted into "You Make Me Feel Like Dancing," and the DJ turned up streams of bright, swirling light. Kids sped up, some weaving like pros, others clinging to the rail. Her elbow nearly caught into Miles as he swerved past.

"Watch it, Mathlete," he said with a grin, not unkindly.

Harriet shot him a look. "You skate like my grandpa."

The pack of guys followed behind, whooping up a chant. They were trying their best to imitate the *Saturday Night Fever* dance sequence made famous by John Travolta.

"Dissed!" Davy said, patting Miles on the shoulder as he skated past the girls. Miles laughed but didn't argue.

The limbo contest started a few songs later. The DJ, decked out in mirrored sunglasses, a see-through green visor, and a glittery vest that shimmered beneath the disco lights, called out names in a voice that echoed off the walls like a carnival barker. The rink lights shifted into bright rainbow streaks as Harriet slid into line with Carli and Trixie. The crowd began to gather, skates clicking and rolling over the wooden floor, the air thick and damp.

Lots of the kids they knew thought they could win. There were amazing prizes: a ten-dollar gift card for the mall, a pack of Bonnie Bell Lip Smackers, a stack of tokens for the arcade, and passes for future skating sessions. The first-place winner would also win an after-school skate session for their entire school. The stakes were as real as could be.

Round after round, the bar lowered. Carli cheered when Trevor knocked it over on the third pass and threw his hands up like a rock star, bowing dramatically to the crowd. Everyone laughed, especially when he exaggerated a limped step with his skates back to the sidelines where Darla waited, arms crossed.

Janet arched herself under the bar with the exaggerated grace of a practiced gymnast, arms waving behind her like she was summoning applause. She blew a kiss to her friends when she cleared it. Trixie didn't make it past the fourth round, flailing and collapsing in a tangled heap of limbs and denim. Carli held out for one more, her face pinched in concentration, tongue poking from the side of her mouth as she shimmied below the stick.

Harriet crouched low, wheels humming beneath her. She could feel the rink vibrating with bass as the crowd stomped and clapped in rhythm to "Another One Bites the Dust." She leaned as far back as she could, arms stretched wide for balance. Her left skate wobbled, catching for a split second, and her stomach dropped.

A flash of panic. She was going to fall. In front of everyone.

Then whoosh! She tipped back her head and her chin cleared the bar. Barely.

The crowd clapped and cheered. Trixie shouted her name, and Carli spun in a little victory dance beside her. Harriet laughed, cheeks burning and heart pounding in her ears. Her legs wobbled as she straightened, the adrenaline racing through her fingertips.

"Nice!" Miles called from the sidelines, a half grin on his face, arms crossed casually.

She wasn't sure if he was mocking her or not. She shot him a shrug and skated off to rejoin the crowd, not giving him the satisfaction of asking. But her face stayed warm for longer than she expected.

Harriet snapped back to the moment, completely back into the automatic mode of the Experience, and at her turn she ducked under the bar, clean. Janet was next and this time didn't keep her footing. She tripped on her own skate and fell, barely catching herself. A collective gasp gave way to polite clapping.

Harriet went two more rounds before falling, a graceful little plop in front of a ridiculously low bar. Truman something-or-another from Bowman Catholic High came in first place in a tight battle. It wasn't a win for Harriet, but it felt like something.

Later, as they lined up for orange slushies, Carli turned to her. "That was seriously awesome. Where did that come from?"

Harriet shrugged. "No idea."

But part of her did. Something had shifted. A thread was pulling tightly between her and these hidden messages of her Experience. Something or . . . someone . . . she couldn't quite name was trying to tell her something.

Something that had started to claw at her. A memory trying to rise to the surface of her consciousness. Something.

She had a shadow of a feeling of what it could be, but did she trust this machine?

Not yet. Not ever.

~

AFTER THE LIMBO CONTEST, the DJ queued up ABBA's "Take a Chance on Me." The rink lights shifted into waves of pinks and purples. Harriet skated to the edge, chest still buzzing from the excitement of getting close to winning, and unlaced her skates at the bench.

Miles stood nearby, holding a soda and watching a group of boys argue over whether Pac-Man or Asteroids took more skill. Harriet didn't plan on approaching him, but he nodded once, like he'd been waiting for her to catch up. He leaned against the rink wall, his duct-taped sneakers tapping to the beat of the Michael Jackson song that came on next.

"You still mad about the mathlete comment?" he asked, sidling up beside her.

She smirked. "Only if you're still sore about losing limbo to me."

"I didn't enter."

"Exactly."

He slurped from his soda.

"Wait . . . how did you even know I was on the team?" she asked.

"I was there."

She blinked. "You were at the meet?"

"Yeah. I helped set up the AV cart and ran the buzzer for half the rounds." He nudged the toe of his shoe against the floor. "My dad wanted me to have a hobby."

"So you saw me there?" She thought about the stupid blazers they had made the team wear.

"Kind of hard not to. You buzzed in before half the questions were even done."

She gave a small shrug. "It wasn't that hard."

He nodded, thoughtful. "No, it was. I tried answering them in my head. You smoked everyone."

"We didn't win against you guys. You're a tough team to beat."

"Not with you slicing through the competition." He snorted. "Come on. I've got tokens."

"Ah, I don't have any quarters left." She reached into her pocket. "And I don't want to use my five-dollar bill."

"Want to play together?"

"What do you mean?"

"You shoot. I'll dodge," he said.

"Ok. Let's try it." She nodded.

Inside the arcade, the lighting was lower, everything buzzing electric hues. Kids lined up behind machines like they were guarding treasure. Harriet followed Miles to a Galaga console. He slid a token into the slot, and she lined up next to the joystick, her hand hovering over the Fire button.

The game started. She wasn't great but she caught on fast. Miles didn't offer instructions. He just played, leaning close enough for her to smell the faint mix of his Dr Pepper and whatever cologne he must've swiped from his father's bathroom. They lost on level three, laughing at how badly they bombed. Literally.

Behind them, Janet skated into the arcade like she owned it, her lace bow clipped high, bracelets jingling with every push off. Her homage to Madonna's *Like a Virgin* album cover was complete with fingerless gloves and a mesh top layered over a tank.

"Miles," she said, voice sharp as her eyeliner. "We need to talk."

He looked at Harriet, then back at Janet. "Now?"

"Obviously." She crossed her arms. "In private."

Harriet stepped away, pretending to study the air-hockey scores.

Janet pulled Miles a few feet over by a soda machine. "You said you'd skate with me during the couples round."

"You were skating with Quintin," Miles said, arms crossed now too.

"That wasn't Quintin. It was a kid I knew from Jefferson." She flipped her hair, bracelets clinking. "Besides, I saw you laughing with *her*."

Miles's face didn't change. "So?"

"So I guess we're done."

"You guess?"

Janet narrowed her eyes. "We're. Done." She spun dramatically and stormed out of the arcade—as much as someone could storm out in rented skates.

Harriet wandered back over, hands stuffed in her front pockets. "You okay?" she asked.

"Yeah, it's okay." Miles shrugged, shaking his hands a little as he lifted them. "She was itchy."

She nodded, biting back a smile. "That is a lot of lace."

He nudged the video game with one foot. "You wanna go again?"

"Yeah. But I'm driving this time."

AFTER THE ARCADE emptied out and the snack bar's popcorn machine fell silent, the last skate of the night rolled on. The DJ slowed things down with "Just the Way You Are," and the lights softened to a golden pink.

Harriet and Miles stayed near the rail. Both had already returned their skates, not talking much. Trixie had already left with her older cousin. Carli was trailing behind Trevor after she had found out that Darla had left early to go home. So much for Trevor being so last week.

"Next year's gonna be weird," Miles said.

Harriet nodded. "High school."

"It might be fun. I mean, we'll be at the same school again." He rested his hands on the top rail and leaned forward like he could see the future on the rink floor. "They say the ninth graders get shoved in lockers."

"I'm not small enough to fit," Harriet said, mostly joking. "I'm kind of tall."

"You could also take 'em down," he said, more serious than not. "Maybe a little better than in Galaga?"

"Most definitely." She laughed.

They watched as the remaining kids skated a last loop together. It wasn't a couple's skate between them. It wasn't a big moment. Just participating from the sidelines, watching a quiet circle slow down with the music low and the rink nearly empty.

As the final song faded, a flicker rolled across the scrolling message board.

REMEMBER: MOMENTUM = CONFIDENCE.

Harriet froze for just a second. *Had the scrolling message board glitched?* It was there for one rotation, and then poof —the message was gone. Back to high scores and ticket redemptions.

What does that even mean?

Miles didn't see it. Or pretended not to. He was picking the last kernels of popcorn from the bottom of his red-and-white bag.

"See you," Miles said, crunching up the bag and tossing it into the trash. "Clementine High, here we come!"

"Yeah. See you." He marched out the door with the group of guys from the old neighborhood.

Janet was also packing up with her crew and noticed Harriet grabbing her sweatshirt from the locker.

"He likes weird girls now," Janet said, tossing her hair with performative indifference. Loud enough to be heard from near the snack bar. "I hope she enjoys second place," she said with a snotty emphasis on "second."

Harriet said nothing. What would Carli say if she were here? How would Trixie react to that rude comment? She could really use her girl group now. It didn't usually matter to Harriet what other kids said, but this felt different. The words didn't need volume. They already echoed.

Outside, the night air felt cooler. Parents pulled up in station wagons and hatchbacks. Harriet waited for her mother outside and felt a woozy chill creep up the inside of her spine. Janet and her social-climbing bullies had gotten to her. It hadn't taken much. Just a few loud whispers near the lockers and one perfectly timed comment.

Now the lights from the Skate Town sign were coming up too

brightly, burning into her retinas, the music cutting off mid-beat as the glass doors opened and more kids left. She found herself checking and guessing at what the other girls were saying about her behind the final sips of their sodas.

The door shut loudly, and she jumped, momentarily worried that Janet and her cronies could bring the drama outside. Earlier, she had wanted to snap back with something clever, something Trixie or Carli would say to shut her down. But by the time Harriet had worked out a comeback about Janet tripping over her own skate, her apparently new nemesis and her crew had piled into the back of Janet's father's navy-blue Suburban.

More kids waited on the other side of the building. A few tossed crumpled napkins at a trash bin near where she was waiting for her ride. Most missed. She looked up to see Davy and Leon were throwing half-melted ice cubes at each other, trying to make them stick. "Like, so mature," she grumbled as one ice cube neared her head. "Could you *not*?"

Quintin walked past Harriet, then doubled back. "Hey," he said, hands stuffed into his sweat jacket. "You, uh, crushed it at limbo. Just saying."

"Thanks," she said, voice soft.

Leon rushed by, avoiding a tossed cup of half-melted ice that Davy threw at him. "Girl, you ducked under that bar. Like, that was so rad," he said, adding extra syllables to the *a* in "rad": *raaaaaad*. "Miles, man, you didn't even try."

Miles followed the pack, hands in his pockets. "Why you dissing me?"

"Yeah, because Miles was trying to hide from Janet," Davy added from behind a bush, grinning and dodging Leon's final ice attack.

"I didn't see you in the contest, Leon."

"I've got bad ankles, dude. You know this."

Quintin looked at her again. "Ignore Janet. She gets like that. She used to live next door to me. It's not personal."

It felt personal. But Harriet nodded anyway, outwardly pushing off the feelings but inwardly whirling like a circus acrobat spinning in the big top. "Oh, I don't care."

Across the lot, headlights flickered as more cars entered the parking lot. Her mother's station wagon pulled up slowly, tires crackling against loose gravel left over from a melted, grimy snow pile. Harriet checked for her sweatshirt, quickly tossing it on, and headed for the car, the laughter and noise of the guys arguing over whether rumors that David Lee Roth would quit being the lead singer of Van Halen were true was already fading behind her.

She was grateful as her mother's car slowed in front of her. She flung open the door and slid into the bench seat, tired and a little dizzy from sugar, skating, and whatever this night had been. Inside, the air was warm and smelled like Fruit Stripe gum and Grandma's anise candy. She buckled her seat belt without a word. Her mother glanced at her through the rearview mirror.

"How was Skate Town?"

Harriet pressed her cheek to the glass, absorbing the calming, cool smoothness. "Fine."

The roller rink building receded behind them, all glitter lights and digital waves as the Experience shifted once again. But the words clung like static.

Some part of her knew this version of life, the middle-school years, the rules of limbo contests and arcade scores, was already slipping into the past.

What would come next was something else entirely.

The skating rink disappeared in a fuzzy mist behind her, and the interior of the car faded and formed the inky-dark void of the Experience pod. A strong smell of sun-dried earth and a hot breeze permeated the dark area, very unlike the sweaty, humid air you could cut with a roller blade that she had experienced moments before.

"That was tragic," she said with sarcasm. "No, scratch that. More like demented and sad, but social." Putting her hands on her hips, she looked around, as if to search for a hidden camera. "Hey, are you up there, Guide Guy? I think I got your cryptic message, by the way," she continued, hoping for a response. Hearing none, Harriet looked at her phone. "Maybe I could reach customer service on this thing?" She scanned the app for any type of contact page, finding none. The green frog bounced along with the bubble, saying, *J-j-j-j-just a minute!* An amphibious version of Max Headroom.

The warm air dissipated, and a smell of cut grass and fall leaves took over. Harriet looked around the room, waiting for the next musical interlude to escort her somewhere new. "Hey, Ted or anybody listening up there?" She shook her phone slightly, as if it were a Magic 8 Ball and she could change her fate. "This preteen torture is really great, but hardly the type of relationship I'm looking for in my wish for a better life. I mean, who wants to relive middle school?"

"Pardon the delay. There is a glitch. We are loading your next memory now," the Guide announced.

She exhaled hard. "Where will the Experience lead to next?" she asked and noticed the tattoo of mountains inside her wrist, glowing in the light of her phone. "Maybe back here? That makes sense for my life goals."

The frog emoji on her phone put on headphones and started to dance.

"You know what I consider a success? Getting out of here without my boss noticing. And getting an all-expenses paid trip to Hawaii. Can you promise that?"

"Hi, Harriet. Ted here. Just stepping in after an unexpected problem with the AI guide. Don't worry, we'll have you back in your regular Experiences soon."

"What about the vacation, Ted? I think I'll need one after all you've put me through here."

"We'll do the drawing for the vacation shortly after your Experience has finished. Oh, the next sequence is now ready! Enjoy your Experience."

"It better be good, and I better get to go to Hawaii. If we don't get to the good stuff soon, I'm leaving this fever dream. One more chance, dude."

But Harriet's Experience had started before he could reply. When she looked at the app on her phone, the frog emoji was pixelated, color squares that shifted back and forth. It put on dark shades and danced to an eighties song about wearing sunglasses at night.

Chapter Ten

Harriet saw the outline of the tall brick school form in front of her and heard the sounds of conversations, radio static, and someone reciting lines from *Fame* spilling over a lawn packed with teenagers. The three-story building wrapped around a patch of green, and the low concrete stairs led to three separate entryways. Wooden doors with square panes of wired glass and scuffed metal handles stood like guardians to the chaos inside.

"Welcome back to high school," the computerized voice above her said cheerfully. "Remember when your life was all about A's, Harriet? Activities. Accolades. Achievement."

"Excuse me?" she said, barely breathing, hesitant as her senses were flooded with new information from this past era.

"That's something you should remember."

Before she could respond, the simulation slowed. Students blurred at the edges. Movements softened. The sound dimmed to a faraway flicker.

Crumpled flyers, cigarette butts, and the remains of vending-machine lunches were scattered over the sidewalks around her. Leaves blew in circles under the gentle swaying leaves of the maples. A Rick

Astley song played from a boom box near the stairs. Just hearing it made her left eye twitch.

Her phone beeped. She glanced at the scene and then read aloud the text bubble that had formed above the sunglasses-wearing frog. "Rickrolled?" she muttered.

She pulled in the crisp air. Raked leaves, aerosol hair spray, and the sting of cold threatening to shut down autumn for the year filled her lungs. The breeze sliced through her oversize cable-knit sweater and stiff, collared shirt underneath.

A janitor dumped a heavy plastic bag into a rolling dumpster. The metal barrel trash can he'd emptied was painted in school colors, black-and-red rings circling the outside like a bull's-eye. He wore gray coveralls and boots so beat up they probably had tenure. He looked her way, just a flick of his work-gloved hand raised in acknowledgment and disgust as he picked up the remains of a fast-food meal.

She tested her movements. She wondered if when the Experience had not fully calibrated, whether she still had some control and could interact. She asked the janitor, "What year is it?"

He crouched beside a shrub, plucking an A&W burger wrapper and a torn math worksheet from the grass. "Gosh-darn kids, don't even know what year it is? For cripes sakes, kid. It's 1987. Now git and learn to pick up after your darn self."

"I'm sure that meal wasn't from me," she said, the flyers pressed against her chest flapping in the wind.

"I bet I'll find whatever it is you're passing around there in every nook and cranny of these bushes. Do me a favor, will ya? Just tell those friends of yours to stop littering."

"I'll try," she said. Her eyes dropped to the flyers, looking over the pages.

HOMECOMING DANCE: SATURDAY, OCTOBER 17
MIDNIGHT CIRCUS
Step right up to the most unforgettable night of the year!
A carnival of lights and shadows awaits! Whether you're dressed to dazzle or

*just there for the Moon Pies and Hi-C punch, this night promises spectacle
and sparkle.*
*Join us under the big top for this year's Homecoming Dance, themed
Midnight Circus.*
Tickets on sale during lunch at the ASB office all week.
Prices go up at the door—so don't wait!
Formal attire encouraged. Unicycles not required.

SHE EXAMINED the hand-drawn pictures in the borders. A leotard-wearing tightrope walker at the top. Sparkling masks, circus posters on a striped vaulted tent, oversize playing cards lining the right-side bar. The lower section was completed with a ringmaster, a lion tamer, and an acrobat.

Her fingers grasped the page with a little too much purpose. Of course she was promoting this thing. And with a snap, the simulation took over, and she began to walk across campus, her body working on autopilot, her mind working in *Valley Girl* lingo, and her social skills working in hyperdrive as she passed out flyers to students.

"Harriet, I voted for you for homecoming queen at lunch today." Raj, a good friend from that era, appeared near the hedge. Circle-rimmed glasses. Straight hair. Wildcat T-shirt. Looking closely at the dials and settings of the camera swinging from his neck. It was all coming back to her.

She tucked her chin and smiled sideways. "Thanks, Raj," she said in a tone so high-pitched it could double as rodent communication. "That's . . . bitch'en."

Oh no. No-no-no. From the viewing chamber, she groaned aloud. What was that? Had she actually said, "Bitch'en"? God help her. It was now confirmed: she had been tragically fluent in *Valley Girl*.

"Can I get your face? For the supplement?" Raj asked, lifting his camera from his chest. His Wildcat mascot tee stretched as he adjusted the strap, the cartoon paw in mid-swipe across his rib cage.

A memory pulsed from inside the Experience chamber. In her gut, she already knew this one.

"Oh no. I remember this. Exactly."

She reached for her phone, the little frog on-screen flipping between freeze-frame glitch and seizure mode. Déjà vu with a death grip.

Maybe this was the opportunity she needed. If she could get her teen self to refuse having the photo taken, maybe she could short-circuit this whole stalker-grade simulation.

"It's kind of a bad hair day," she heard herself say. She willed words to form, movements from her fingers, the direction of her nod to say *no*. Any little thing to override this moment.

She felt a twitch in her left hand. *Yes. Good. Stick to it. Say no. Say you'll do it later and then walk away.*

Harriet's teenage hip shifted. One hand slid to the waistband of her jeans, thumb hooked in the pocket. "Alright. Just one. We can always retake it, right?"

"No, no, no." She felt the words bounce uselessly in the dark. The Experience was in full presentation mode. She couldn't stop this stupid thing. Not even close.

Raj smiled tightly, squinting behind his lenses. "You're such a babe."

Harriet wanted to scream. She did scream. But nobody in this frozen flashback could hear her. To her right, the grumpy janitor lingered in the background, raking up snack wrappers and complaining under his breath, rake bristling with full Freddy Kruger vibes.

"Is it true?" Raj asked, peering through the camera viewfinder as he adjusted the aperture. "I heard you got Splat Rocket for the dance."

Harriet's fists curled tightly with excitement. "It's true."

"Really? Awesome!"

He snapped several more pictures while she flipped her hair instinctively, the scent of her apple-sweet hair spray wafting up with the movement. Grown Harriet winced somewhere in the shadows of the chamber but had to admit it: her younger self didn't lack confidence. At that age, Harriet had snapped into a high-performing, high school self with ease, riding the wave of belief that she could, in fact, make a difference in this world. A wave she now understood would eventually have to crash.

Teen Harriet smoothed her sweater, stepping into her role as student government representative once again. She pointed across the quad. "We're also opening the auditorium for a black-and-white noir film screening."

Raj grinned, shaking his bangs out of his eyes. "Now that's artful. Not all that metalhead hair-band stuff."

"Some people like that," she replied, watching a group of students bunny-hop their bikes near the steps. "There's a DJ in the small gym. Metal, new wave, top 40, probably some hair-band stuff too."

"Not for me. But it's totally radical what you're doing here." He snapped another photo. "Might be the best dance ever."

"The committee's doing a ton of work," she said, nodding toward a cluster of students under a tree, balancing paper bags on their laps and talking through mouthfuls of food. "Thank them."

"Oh, I know. But you . . . the girl with the huge stack of flyers and no free period, you're the one making it happen." He let the camera drop to his chest and turned toward the school's brick facade. "I'd help, but these photos aren't going to develop themselves. See you around, babe."

She lifted her hand in an artsy kiss-blow, which he answered with an elbow-lifted wave. The stack of flyers at her side flapped in the breeze. One had already escaped, tumbling toward the skater crowd congregating at the far end of the steps. She stepped off the path to retrieve it. Whatever else she was, and despite what the janitor claimed, she wasn't a litterbug.

Harriet took a few steps across the lawn, chasing the loose flyer. A couple passed by, heading toward the cafeteria entrance. Trevor, blond and braces-free now, walked alongside Janet, who was sporting a glittery spiral perm and bold blue eye shadow.

Janet's eyes narrowed as they crossed paths. She tugged Trevor's arm tighter, as if to steer him away. Harriet could feel the stare, the unspoken grudge from the Skate Town incident still flickering like static between them.

"Love the hair, Janet!" Harriet chirped, her tone bright but not biting. "Where'd you go for the perm?"

Janet ignored her and pulled Trevor toward an outdoor table where students were unwrapping sandwiches. *Same old games,* Harriet thought. *New school building, same middle-school drama.*

Harriet felt a shift. The wind tugged at the edges of her flyers. She watched Raj disappear behind a group of upperclassmen holding neon water pistols like they were undercover agents. The world slowed around her. The air thickened.

A burst of motion broke through the slowed reality. A sophomore in a black trench coat launched herself from behind a hedge, wielding a blue plastic water pistol. "Water-gun takedown!" she cried, aiming it straight at Harriet.

Harriet lifted the stack of flyers like a makeshift shield. "Don't even think about it. Go spray someone else. I'm a senior. Hit me and you'll regret it."

"Oh yeah?" the girl challenged, squinting through the beads of the sight from beneath the brim of her fedora.

"Try it. I'll have the D&D club recruiting you for life."

The girl backed down, scampering away just as a swarm of upperclassmen emerged from the courtyard. They charged past Harriet, plastic water guns raised like Cold War-era spy gear, spraying unsuspecting underclassmen with triumphant shouts.

"She should've chosen more wisely," said one tall boy with spiky hair, holstering his water gun like a cowboy.

Harriet barely sidestepped another blast. One of the boys used her as cover, ducking behind her just as water sprayed past. In the shuffle, he stepped hard on her foot.

"Ow! Get bent, jerk!" she yelled, hobbling on one chunky penny loafer. Her other hand reached toward the spilled flyers that now danced over the grass.

A redheaded freshman hustled toward her, scooping up the runaway flyers. "Here. Want help with the rest?"

Harriet blinked. "Thanks, Sandy. I think they're all accounted for." She looked across the quad where others were now grabbing at the scattered papers.

"Want me to tape some up?" Sandy offered, holding the flyers close to her chest. "I can do the front entry. There's barely anything up there."

"That'd be amazing." Harriet handed her a roll of tape from her pocket.

Sandy gave a small smile, her glasses slipping down her nose. "Hey, Harriet, can I ask you something?"

"Sure." She felt the simulation tilt slightly again. The sound around her softened, her vision narrowing.

"I'm running for freshman president. Would you endorse me?"

Harriet hesitated, watching the girl's bright hoop earrings swing as she waited. Then she smiled. "Absolutely. I think it's awesome you're getting involved. You'll make a great student president."

"Thanks!" Sandy clutched the flyers tighter. "It's for my college résumé. See you around."

Harriet watched her walk off, then she turned toward the skater crowd as another flyer caught the wind.

The scene glitched again, freezing momentarily, and she glanced at her phone. The frog delivered a new message: *Parallel lines. Parallel lives. To show you how good your life has been.*

"That's debatable," Harriet said. "Parallel lives or paralyzing lines? This whole thing reeks of weird. And I want out. I'm serious."

Above her, the AI voice popped in "Harriet, sorry for the delay. We will be online again soon. This is all part of working out bugs in this new technology. It takes a little time to read your memories."

"Read them? That's so creepy. And this version of me . . . it isn't even who I became. I wasted years burning out on stuff no one even remembers."

"I see this memory still resonates with you. That's a good sign."

"Good for who?" she shot back. The words spun in her chest like loose debris caught in wind to be swept away by some old curmudgeon. "You can't keep me here. I mean it."

"Please be patient. Your perception of time will soon take you back."

"I don't trust you, bucko."

And the Experience snapped back to the lawn of Clementine High School.

Chapter Eleven

Skaters took turns launching off the low stairs, some barely landing, others biffing it completely. One girl on a BMX spun out a clean wheelie and landed with a flourish. Applause broke out from the crowd as she rolled to the edge of the steps.

Then came the boy with the wild grin and grip-taped skateboard. *Smiles.*

He hugged the biker girl with one arm and kicked his board into position with the other. The name *Smiles* was scribbled in big block letters on the board beside a field of Mr. Yuk stickers. The neon-green faces frowned back, like they knew something no one else did.

Miles, as she knew him, flew off the stairs, kick-flipped, and landed. He rolled over to the group that was watching.

"Did you see that?" he asked, eyes flicking to the girl with the spiky bleached-blonde hair. His voice didn't mask how much her opinion mattered.

"Nice one, Smiles!" Carli leaned against her handlebars, arms crossed. She cracked her gum and gave him a grin like she could own the whole school if she wanted.

"Dude, you nailed it!" Davy called, flicking ash from a cigarette while perched on his board.

"Yeah. Bodacious," Matt added, waiting at the top of the stairs.

Harriet watched from across the quad as a few remaining papers scattered in the breeze. Behind them, Sandy was handing off flyers to the ASB crew while the skaters claimed their corner by getting scrapes and bruises and doing tricks. Harriet watched from the sidelines, picking up the remaining flyers in the area.

Leon wiped out at the top of the steps, then tried again with a stubborn huff. The group cheered him on. "Come on, man. You've got this!" Davy gave a hearty clap.

Smiles was next and dropped into a clean 360. He landed it with a slick thud and flipped his board up into his hands. He turned toward Carli with a proud half smile and held the board between them. She smirked and ruffled his bangs before he stole her lighter from her hand. A quick gesture.

"Hey, don't touch! You'll mess up my hair," he warned, snapping the lighter into life.

"I'll need that back." Carli winked and rolled her bike down the steps with a soft bounce. Smiles lit a cigarette, shielding the flame from the wind. He cupped his hand, took a drag, then followed her down.

"It's way too nice to be stuck in algebra," Carli said.

"I couldn't agree more." Smiles exhaled and adjusted his grip on the board. "Algebra sounds terrible. Let's skip."

They walked side by side, her hand in his back pocket, his hand sliding the lighter back into hers. They melted into the stream of students wandering off campus, slipping between parked cars like shadows.

Harriet zipped her remaining flyers into her backpack. She watched the pair disappear through the back gate, a slow, familiar ache tightening in her chest. Once upon a time, Carli had been her best friend. She had been the girl who had stayed up with her making prank calls and trading secrets under a blanket fort. Now Carli was carving out her own legend, one wheelie, one skipped class at a time, while Harriet handed out flyers for the Honor Society and tried to keep her GPA perfect.

Maybe that was just how it worked. People split off, took different roads. And sometimes, no matter how far you looked back, you couldn't trace your way to where it all had shifted.

Grown Harriet muttered under her breath, "Back-pocket mall grab. Really, Miles?"

Still, there was something about her teenage self in that moment. The movement, the voice, the certainty, that made her pause. Maybe this whole simulation was about rediscovering whatever fuel that girl had been running on.

THE SCHOOL BELL RANG, echoing across the quad, muffled through the trees. Harriet made her way inside, climbing the stairs to the third floor. She moved from bulletin board to bulletin board, layering her flyers over outdated announcements. As she stepped toward the stairwell again, a hall runner skidded to a stop beside her.

"Harriet! You're seriously hard to find. Coach Elliott wants to see you." He handed her a blue pass.

She eyed the slip like it had insulted her mother. "Why? I'm excused. This is school business. It even says so on my Student Government Hall Pass."

The runner shrugged, his chains clinking against his football jersey. "I'm just the messenger. He's in his office."

She groaned, loudly enough to turn heads. "Of course he is. For a gym teacher, he sure spends a lot of time behind a desk."

"I'll let him know you're on your way," the runner said as he bounded down the steps. "You don't want to disappoint Coach."

"Yeah, yeah."

Harriet shoved the remaining flyers into her backpack and pocketed her stapler. She took the stairs down two flights, passing the stone carving of Joan of Arc, the patron saint of overachieving students everywhere. Or at least at Clementine High. The building transitioned from Gothic to grafted-on seventies modern as she reached the athletic wing.

Coach Elliott's door stood open across from the locker rooms. She knocked once and stepped in.

"Harriet Last. First in a lot of things," Coach said without looking up. "But not in my class. Sit."

"Come on, Coach. You know I love your class." She dropped into the armchair like it had betrayed her.

"Cut the comedy. You're skipping."

"I'm working. For the school."

"You've got plenty of time to tape up flyers when you're not supposed to be in PE. That's what teammates are for. Teamwork. Heard of it?"

"Awesome. A speech."

"I'm sparing you the speech. You know what you need to do."

She raised her eyebrows. "I do?"

"I counted. Thirteen unexcused absences. That's a quarter-letter grade per day. Your A is now a D-plus."

Harriet sat up straighter. "A D-plus? That's criminal. And it's gym class."

"Exactly." He leaned back in his chair, rocking slightly. "You see the problem."

She crossed her arms. "I'm on the tennis team. I show up for practice. I go to every meet."

"C-team. Doesn't count."

"That's brutal."

"Good thing I'm offering you a deal: one week after school. You help with a tennis outreach program I run. Teach neighborhood kids some basics."

"I'm not qualified to teach tennis."

"You're qualified to learn. Fast." He slid a copy of *Tennis for Beginners*, a VHS tape, and a mimeographed schedule across the desk. "It's about time spent with the kids. Building relationships. Showing up."

She eyed the materials. "So . . . this is a punishment?"

"It's a second chance. Better than detention or losing your grade. You interested?"

"Do I have a choice?"

"Sure. Take the D-plus."

"You know that's not happening." She scooped up the stack with a sigh.

"Starts today. You won't be doing this on your own. I have one other volunteer."

She got up to leave, nodded to the coach, backpack slung over one shoulder. "Next time you send your football henchmen after me, maybe tell them not to ambush me with a hostile takeover of my afternoon."

"Glad to see your sense of humor's intact. Because there won't *be* a next time." He picked up the phone, chuckled, and waved her off. "Now get out of my office."

Harriet raised two fingers in a peace sign and backed out into the hall. Her voice echoed down the tiled corridor. "How am I supposed to teach tennis to little kids? I'm supposed to meet my study group at the library."

The bell rang again. The large metal doors of the gymnasium opened, and the halls filled with students in gym clothes, T-shirts, and shorts with their marker-scrawled names on the swoosh right below the Wildcat mascot.

"This sucks!" she shouted just as someone called out to her from near the pay phones. *Miles*—as she simply would never call him that other weird name—leaned against the wall, a crumpled slip of paper in one hand and a pile of change in the other.

"What's your major malfunction?" he asked. "Some of us are trying to make phone calls over here."

"Mind your own business, creep."

"Wow. Bad day?" He slid a few nickels and a dime into the slot and lifted the receiver.

"Why would you assume I'm having a bad day?"

He held up a hand in surrender. "Because you're yelling in the hall-way. And now the entire gym wing is part of your soap opera. It invites commentary."

She groaned and checked her watch. "I'm late for Spanish. Not that it's your concern."

Miles returned his focus to the phone attached to the wall, but added, "Well, I hope your day improves."

"Whatever, *skeezoid*." She stalked off toward the main hall, grumbling under her breath.

He watched her go, shaking her curls with a final flick as she turned the corner. "Theater kid," he muttered, then dropped another coin into the phone. "Hi, Carli? Yeah, I can't meet after school. Got stuck with some tennis thing . . . No, not because I skipped fifth hour. Because I got caught smoking in the locker room . . . It was a bet." He twisted the cord around his finger. "I know, I know. I'm disappointed too. So, what's on *The People's Court*? I can't wait to hear all about it."

Chapter Twelve

The tennis courts were surrounded by a tall chain-link fence and shaded by a few shaggy-looking elms. Shadows from the late-afternoon sun stretched across the cracked pavement as Harriet arrived, clutching her clipboard and trying not to look completely lost.

A dozen kids fidgeted near the fence while a curly-haired teen handed out rackets like they were candy canes. Most were using them as swords.

"Hey, buddy, no poking," Harriet said to a boy tapping his friend's arm with the edge of his racket.

The kid grinned, clearly unbothered. Another tried to lift the hem of a girl's tennis skirt with the frame of his racket. She slapped his hand away. "Don't touch me, asshole."

Harriet blinked. "Second grade? Really?"

She caught sight of Miles across the court. He looked like he'd walked into a comedy sketch, dodging wild swings and plucking rackets from midair. He spotted her and stifled a laugh. "Tough crowd," he said, stepping over a racket like it was a land mine.

"Tell me about it. This isn't exactly my idea of fulfilling community service."

"How'd you get roped in?"

"I'm paying for missing gym." She squinted at him. "What's your reason?"

"Caught smoking in the locker room." He shrugged. "It was a dare."

Harriet gave him a slow blink.

"I know. Real mature. But honestly, I've seen our drama teacher sneak a puff outside the theater. Where's the justice?"

"Do you have the schedule?"

"It's in my locker."

She held up the clipboard. "You left your schedule in your locker?"

"Yep."

Harriet sighed and handed it over. "Ice-breaker game first. Then teach them how to hold the racket. You ever play?"

"Yeah. With my mom. Coach said I just had to help wrangle them. You're the brains here."

"Terrifying." She clapped twice. "Alright. Let's learn some names."

A boy piped up. "We have name tags."

"Even better. Let's go around. Name, grade, favorite animal."

Miles added, "And if anyone remembers all of them at the end . . . ice cream on Coach."

Harriet raised an eyebrow. "Do we have ice cream?"

"We'll figure it out."

The kids shouted out names, grades, and animals. Harriet tried to keep track: Sharks, lions, owls, and a unicorn made the list. Miles whispered sarcastic commentary at the end of each one, and a few of the kids started copying him. By the time the last kid spoke, Harriet was already reading the next line on the clipboard. "Okay, the next part says, 'Play tag.'"

Miles perked up. "Now, this I can do." He whistled to get their attention. "Alright, little racketeers. Time to stretch those legs. Tag rules: No hitting, no using rackets, and no screaming unless you're having fun."

They picked a volunteer to be "it," and chaos unfolded. Little feet pounded the court while kids shrieked, darted, spun, collided, and then kept running. Harriet turned back to the clipboard, searching it as if her life depended on it.

"Fundamentals," she murmured. "Today: grip and wall work."

She glanced up. A boy was using his racket like a pogo stick. Another used his as a shovel.

"Miles?" she called.

"On it." He jogged back to the group. "Alright, stop the madness. Pete and Thompson! Rackets down at your sides, guys. Everyone else, grab yours and line up along the fence."

They obeyed and slowly found spots on along the chain-linked wall. Sort of.

Harriet held up her racket. Kids leaned in to see what she was doing. "See the handle? It's not round. It's shaped like a long octagon. Your job is to put the flat side between your thumb and finger, right where that webby bit is."

Miles added, "The 'webby bit' is official tennis lingo."

Harriet sighed and smiled. "Watch me, then try it."

They demonstrated. Kids followed. Sort of. Miles walked the line, adjusting grips, making jokes, showing off his own technique. Harriet followed up with corrections, praise, and patient redirection. Progress was slow but real.

Miles stood at the center of the court and raised his voice over the chatter. "Okay, rackets down again. Let's move to the wall. Time to see if we can hit the ball and not each other."

The kids cheered and scrambled after a bucket of balls. Harriet positioned herself near the wall and held up her clipboard, holding it out of reach just above their busy bodies.

"Find some space. One arm's length apart," she said. "We're practicing controlled hits: bounce, hit, wall, bounce, hit again."

Some of the kids nodded, chins tipped in her direction. Most just started swinging. Pete and Thompson immediately resumed their sword fight, this time with balls flying.

"Arms out like a *T*," Harriet instructed. "If you can touch your neighbor, you're too close."

The boys laughed and spun in circles, trying to outpace each other's twirls.

"Careful," Miles warned. "You're gonna . . ."

Thwack!

Pete's racket smacked Thompson square on the bridge of the nose. Blood streamed down Thompson's face. He screamed. Pete screamed louder.

"Oh my God," Harriet gasped. She dropped her clipboard and jogged over.

Miles was already there, crouched in front of them. "Breathe. You're okay," he said gently. "Thompson, tilt your head back. Pete, buddy, you're not bleeding."

"But I saw it!" Pete cried, hands flailing.

"You saw his blood. Yours is still inside you. Deep breaths."

Harriet waved at the other kids to take five. "Practice swings only, okay? I'll show you again in a second."

Miles helped Thompson to the fence and grabbed the first aid kit from the gear bag. Pete clung to his arm like he'd just witnessed a murder. When Thompson was patched up and safely seated against the fence, an ice pack in hand and Pete by his side for support, Harriet returned to the group.

"Alright. No more spinning. No more duels. Just aim for the wall, one bounce, and try again."

A girl named Sandra stepped up. "What if the wall hits back?"

Miles, taken slightly back by the child's comment, threw her a look of sarcasm. "Then it's learning to respect boundaries. Try it anyway."

The group looked around, confused, but the girl's tension turned into determination. Sandra gripped her racket correctly and sent the ball in a clean arc toward the wall. It bounced once, then twice, and she returned it with a proud grin.

Harriet clapped. "Nice! That's exactly it."

Sandra gave a small shrug but danced in place like she'd just won the lottery. Another girl stepped up and copied her grip.

Miles wandered along the row, tossing encouragements and miming exaggerated technique. "Thumb up, elbow out. Pretend it's a light saber. No actual slicing."

By the end of the session, most of the kids had managed at least one clean bounce. Even Pete and Thompson, now side by side with a paper towels taped under Thompson's nose, managed to gently volley a ball together.

When the final bell rang and the last kid was picked up, Harriet let out a long sigh and leaned on the fence. Miles handed her a bucket half-full of stray balls to collect the rest. "One day down," he said.

"Four more to go."

They both laughed.

Harriet added, "I don't know if we're going to survive."

THEY REACHED the shed and returned the rackets to their hooks. Harriet lingered a second longer, hanging up the last one. A small puff of dust rose from the old wooden walls. She shut the door gently, like it might collapse if she slammed it.

"Want to get a slice of pizza?" Miles asked, rubbing the back of his neck. His curls were damp with sweat, and he looked like he'd already mentally checked out for the day.

Harriet zipped her hooded sweatshirt halfway up and glanced sideways. "Seriously? After all that blood, sweat, and second-grade swearing?"

"My stomach doesn't discriminate. I'm starving," he said. "Also, I'm ninety percent sure those kids said things that will haunt me into my twenties."

"I should study. Big trig test tomorrow."

"But will you? Or will you fall asleep on top of your notes and wake up with graph paper imprinted on your forehead?"

She made a face but smiled. "What's wrong with being prepared?"

"What's wrong with getting some study fuel? You've got to eat, don't you?"

"I'll eat some soup at home."

"I hate soup."

"What's so wrong with soup?"

"It's absolutely boring, Harriet."

"At least I'm making a future for myself and while eating a delicious bowl of chicken noodle soup."

"Ouch. That hurts. How do you know that? You can't really think

I'm building a future on teaching tennis, right?" He patted his heart in mock pain, "Really, I'm a sensitive guy, you know."

They walked together toward the parking lot, tennis bags slung over their shoulders, the sun now a warm blur behind the school's brick wall, casting long golden lines across the asphalt.

"Smell you later, I guess," Miles said, swinging his duffel bag over his shoulder and giving her a lazy salute.

"Yeah. See you tomorrow."

Harriet reached her car first. Her sneakers scuffed the faded parking lines as she pulled her keys from her sweatshirt pocket. She climbed in and turned the ignition.

Click.

She frowned. Tried again.

Click-click.

Miles paused mid-step, already pulling on a sweatshirt over his gym T-shirt. "That doesn't sound promising," he said from the nearby motorcycle parking area.

Harriet groaned and slumped forward, resting her forehead on the steering wheel. "Come on. Not today."

"You know what you're doing?" he called, setting his backpack on the seat of his bike. He casually walked toward her car, arching an eyebrow.

"I can drive the car. That's about it."

He jogged over, dust kicking up under his shoes. "Pop the hood."

The late sun was dipping lower now, and the air had cooled enough that the metal of the car hood felt almost cold to the touch. They both stared at the front end of the car like it might grow fangs.

"Alright." She reached just above the grill and yanked the lever with a tired sigh. They lifted the heavy lid that emitted a metallic grinding sound that hurt Harriet's ears, and she asked, "Do you know what you're doing?"

"For sure," he replied and began a slightly random search for something obvious. He tapped the battery. "The click can mean the battery isn't getting any power to the starter." He wiggled the connectors. "Try it now."

She got back into the car and turned the key. The engine groaned, clunked into life, and grudgingly started. "Hey! It started."

"Shut it off!" He pulled his head from under the hood to shout over the loud rattling, "I think it needs oil!"

"I've got oil in the trunk," she said. "My dad painted the cap orange because I poured it in that dipstick place once." She pointed to a looped metal handle under the hood that projected from a thin tube attached to the engine. "And now I forget. And I have to explain it to anyone who looks under my hood."

Miles chuckled. "That's . . . responsible? In a cautionary-tale kind of way."

"More like humiliating, but yes. Now I can never live that down."

He pulled the dipstick, wiped it with a paper towel she found in the glove box. "You're down a quart."

"But I added some this week."

"Then your car's a thirsty beast. Let's feed it."

She fetched the can of oil from her trunk, along with a can opener and a funnel. Miles popped a square hole on one side and a triangle hole opposite for pouring. He poured it in with the kind of caution reserved for old machines and new relationships. When he finished, he stepped back, wiping his hands on a clean spot of the paper towel, nodding at the driver's seat. "Try it now."

Harriet slid in and turned the key again. The engine coughed, sputtered, and then roared to life with a guttural rumble.

"Victory," Miles declared, tossing the towel into a barrel trash can. "And by the way, maybe keep a can of Coke in the trunk too."

"I'm going to put Coke in the engine?" She pulled back with a quizzical look. "I know that doesn't go in the oil thingie."

Miles chuckled. "Not in the oil. Don't do that. I saw a guy pour some Coke over the connectors when the battery is a little corroded. It cleans it up pretty quick." He removed the bar holding up the heavy hood and lay it in a groove on the inside edge of the fender. Then he dropped it down with a *thunk*. "Piece of cake," he said, dusting off his hands.

The engine was rough, but it complained less. Harriet sat leaning against the open window of her car. "I owe you. Want me to buy you that pizza?"

He flashed a grin. "Thought you'd never ask."

"Angelo's, okay?"

"Is there anywhere better? I'll race ya there. The first one there will buy the sodas."

"Race?"

Harriet watched as Miles trotted to his bike and threw on his backpack. He put on a painter's cap with the lid facing backward, his bangs poking out over his eyes.

"It's only a couple of blocks up the road!" she shouted.

He held a hand to his ear, grinning as if he didn't know she was definitely not up for a race, and he started his bike. "See you there!"

Chapter Thirteen

M iles revved the handle of the motorcycle, lifted his feet, and took off from the school parking lot, the engine spitting out a low snarl as he accelerated. He grinned into the breeze, dark glasses holding back the parted bangs that flopped in the wind, weaving past slow cars like it was a sport.

Behind him, Harriet slowly backed her bus of a vehicle from her space, easing past a few students still loitering near the bike racks. Her turn signal clicked like a metronome that couldn't be rushed, and she moseyed her way out of the lot like she had all the time in the world. She didn't rush and, unsure of the road as a new driver, gave the right of way to anyone near her lumbering behemoth of a car she treated like the one the B-52s sang about, a beloved whale on wheels.

Miles, meanwhile, ran his bike over the curb with the reckless grace of someone who'd done it a dozen times and only wiped out twice. He cut across a patch of loose gravel, fishtailing slightly for flair, then wove around a line of stopped cars idling at the light on the hill. The warm evening breeze whipped past his face as he leaned into the turn, letting the hum of the engine echo off the buildings as he coasted up toward the familiar glow of the uptown neighborhood pizza place.

He rolled to a stop beside the brick building, parking neatly beneath the old hand-painted ANGELO's sign stretched across the second-story bricks. The cartoon chef above the door still held up his oversize pie like it was a trophy, though his mustache was chipped and the once-vivid colors had faded into something like the inside of a rusty lunch box. Still, there was a comfort to it. The whole place looked like it had been dipped in marinara and sealed with a layer of parmesan dust.

Miles didn't care what the outside looked like. The air smelled of yeasty dough and pepperoni, and somewhere deep inside, he could practically hear the flattened dough circles flip as the chefs punched them up over their heads with a spin. He had seen it a hundred times, as had most students at Clementine High. If pizza was not what one was hankering for, the lure of Angelo's famous garlic knots was impossible to ignore. They drew in customers the way bug zappers drew flies, except with slightly more dignity and a lot more carbs.

He swung one leg over his bike, standing beside it with his hands in his pockets, scanning the street for signs of Harriet's car.

A minute passed. Then another.

Still no Harriet.

He took in an exaggerated lungful, rocking back on his heels. "Of course," he muttered, glancing at his watch. "She's probably measuring parking spaces for tire alignment."

Across the street, Harriet had clearly decided the tiny parking lot beside Angelo's was a no-go. She drove past a stack of pallets and a massive dumpster, bumping over a curb into the adjacent Piggly Wiggly grocery store lot. She rolled slowly, deliberately, through two rows of faded white lines, her head tilted in concentration.

Miles crossed his arms.

Harriet circled once. Then again. She seemed to be searching for two empty spaces end to end. Finally, she parked far away from the entrance, away from any other vehicles, and got out. She walked around her car, surveying it like she was checking a spaceship for landing damage.

"Come on!" Miles yelled from beside the restaurant. "You said you had to study! And I think my stomach is literally eating itself."

She ignored him. Took one more look at her front tire. Then

headed toward the smell of oregano and melty cheese. Harriet carried her backpack across her shoulder as she approached where Miles leaned smugly against the brick wall, one foot resting on the low ledge near the doorway. He glanced at his watch with theatrical impatience. His stomach groaned in protest. The Angelo's cartoon face smiled down at them, flaking paint above the billboard-size pizza pie that he momentarily wished was real. "What does a guy have to do around here to make good on a hard-earned slice of pizza?"

"Take a chill pill, dude. I'm good for it." She laughed.

Harriet wrinkled her nose and smiled. "Smells better than those little kids."

Miles inhaled deeply. "And like success. Hey, we did pretty well today."

A bell above the door jangled as they stepped in. Angelo's was a neighborhood staple with framed Italian sceneries and signed baseball cards for decor. A flickering neon sign in the window blinked HOT SLICE like a dare. Two middle-aged men chuckled loudly at some joke, seated at the counter as the chef, wearing a white T-shirt beneath his tomato-stained apron, pressed dough on to large silver trays. A baseball game played from a chunky TV set above the drink fountain.

Harriet pointed toward a booth along the far wall, past the worn arcade games and next to the jukebox. "Third one."

Miles tilted his head. "That's oddly specific."

"It's my lucky booth."

"What, did you win a scratcher here?"

"Scratcher? What's that?"

"Never mind. It's something my uncle introduced me to."

"Okay. Well, if you must know. I got a B-plus in chem after studying here once." She slid into the cracked vinyl seat, casually nudging her backpack over a tear in the upholstery.

"A legend is born," he said, dropping into the seat across from her. He thumped the laminated menu like a conga drum. "You're a strange one, Harriet."

"That's not very nice." She took the menu, half-ignoring his comment.

A gum-snapping waitress with dyed red curls and a MANDY name tag sauntered over, chewing hard. "What'll it be?"

Miles leaned forward. "Two slices of the special and a Dr Pepper."

Harriet scanned the smudged menu, brow furrowed like she was reading legal fine print. "One special, but light sausage, extra pepperoni. No onions or green peppers."

Mandy raised a penciled brow without lifting her pen. "So . . . sausage and pepperoni."

Harriet lifted one shoulder. "With the veggies on the side."

Mandy turned and pointed at a hand-scrawled sign taped to the back of a flattened pizza box above the counter. The marker ink had bled slightly into the cardboard fibers. "No substitutions. It's the special."

"Fine." Harriet exhaled slowly, adjusting her backpack farther into the corner of the booth. "Regular it is. And water, please."

Mandy gave a theatrical shrug like Harriet had just asked for sushi at the bowling alley, then walked off. She shoved their order onto the spinning silver wheel. "Order up!"

Miles raised both hands in mock surrender, leaning back in his seat like a man under investigation. "Complicated much?"

"I like what I like," Harriet said, folding the laminated menu closed with careful precision. Her voice had a dry edge, but her eyes sparkled like she kind of enjoyed the pushback.

"Must be exhausting being you." He smirked, then turned his attention to the condiment tray. In a smooth series of movements, he began stacking jelly packets and creamers into a lopsided tower like it was a high-stakes Jenga match. The grape jelly wobbled on top, slightly askew.

"Keep talking and I'll knock it over," Harriet warned, narrowing her eyes as she leaned forward, pointer finger hovering just above the fragile tower. She moved slowly, dramatically, inching across the table like a game-show contestant making the final move in a televised showdown.

Miles raised his eyebrows but didn't flinch. He reached over, plucked a sugar packet from the tray, and, with all the flair of a magician, balanced it delicately atop the teetering structure. The tower swayed slightly.

"Oh no," he said. "My entire architectural legacy is in your hands."

"Think I won't?" she replied.

"I know you will." He looked up. "You don't back down from a challenge. I like that about you."

Their eyes locked in mock-serious tension as the sugar packet leaned just a bit too far. Harriet's finger twitched. Then she pulled back with a smirk, letting the structure wobble on.

"Did you bring in your homework?" Miles asked finally, pushing the salt and pepper shakers out of the way like clearing a chessboard.

"I did, just in case, but it's better if it stays in here," Harriet said, patting the top of her bag. "Didn't want Dostoevsky soaking up pepperoni grease."

Miles let out a theatrical gasp. "Excuse me, scholar."

"Some of us like our suffering Russian and slightly dry."

He leaned forward, resting his elbows on the table. "And some of us like our homework wrinkled and smelling like mozzarella. It builds character."

"It builds a tragic GPA."

"Which is still more optimistic than *Crime and Punishment*, so . . . you're welcome."

She rolled her eyes but smiled, reaching for the last jelly packet like it was a prize and aiming it at him.

Their food arrived quickly: three oversize slices balanced on two red plastic trays. Miles immediately dusted his with red pepper flakes. Harriet began meticulously blotting hers with napkins, pressing into grease from every angle like she was documenting a crime scene.

"You've done this before," he said, mid-chew.

"I've seen the oil pool under that slice. I'm not letting it into my body."

Miles tilted his head. "Tell me something. Why are you really throwing that Gatsby party?"

Harriet paused, mid-blot. "Because I do some kind of end-of-the-year party every year. And because it's fun?"

He looked at her through the lower half of his eyelids. "Is it? I mean, what does one do at this Gatsby party?"

"Not everything is about skipping class or brewing existential dread over pizza. Some of us like finer things. We sip bubbly drinks, have a bonfire, and play good music."

"Touché. That does sound kind of cool." He took another bite. "You're not what I expected."

"I get that a lot."

The jukebox shifted records to a song by Lionel Richie. Something warm and familiar. Harriet slid out of the booth and pointed toward the hallway near the kitchen. "Bathroom break. Don't let the sugar packets unionize while I'm gone."

"Copy that." He looked longingly at his nearly empty plate.

The hall smelled like bleach and marinara as she walked past the kitchen into some dark corner with poor lighting. She nudged the bathroom door open with her elbow and winced. Exposed pipes rattled. A roll of paper towels sat sagging on the sink, and the mirror bore a piece of masking tape that read, *You're beautiful. Don't listen to Chad.*

When Harriet returned, wiping her damp hands on her jeans, she found the table transformed into a miniature tennis court. Miles sat with one foot over his knee in the booth like an overly confident game designer, surveying his creation with the quiet intensity of someone who'd clearly taken this too far. Jelly packets stood upright like lopsided players, grape on one side, strawberry on the other. Sugar packets had been lined up with precision across the center, forming a makeshift net. Napkins framed the boundaries, torn edges fluttering slightly every time someone opened the front door.

"What is this chaos?" she asked, sliding back into the booth and eyeing the scene like she was about to call in a referee.

"Tactical layout," Miles said without looking up. "For tomorrow's lesson. Kids will be here. We'll be here. Ball goes here. Blood probably here." He punctuated the sentence by dramatically flinging a ketchup packet off the edge of the table like a casualty of war.

Harriet snorted. "You used the condiments as civilians?" she asked, playing along.

"Only the brave ones."

She reached for a creamer, turning it slowly in her fingers. "This one's me?"

"Obviously."

"You made me too tall," she said, inspecting the creamer's towering shape with a dubious frown.

"I was being generous," he replied, stacking two sugar packets beside her creamer as if building her fan club.

She tucked the creamer carefully into the back corner of the napkin court. "Fine. But I will teach the serve first."

Miles squinted at her. "You always have to be in control?"

She met his gaze, deadpan. "You don't?"

He shrugged, flicking a salt packet into the spectator section. "Not when it's someone who rewrites the rules every five minutes."

She smirked. "That's not control. That's adaptation."

They sat there for a beat, the booth glowing softly with the flicker of the neon sign outside, caught mid-blink somewhere between HOT and OT. The red light filtered through the window in lazy pulses, painting streaks across Miles's cheek and the laminated tabletop.

"Thanks for helping with the car," she said finally, her voice quieter now.

"Thanks for not quitting after the first bloody nose," he replied, giving a small nod toward the imaginary battlefield. "I just could not stand one more Saturday detention."

She leaned back, hands folded behind her head like she was already ten years more mature and had her future entirely planned out. "I've got four more days to decide."

Miles took a long sip of his soda, letting the straw squeak against the ice. "We'll see if you survive."

"I'll survive," she said, sitting up straight again and brushing crumbs off her jeans. "Question is . . . will they?"

Miles grinned but didn't argue.

Outside, the sign blinked again, casting red-and-white shadows in uneven beats. Inside the booth, neither one moved to leave. The jelly players waited silently on the court, sugar net still standing.

Chapter Fourteen

The world around Harriet shifted again. The flash of the sign stayed with her the longest as the restaurant faded away. In the new scene, she heard the harmonies of a choir and a random metal folding chair scraping along the floor as one of the many faces around her adjusted in their seat.

She blinked and found herself seated among a sea of black robes. Her hands clutched a small purse and a folded graduation program. A red-and-white tassel swayed at her cheek with every turn of her head. Someone in the stands coughed lightly, the auditorium lights shining brightly over rows of families packed into the bleachers. The muggy air buzzed with the well-rehearsed harmony of high school choir students nailing a four-part arrangement.

"Hey, Trixie. How much longer before we walk?" Harriet felt a sensation in her pinky, and she willed it to move. It jiggled a little to the right. She just had to try to interact, if getting out of this thing was futile, at least she could mess around with it. Her own past she was being forced to relive. It was only a simulation, after all.

Trixie held up her own program and whispered, "After this song and Dr. Kenyanson's speech. Which I doubt will be half as interesting as yours."

~

GROWN HARRIET GROANED INWARDLY. Oh God. That speech.

She glanced down at her phone. The screen was grayed out, the frog from the app frozen mid-smirk.

"This is so cringy," she muttered under her breath, "I think I quoted U2 and told everyone to love themselves. Like, unironically."

Her pinky twitched, and she tested her ability to move. She managed to raise and lower it with the beat of the music.

"Yeah," she whispered to Trixie, playing along now, hoping to get out of this one way or another. "I think the principal opens with a mic fumble."

"What?" Trixie paused, a digital twitch flashing across her face.

"Dr. Kenyanson. Watch. He'll drop the mic adjusting the stand."

Seconds later, the principal fumbled with the podium and knocked the mic off its stand with a hollow thud.

Trixie turned, wide-eyed. "How did you . . ." Her face twitched again, a subtle tic.

Harriet straightened in her seat, feeling more volition. Maybe this was it. Maybe she could push back. She poured all her mental energy into changing the dialogue, breathing deeply from within the Experience chamber.

"This isn't real," she said, locking eyes with Trixie. "You're not really here." She looked down at her flexed pinky, and a knowing smile crept across her face.

The moment shattered. Trixie blinked once, then her smile flickered beneath her graduation cap. Her image blurred, then reset into the darkness of the Experience chamber. And Harriet was alone again. No choir, no audience. Just blackness and the faint glow of her frozen phone screen.

"What now?" she said, her voice a whisper, low and calculating as she planned her next highjacking of the Experience. She couldn't rely on this bug-filled simulation to figure out her future life. She didn't need this level of intervention. She knew her life was a product of the choices she had made, and none of them had been that terrible.

It was eerie how specific these memories were. Eerie and invasive, in her opinion, and she had seen enough. It was ironic how she had been accepted to the top university of her choice, made speeches like these, joined all of the right organizations, pulled in high enough grades, and yet it was simply unfortunate that she didn't qualify for enough financial aid to make that plan work. Her hours of volunteering were simply not going to foot the bill and ironically, her ideal of college life was simply going to be…different than she had imagined. She had let this machine extract enough from her. It was time to take control and get back to her own, mundane life.

A speech bubble popped up on the phone screen, the frog's pixelated flipper patting its light-green chest. *Under repair. My bad.* The phone screen went blank with a digital snap, but only for a moment.

The frog reappeared and snapped a fly out of midair.

Again. The buzzing fly and *snap!*

And again with a text bubble. *Grabbing your young-adult memories now. Prepare for our next Experience!*

"Oh, for crap sakes!" Harriet narrowed her eyes. "I am not doing this again. How do I get out of this thing?!"

Chapter Fifteen

L ight bloomed through the blackness as Prince shrieked mid-song. The sound pierced the air of the Experience, jolting her to attention. Harriet found herself standing on the back lawn of her home, the fixer-upper her family finally finished, wearing a silver flapper dress with fringe that danced every time she moved. "Oh, I loved that dress," she said as the memory enveloped her senses and immersed her in the scene.

The backyard glittered with fairy lights and dime-store lanterns strung between trees and fences. A folding table draped in a lace thrift-store curtain sagged beneath towers of plastic cups and a punch bowl filled with ginger ale and floating green grapes. A stack of paperbacks with a sign in front that read, TAKE ONE! sat beside a makeshift photo booth. A coat rack next to it featured a smattering of secondhand hats, including straw boaters and fedoras. On the table lay an assortment of feather boas, all props to use in front of the painted cardboard cutout.

The cardboard was cut into the shape of a yellow car with the words *Old Sport* painted in cursive. For good measure, Harriet had insisted that a large poster board with circle-framed eyeglasses from the novel was also hanging from the second-level window above it.

The Gatsby eyes of God were watching over this senior party. And it was going to be the best.

Claire from her English class sat on a stool, holding a Polaroid camera, ready to get group pictures. She was eyeing up the paperbacks. Janet and Trevor, now over the drama after surviving AP Econ together with Harriet gave them a type of respect old war buddies could have, were nuzzling into the seats behind the convertible photo prop, waiting for Claire to take another shot, while Harriet walked the perimeter of her parents' lawn in low heels. She straightened tea lights and repositioned the record player, an old-timey one she had borrowed from her great-aunt, the one that skipped the record every time someone bumped the table. The Gatsby party was in full swing—no alcohol, but plenty of fizz and posturing.

Harriet blinked against the warm breeze and sipped from a cup of ginger ale. It bubbled up her nose, and she sneezed. She wore a beaded headband across her forehead. Her hair was swept into a low bun with finger waves attempted with a super-sticky gel, and she wore the best vintage-style dress she could borrow from Trixie's old dance costumes.

A boy wearing a sparkly gold suit coat tossed a Hacky Sack into the air. A small circle of suit-wearing seniors tapped at the crocheted ball, flipping it between them and keeping it from falling to the ground. Another tripped over a lawn chair, laughing as he spilled his drink.

Carli was near the fire, in charge of the s'mores-making and the mixtape music. A cassette from Journey was playing on the oversize boom box, and she started belting out lyrics to "Don't Stop Believin'." It was famously off-key but with enough enthusiasm for all the others around the bonfire to join in singing the power ballad—the cluster of seniors linking together, arm to arm, before jetting off to the next stages of their lives.

"Hey," Harriet said casually, approaching a knot of half-lost souls near the lilac hedge. One kid had a bottle of nasty-looking schnapps poking out from his trendy suit jacket pocket. "Thanks for coming. Don't get caught, okay?"

They raised their cups in vague agreement, and she recognized Juan Pablo under the slicked-back hair. They had worked on a project together this year in stats class, but rarely spent time together outside of school, adding to the awkward request.

He assured her, "Yeah, he hasn't had this stuff before. We'll keep an eye on him."

"Nice party, Harriet," Quintin said politely, his hair sliding over and back in a sharp side part.

"Thanks. You guys should get a picture." She pointed toward Claire, who waved back. One of the boys darted to the edge of the lawn and threw up behind the lilac bush with the urgency of someone betrayed by bad drinks and teenage bad choices.

"Is he okay?"

"Taco Bell," another replied with a shrug. "He'll live."

Juan Pablo took him under the arm and ushered him to a lawn chair, where he flopped down, a little green. Quintin walked to the photo booth and posed behind the car with the crew, smiling like Gatsby himself, Leon sitting next to him but refusing to smile for aesthetic reasons. Claire happily snapped the picture, and then they waited as the film developed. She gently waved the photo as they all watched the image slowly materialize.

As Juan Pablo wrangled their vomiting friend, a fifth guy approached the snack table. His hair was lacquered back with an appropriate amount of hair cream, and he wore a Black Flag tee tucked into baggy jeans like it was a statement. Harriet paused. She hadn't thought he would follow through on his promise to come to her "literary party."

"Hey, Miles," Quentin said from across the patio with a conspicuous grin. "Nice to see you made it. How did your breakup go?"

Miles. Miles, who seemed to have given up on the *Smiles* bit now that they were all leaving high school. He waved off the comment and turned toward Harriet, laughing lightly. "Thanks, Quint."

She pushed her long bangs to one side of the headband. "Didn't expect you to show."

"Chuck and Juan Pablo made me. Heard it was something I had to see to believe." He smirked and looked around at the flickering lights. "I like the ambiance."

She glanced at his shirt. "Very 1920s."

He held up a plastic cup. "Is this the fake champagne?"

"Yes. Ginger ale."

They stood near the edge of the firelight, an art deco poster plastered to the window behind them, awkwardly aligned just outside the conversation circles. The music from the record player shifted to something tinny. Near them, Ella Fitzgerald piped through the wooden cabinet as someone hand-cranked the antique player into life.

"So," she asked, "you sticking around or taking off for college?"

"Taking a semester off and living at home. Working at Best Buy. Saving money."

She nodded. "Makes sense. College is expensive."

He nudged her cup with his own. "What about you?"

"Community college. Staying local. The Olds still runs and I can live at home." She gestured behind her. "My mom's happy and thinks it will keep me out of frat house basements." A weak, but somewhat true joke.

"Gatsby would be proud."

"Hardly. But I have my classes already. A bunch of pre-reqs." She sighed and took a sip.

"Moped Guy?" Miles asked after a pause. "If you don't mind me asking . . ."

"No problem. It's fine. Actually, we broke up." She took another sip. "Gone. After prom. Long story."

He tilted his head, his voice quieter now, grinning slightly. "He wanted to have sex. You didn't."

Her eyes widened. "Who told you that?"

"Just a guess."

Harriet stared toward the fire pit, now more ember and flicker than a raging burning of all their past notebooks and assignments. "You're not wrong."

"Good for you," he said. "Also, my girlfriend went to prom with a college guy. So we're both free agents now."

Harriet smirked. "How poetic."

They stood in silence, watching Chuck stagger toward the fire again, his shirt askew and a feather boa now tied around his forehead like a crown. The mixtape that she and Trixie had painstakingly curated to include all the high school favorites stopped suddenly at the end of the cassette. They heard someone near the fire tune into the local top 40 radio station, overpowering the Ella Fitzgerald song from the crank record player with a bouncy Cyndi Lauper tune about girls just wanting to have fun.

"I was going to do paper lanterns, the kind with real candles," she said, changing the subject, "but I was worried someone would set the neighbor's shed on fire."

Miles gestured toward the string lights and his boa-wearing friend wandering a bit too closely to the flames. "I understand your concern." He took a sip. "Nice party, Harriet. It's already better than prom."

The firelight danced along his jaw, softening the edges. He looked older. Not in a bad way. Just farther along in something Harriet hadn't caught up to yet. She felt the space between them waver in her chest like the cling in cellophane, hard to sort out.

He turned to go after Chuck, who had tripped into the garden again. "I think me and the guys will be going."

"Hey!" she called after him. "Thanks for coming."

He paused and grinned over his shoulder. "Thanks for inviting me, Daisy Buchanan."

AS THE LAST of the party friends had left and the string lights twinkled above her, Harriet turned toward the hedge where the boy had thrown up. She grabbed the hose from the garden and turned the nozzle to spray away the evidence, then noticed the scene start to shimmer. The grass dimmed. The fire slowed to a motionless flicker.

The Gatsby party flickered out like a burned-out bulb, and the ambient light dimmed around Harriet. The last echoes of laughter faded as people left for their cars parked along the front lawn, as if the whole memory was being played back on a phonautograph.

Harriet stood in the dark. The blackness wasn't empty. It was too quiet, like sound was being held back by something just out of reach. She glanced at the phone for the frog's next announcement. But the void stayed quiet.

The air stilled. Then a voice filtered through it.

"Parallel lines. Parallel lives. Always the same distance apart."

Harriet turned sharply. "Ted? Is it you? Can you tell me what's going on here?"

No response. Just the digitalized sound of the frog app booting up again. It opened its mouth, and the message repeated above it.

Parallel lines. Parallel lives.

"How cryptic," she grumbled. Her phone buzzed in her hand, and the image changed. The frog turned to face her with the blocky message *We'll be right back!* floating above it.

She groaned. "Seriously? Another glitch? The Experience is taking me straight to the loony bin." Her voice echoed, but the world didn't shift. She waited in the darkness, losing her last ounce of patience.

"Why are you showing me this?" she asked aloud. "What's the point?"

"Young-adult sequence is now finished loading. Prepare for your next Experience!"

Her phone buzzed, announcing her next transition. Overriding her complaints as a bystander in her own memory loop. This was nothing like what she had expected. What had she expected, exactly? Nothing like this.

Harriet stood in the darkness, the phone now glowing faint green in her hand. The frog blinked lazily.

"Let me out of this," she said, trying to steady her voice. "Enough is enough."

Still nothing. Just the frog now bouncing corner to corner in looped animation.

She squinted at it. "You're not funny. You're not helpful. You're not even cute."

No change in the chamber around her, just her growing sense of distance between her and the life she had had.

The voice above her returned, softer now. "You're remembering. That's the first step."

"First step to what?" she snapped back.

"We have to go back a little more. Be patient, Harriet. The futures are worth waiting for."

"What if I just want the life I was used to? Can I just stop this thing right now?"

"Sorry, the sequence has already been uploaded. Enjoy your Experience."

And a light fog swirled around her as the new scene blurred into view.

Chapter Sixteen

T he image of a science lab formed around her as she and a group of students watched the top of a large speaker. It was covered in a thin film, and a guy from class was pouring a silicon-like sand over the top surface. The music went from whimper to blast as the students gathered around, fingers tucked into their ears as they leaned over the speaker for a better look. The bass increased to a chest-thumping growl, and the sand began to dance. As it bounced, it re-formed into patterns, circular and alive.

What is that? She leaned in to look closer at the image that was blurred around the edges and narrowing its focus onto the speaker and the bouncing sand.

Sound. It's about sound.

Compression. Rarefaction. The words were written on the board behind them and progressively blurring into the background. She heard the droning soliloquy of her college physics professor explaining the properties of sound waves.

The peaks and valleys in waves. Always moving forward, never touching.

Like me and Miles? What's the pattern here? What's this whole Experience thing about, anyway? One thing was sure: If she was going to get out of this thing anytime soon, she would have to focus on keeping her head.

Cool as a cucumber, Harriet.

She took one breath. Then another.

The void stretched around her again as the image melted away from her. That damn frog blinked up at her from the phone's screen, its little belly rising and falling like it had lungs. Like it was waiting patiently for her to enter the next stage of this crazy fever dream with its mischievous smile that was wearing on her. After a moment, the message appeared: *Initializing sequence.*

"Okay," she whispered, softer this time. "Where to now?"

A low hum vibrated the floor under her feet. Light began to bleed into the darkness, not from above or around, but from beneath her. Like stage lighting through fog.

Her shoes weren't the clunky loafers from high school or the low heels from the Gatsby party. She was barefoot. And the smell in the air had changed.

Not hair spray. Not cafeteria pizza. Not smoldering homework pages in a bonfire.

Salty air.

The hum shifted into the tonal sound of ocean waves, soft and slow.

Finally! She sighed and relaxed just a tiny bit.

The light solidified. Sand appeared under her feet, soft and pale gray in the dim moonlight. Harriet looked up. The stars weren't ones she remembered, but fixed in place and symmetrical.

She stood at the edge of a beach. The moonlight was reflected in a way that made her feel more like she was on a Hollywood set than at a real ocean. The water appeared to stretch endlessly, quiet and dark, movement subtle and soft. She felt no wind, no cold. Just the weightless hush of being very far away from everything that had once mattered.

Her phone beeped once. *Memory set complete. Initializing parallel track*, the frog announced within its neon-rimmed speech bubble.

"What parallel track?" Harriet's stomach dropped. She looked closer at the phone screen. "What track are we doing now? This one is just fine. Where is the Pause button on this thing?"

The words faded and the frog waved a goodbye. Huh. That was unusual, as if anything she had gone through in the last who-knows-how-many hours had been anything but highly unusual.

A figure stood down the beach, barely visible, facing the water. Still like the barely moving waves. Familiar like the memories, even detached and disjointed as they were.

Harriet started walking, "Hey, you over there?" She could walk freely in this Experience, not like one of her preset memories, she determined. She was willing herself to walk, and she was walking. "Hey, you! I need to ask you a question."

The man turned his head slowly, his face just an outline in the moonlight.

Just as she took another step, the image jolted like a scratched record skipping mid-song. The ocean blinked out, back into the dark-ness she had begun to hate. On her phone, the frog had been replaced by a clunky boot-up screen that read, *Error 409: Reality Misalignment.*

"No! Just stop this." Harriet shook her phone. "Why can't I have nice things?"

The frog on her phone popped back up, now holding a rubber chicken. It grinned maniacally. *One moment, please!* its speech bubble read.

Harriet stared at the screen in the quiet. She had no recourse, no contact phone number to complain to, no way to storm out. "One moment, please," she read aloud. She was on the verge of laughing but wasn't sure that tears wouldn't soon follow if she did.

"Psych." Above her, light computerized laughter followed. "Just kidding. It's just a little temporary setback."

"Psych?" Harriet blinked. Hard. "What kind of computer system would say that?"

The beach was gone. The sand, the stars, the whole poignant moment erased. But that voice . . . the intonation . . . the awkward coughs and pauses as if someone were reading off a script they hadn't rehearsed.

"Who is running this thing?" she questioned aloud. "Ted? Was that you just now? I thought this was a noninvasive AI guide that led me through my scenes and was deleted when the Experience was over. You said that!"

But the darkness gave way to a blur of scenes as if the machine was confused and blending her visions into one. She braced herself mentally for whatever came next.

The blending scenes landed on her standing in the middle of a blank school hallway, holding a plastic cafeteria tray, and staring at a motivational poster about excellence. There was an overwhelming feeling of déjà vu due to being ripped away from the first calming moment she had had in a decade.

Her phone buzzed again. The frog's speech bubble read, *Reinitializing emotional sequence. Please hold.*

She sighed, looked straight up, and said, "Seriously, I don't know how much more of this I can take."

The frog winked, the speech bubble faded, and he face-planted.

"Now I really feel like you're just messing with me." Harriet stared around the school hallway that faded once again. "Who's up there running this?" she shouted. "I need an answer!"

But there was no reply.

PART II
Sound Waves

Chapter Seventeen

M iles sat in his home office, several large monitors casting a cold glow into the dark room. His keyboard rested at a precise angle, the mouse to its right nestled beside a cracked picture frame that wobbled slightly on its bent corner. The glass was cool to the touch and dust-lined, like it hadn't been moved in months. A relic of a memory he couldn't quite let go of, no matter how hard he tried to clean around it.

Streams of information coursed across his screens. He was the type to make only the most informed of decisions. He had built his career, his reputation, his whole life on this principle. As the screen pulsed with new data, he muttered, "I kept thinking we were just running side by side, always just missing the slight opportunity to ignite any sort of spark. But we weren't side by side, living our own lives completely compartmentalized. We were like pushing the air between us, something static that reoccurred, connecting us and reconnecting our lives. Every meeting, every near miss. All compression and release. Like sound waves."

He opened a new notebook, energized by the epiphany, and quickly jotted down the phrase: *Longitudinal Patterning—Predictive Modeling of Emotional Frequencies.*

The photo in the frame showed him grinning at the top of a mountain, blue weatherproof jacket zipped to the chin, sunglasses reflecting a bright sky. The other half of the photo was shoved beneath the glass, where he had hastily ripped it, but couldn't bring himself to throw either part away, like he had started to erase the past but stopped short. A woman's mitten peeked from the torn edge. A clumsy farewell.

Last night—or, technically, very early that morning—Miles had finally taken the photo from the shelf where it had been sulking beneath a layer of dust. He had intended to deal with it once and for all, but it had ended up back on his desk.

The photo wasn't logical. It no longer served a purpose. He knew it, but he couldn't reconcile the feelings holding him back. The feeling of being stuck in a loop that he couldn't resolve or find a better way to live.

He grabbed the photo, turned it once in his hand, hesitated for half a breath, then tossed the whole frame with a dull clatter into the metal trash can beside his desk. The glass didn't break, but the sound still felt final.

He didn't look back at it. Instead, he leaned forward, elbows pressed to the cool edge of the desk, eyes narrowed at the glow of the monitors. Lines of code and data models pulsed faintly in blues and greens, the only light in the room in the wee hours that had snuck up on him once again. His fingers hovered over the keyboard for a moment, then resumed their work: searching, sorting, recalibrating. It was like he could code his way out of his memories.

At first, he'd only analyzed his own life.

That had been the safest place to start and the only set of variables he truly understood. All those years spent building systems to diagnose other people's inefficiencies, designing tools to optimize behavior, to tweak performance or engagement or retention, it had always been about external solutions. Apply logic. Find the gap. Fill it.

But this time, he had turned his focus inward.

He had mapped timelines. Traced decisions. Flagged inconsistencies in how he had showed up for others, how he had backed away at the wrong moments or pushed too hard at the right ones. Taking what he knew from decades of solving other people's problems through technology, he had turned that same relentless thought process on himself, his relationships, his silences, his well-constructed walls.

If patterns could be broken, then loneliness could be too. That was the theory, at least.

He wasn't coding toward happiness, exactly. He was just trying to understand how he had gotten here. This drifted version of himself was who he was now, but somehow also not himself: brilliant developer, but alone. What were the keystrokes that led to isolation? What algorithms of avoidance had he run so often that they'd become automatic? Why couldn't he find a balance of push and pull that wouldn't tear apart his most important relationships?

The answer, he hoped, was somewhere in the data. The determination—stubbornness Claire would have called it—was his quality that helped him build this company. That need for control and avoidance of chaos had brought harmony to their inventive ventures, but they also built walls that blocked intimacy and emotional depth with the people closest to him.

It wasn't just Claire, or Emma, or Tina. When did he last reach out to a buddy from the old neighborhood? Or pick up the phone to call his father? His relationships were simple, functional, and compartmentalized to mostly work. Anyone else in his life could claim their relationships were splintered and fractured and weathered by the lack of upkeep. He chose to focus on his patterns that led to relationship neglect and the data to be his lens. And if he could find the proper break points in his own life, maybe he could do more than just fix what was broken.

Maybe he could build something worth keeping.

He built a database of his own life. Hundreds of files. Digitized yearbooks. Neighborhood maps. Archived social media photos. All to chart his own behavioral drift and emotional highs and lows.

The Experience App was supposed to be personal. It was going to be clean and contained. Nobody wanted that level of personal information out in public. Most people cringed at knowing about their true patterns at all. And yet, he was making a machine to reconstruct his most intimate thoughts and emotions in order to predict how he would behave in the future. And . . . hopefully avoid the same pattern of mistakes.

He had finally admitted to himself that it had started the night Claire had ghosted him.

They were supposed to grab Thai after her Wednesday yoga class, just like always. A standing date. Nothing fancy. But when she didn't show up, didn't text, didn't even send one of her trademark "Running late, save me spring rolls" messages, something in him shifted.

At first, he'd tried to rationalize it. Traffic. A dead phone. A momentary lapse. He waited on the bench outside the restaurant, watching condensation gather on the inside of the entrance window, trying to convince himself it wasn't what it looked like.

But by the time the string lights clicked off above the patio and the restaurant staff began stacking chairs, it was obvious. She wasn't coming.

When her message finally arrived two days later, it was short, cool, and final, and it hit harder than he had expected.

I'm sorry. I need space. Your moods are too hard to guess lately. I can't keep orbiting you like this. Please don't make this harder.

He read it twice. Then again.

She called it *space*, but he knew it was something else. A fade-out, clean and quiet. She didn't want to talk it through. She didn't want to fix it. She wanted out.

That night, as he sat alone at his desk, her used chopsticks from weeks ago still in the kitchen sink, he had wanted to know what had gone wrong. Not just with her, but with the others too. Why his patterns kept looping into the same lonely conclusions, why every relationship seemed to collapse under the weight of his own precision. The harder he tried to stabilize things, the more brittle they became.

"What time is it in London right now?" he asked.

His laptop responded, "It is ten-oh-three a.m. in London with cloudy skies. A bit balmy for March, with a temperature of twelve degrees Celsius."

He toyed with an intuition, an instinct that his business partner would be ready to entertain this radical idea and consider putting the company's resources into developing it. He urgently felt he needed her support; he had to dive in and launch a prototype before this idea bounced away from his drive to do the unspeakable. If he was going to make a public version of this process to work for others who wanted clarity in their lives, he couldn't do it alone.

He shoved in his earbuds and called Adriana using a voice command. The search engine refreshed, splashing his screen with therapy ads and self-help blogs. Her face blinked into the corner of his screen.

"Top girlfriend problems," he muttered, typing.

"Hello, Miles. I'm doing fine, thanks," Adriana said dryly, not looking up from her spreadsheet. "What can I do for you at, what . . . three in the morning your time?"

"That. Right there." He shared his screen. "This is the problem we should solve."

She exhaled, nudging her glasses up with a knuckle, her expression hovering somewhere between mild exasperation and fond resignation. Behind her, a ficus stood tall against a sunlit window. "Miles, you and Claire only broke up a couple of months ago."

"It's not about Claire."

She raised one palm, flat and steady. "You sure about that?"

He didn't pause. "It's a pattern. Relationships fall apart. People fumble through the same messes. We could actually help. Isn't that what we said we wanted? Back when we still believed we could change the world?"

Her gaze flicked from the spreadsheet to his face. "Sure, relationships are an evergreen concern. Great for creating buzz around products. And solving problems around them will always have a special appeal to the public. But have you thought this through?"

"I have." He spun in his chair, the bearings groaning. "And I need to fix that squeak. It's going to drive me mad."

He ducked under the desk. Adriana listened, leaning back in her chair as he pulled the can from a desk drawer. From beneath, his voice floated up, low and certain. "Not a dating app. Not another swipe-your-soul-away startup. Something else." He paused, hands still over the chair's base. For once, the idea didn't feel like desperation. It felt like clarity.

She lifted her mug, the company logo beneath British and American flags catching the screen's glow. After a sip, she set it down and tilted her head. "Alright, then. What are we building? This . . . memories reconstructer."

"Something that shows people the truth about their life experiences. Not curated feeds or motivational quotes. Actual playback from people's real lives. Honest reflection on what they have really done. A forced moment of reflection to cause them to pause and think about the consequences of their next action before moving forward. Moving forward into a more thoughtful manner."

Adriana raised a brow. "That's either revolutionary or wildly naive. And possibly both."

He straightened up. "We haven't made anything new in years. This could be it."

"I've been meaning to talk to you about that."

"Then let's talk. Now. Because I think this one could actually matter."

"Alright." She folded her arms behind her head. "Alright, genius. Pitch me."

"We document everything: social media, emails, photos, journals. And people make bad decisions. What if we used that to let people look back and actually see the patterns? Not months later, but now."

Adriana lowered her glasses. "People don't want truth. They want dopamine."

"And look where that's gotten us."

She studied him. "Been doing a lot of reflecting, have you?"

"Didn't have a choice."

She nodded, the hint of a smile tugging at her mouth. "Reflection is the sandbox of life. Build something. Knock it down. Build again. But what you're suggesting is that we code a moral compass."

"No. Not morality. Just cause and effect. Show people their lives like an immersive movie, then offer alternate versions. Let them see what could come next, dependent on their patterns and how they choose to repeat them. Or not."

"So we feed their data into a story engine. And use some kind of GPT?"

"Exactly."

"Sounds like a lawsuit waiting to happen."

"Encrypted. Completely private. No servers. Just local and in their own private space."

"Still not therapy-certified. Still sounds like a robot-led intervention."

He glanced at the trash can. "It's always too late to do the right thing. What if it didn't have to be?"

Someone spoke off-camera on Adriana's end. She nodded at them and turned back, holding up one finger as if to signal that the call would soon be finished. "I wouldn't want to relive my past. It was brutal enough once."

"Even if you could improve your future?"

"That's exactly how time-travel movies start, and there is always a cost to messing around with time continuums." Adriana looked back at her screen, losing interest, but letting Miles finish.

"I don't watch movies. Waste of time."

"That tracks. You're the only tech guy I know who still hasn't streamed a single series. And besides, my life is absolutely perfect right now." She waved again toward the woman with a bobbed haircut who appeared from the door behind her. The woman gave Adriana a squeeze and a kiss for a moment on-camera and said, "Hi, Miles. Jeez, you're up late. Working long hours again?"

"Hi, Tanya. Yes. I have to work when the ideas do."

"Don't forget to get some sleep!" She waved and turned to leave. "We've got a luncheon to go to soon. Hope you don't mind."

"I'll be off soon, I promise," Miles said with a smile. Tanya was always the cheerful counterpart to Adriana's steely, serious nature. "It's good to see you."

Adriana leaned into the camera, getting down to the business aspects of Miles's next big idea. "So who's signing up for this? Most people already believe the lies they tell themselves for free."

"Not everyone. Some people are ready to know how their patterns are self-sabotaging their lives. They need to know. I'm telling you, this thing will sell."

"It's honest at its core, I'll give you that. But it's also creepy as hell."

"Maybe creepy is what people need." He was not ready to let this project get lost in some emotional debate when all it really was was binary code. A tool to help people make better decisions.

She tapped her glasses against her chin. "Fine. We'll talk about it tomorrow. Just don't wake us up again at five a.m like last week. Tanya already gave me the look. So it's time to sign off."

"Duly noted." Miles waved as she stood and backed away from the camera. Adriana gave a small wave and clicked her keyboard.

The call ended.

Miles sat still, staring at a blinking cursor on a blank screen. The hum of the hard drive's cooling fans filled the silence, steady and indifferent. The room felt colder now, like the air itself was waiting for him to move. Then he opened his photo archive and started selectively reviewing his past.

Claire on a hike. Forced smiles with coworkers. Blurry bar nights with names he barely remembered. And one grainy shot of him alone on a balcony, city lights behind him, his expression unreadable.

Then: a folder marked *Personal*. Essays, journal scans, documents from the late nineties.

What patterns do we miss while we're living them?

What if something could show us?

He was going to find out.

Chapter Eighteen

"Am I your guinea pig?" Harriet shouted, stumbling once more through the dark, glossy void of the Experience chamber. Her phone pulsed dimly in her hand, the frog logo spiraling at a crawl, slower than before, as if mocking her. "Dude! I didn't sign up to be part of your science experiment!"

A faint odor of drying clay and coconut swirled around her, cloying and unplaceable. It mingled with the creeping nausea she'd come to associate with these transitions, like an elevator dropping mixed with vertigo. She pressed her palm to her forehead and groaned, the sound tight in her throat. "I'm going to sue. For mental stress. And stuff."

"Don't worry, Harriet," came the voice. Smooth. Synthetic. Gratingly calm. "It's only your memories. They are encrypted so only you, the user, can experience them."

"Right," she snapped, pacing in slow circles. "So how do you know about the graduation party? Or the conversation I had with Coach in high school? That was before this technology even existed!"

Her thumb jabbed at the screen, hard. Nothing responded. The frog winked at her, unbothered as the text bubble flashed, *Just a moment!*

"This is stalker-level creepy," she said. "Simulation or not, I'm done. I'm taking legal action, buddy."

"I am a computerized guide and part of your journey," the voice replied. Its inflection remained flat as glass. "When your journey is complete, I disappear with it, I assure you."

"I'm not buying that. A minute ago, I heard that guy, Ted. The guy who convinced me to try this thing in the first place."

"Harriet, you gave your consent to participate in the full Experience," the voice continued, unmoved. "Some minimal human interaction is integrated for user safety. We certainly don't want you to feel . . . uncomfortable."

A pause, then a faint, artificial sigh. "Harriet? This is Ted. I'm sorry, but I had to step in a little, especially while moving through some of the recalibration. Remember, this is part of the beta. Bugs are to be expected. Trust that this is all about you. You will return to your regular life shortly."

"Unless I choose to try something else, right? To try something more aligned to my hopes, dreams, skill set," she muttered. "Isn't that the point of this Experience?" She crossed her arms tightly over her chest, the phone trembling slightly in her hand. Her pulse pounded in her wrists, her breathing shallow and uneven. Anger and dread tangled inside her like tree roots beneath a sidewalk threatening to upend entire squares of concrete. Quiet but powerful.

The sense of being observed was overwhelming. Like something was peeling her open from the inside. She couldn't explain it. Not quite. But it scraped against her bones, charging against them with sharp energy like static. Too invasive to ignore. Too intimate to forgive.

They were just memories, yes. But they were hers. And this machine, this thing, had no right to have them, nonetheless drag her through them like this.

"The simulation requires one final adaptation from your young-adult years," the voice said. "Only then can your alternate life outcomes be generated. It would be a shame to miss your world adventures."

Harriet's eyes dropped to her wrist. The small tattoo of mountain peaks stood out in the dim glow, black lines smudged slightly over time, like memories faded at the edges. It was supposed to symbolize adventure, dreams, a version of herself that had once said yes to the unknown. Now it just made her feel left behind.

"Fine," she whispered. "Let's get this over with." If she could survive a week of performance evaluations, backlogged insurance claims, and communal microwaves that made everything smell like fish tacos, she could survive this. Probably.

She backed farther into the void, retreating inward to that mental bunker she'd built as early as in grade school, where she went during awkward moments, social events her parents dragged her to, and long evenings reading dry textbooks while the twins played make-believe in their shared room. It was a kind of invisible cloak, a disappearing act without leaving the room.

Maybe the guy was telling the truth. Maybe there was some value in all this. Maybe Ted hadn't totally scammed her. He had said there would be three possible life outcomes.

And she *was* curious. She had watched snippets of her past that were at minimum technologically fascinating; at least she could see what nonsense this machine came up with for her life. It was the same morbid curiosity people held for car crashes or bad reality TV. She needed to know if, according to this machine, she was doomed to become the woman who filed forms until retirement at seventy-three, died alone, and was found three days later with a half-finished yogurt in the fridge and a phone full of unread emails.

She closed her eyes and imagined herself somewhere else. A hut near the ocean. Sunlight warming her face. No clocks. No bosses. No calls to return.

"This next one better be worth it," she grumbled. She traced the edges of her tattoo again, grounding herself. "I can go anywhere on vacation if I finish this thing, right? Like Machu Picchu? I never made it that far south."

"Sorry," the voice chirped. "Sweepstakes valid for continental US only."

"Wait. Not even Hawaii?" she gasped. "Why are you messing with me? I don't understand why I can't see something better, something I didn't already live through. I can't control anything here. I can't leave."

"Please trust the process, Harriet."

She looked at her phone. The frog at the center of the screen, with that stupid grin and that stupid message: *Just one moment!*

"Listen, Ted—or whoever you are—this is not what I signed up for. The app's called the Experience. The very least you could offer is a fantasy ending in Maui. Or a margarita. Something."

"Hold for your next memory," the Guide said, overriding her. "We will check on the vacation specifications. They are in the terms and conditions."

"Thanks for nothing," she muttered.

The void rippled. Her surroundings grew lighter, as though someone had switched on the world behind a curtain. The blackness thinned like tissue paper, shifting, wavering, then tearing open into . . .

A college lecture hall.

The light conversation from students filled the air, layered with the screech of chair legs and the scratchy work sounds of mechanical pencils. Rows of faded-orange seats were packed with bodies half-unwrapped from bulky winter coats, scarves tossed across the backs like shed skins. There was a smell Harriet instantly remembered: wafting chemicals from the adjoining lab, dusty chalk, and the faint echo of that strange wax they used to polish this floor.

At the front of the room, a lanky, bearded professor, one of those types who probably lived in his office, was setting up a tabletop catapult using duct tape, a ruler, and what appeared to be the campus mascot in plush form. "So," he droned, "when we factor in angle and force . . ." He spun toward the chalkboard, unleashing a cascade of formulas in chalk, his arm a blur.

"Ted!" Harriet hissed, clutching her phone like it might lunge at her. She resisted the urge to throw it into the nearest virtual trash can or imaginary vortex. Instead, she jammed it deep into her purse, as though burying it might make the whole thing stop.

"Oh my gawd. Physics 101," she muttered, her sim-self lowering into a plastic seat that hadn't existed a moment ago. "When will the humiliation end?"

Chapter Nineteen

Harriet squinted toward the front of the lecture hall, her eyes half-closed with sleep, trying to make sense of the chalkboard mess. Letters, angles, velocity vectors, arrows pointing in every direction. The professor mumbled something about catapults and parabolic arcs while holding up a stuffed animal like it was the holy grail of Newtonian motion.

She sank lower in her seat. A chill ran through her, the type you get when you think something bad is going to happen and not just because you sloshed your way through a midwinter morning to get there.

Her coat was still on, zipped to her chin. She hadn't planned to stay long, just enough time to count for attendance and to grab the new handouts. As it was, she had been late and was stuck taking a seat to close to avoid the scrutiny of the professor. She hadn't even meant to come to class, honestly. But something about the ritual of trudging across campus, the sound of her boots on salt-scattered concrete, to see this semester through had pulled her here by inertia alone.

The cold plastic seat beneath her was less unforgiving than the late-work policy in this class. She could feel every vertebra with each slouch of her spine, every ache from the previous night's shift at the pub. Her back hurt from carrying trays of beer-filled mugs. Her hands smelled faintly of bleach and fried food no matter how often she washed them. There was a small tear in the hem of her sweats that she hadn't had time to sew.

She was here. But she didn't know why she was here.

Not just in this class. In college. In life.

Her pencil rolled off the long table stretching the length of her row of seats. She didn't reach for it. It clattered to the floor and rolled right to the front of the room.

"Hey."

The voice was too close and unmistakably familiar. She didn't need to look up to know it was him. His hair was longer, a little shaggier, and he wore an army-green painter's cap and light sweater that made him look more like a casual TA than a college sophomore. A canvas messenger bag sagged at his side, weighed down with God knew what —floppy disks, maybe. Graph paper.

He looked . . . at ease. As if the campus were his natural habitat. A mini-professor in the making.

THEY'D PASSED each other maybe once by the library steps. A quick recognition and rush off to other buildings and study groups. Once they had bumped into each other near the vending machines. But not a single word beyond "Hey" and "Nice to see ya." No shared classes. No planned study sessions. Just distance, stretched thin across time and coincidence. And to be honest, she hadn't noticed. Until now.

And now here he was. Sitting next to her in her simulated physics class from ages long gone.

Miles slid into the seat beside her with the confidence of someone who wanted to be there. His coat was already off, revealing a lanyard that said something about a coding symposium. His notebook lay open, lines of blocky handwriting crammed into every margin. He smelled like coffee and clean laundry.

"I didn't know you were in this section," he said.

Harriet gave a vague shrug. "I'm usually not."

"Fair. The guy sounds like a sleep mantra with a caffeine addiction." He laughed. "But he's not a bad guy, really."

She allowed herself a twitch of a smile. "He's got the catapult again."

Miles leaned forward, elbows on the desk. "I love the catapult. That's the good part. He launches that stuffed bear at the end and pretends it proves something about thermodynamics."

She glanced sideways at him. His face was flushed with excitement. He was actually into this. Harriet didn't even know what major she was supposed to have. She was technically undeclared, a title that felt like a cosmic insult.

In high school, she had believed that just getting into college meant everything would fall into place: a good job, some tightknit friends, a steady guy and a clear path to making a quaint little life with a brightly painted house, two and a half kids, and a dang dog. What she found was a muddy existence without the excitement she once had for dreams she wasn't sure she wanted, commuting between the extension college for classes, slinging beers at the local pub to pay for it, and her makeshift basement bedroom at her parent's house just to get by.

Miles nudged her notebook with his pen. "What're you working on?"

She blinked at the page. She hadn't written anything. Just a line of doodles along the margin: mountains, spirals, a coffee mug with wings.

The chalk screeched again and Harriet flinched. The professor was droning on. Something about trajectory. She didn't take notes. Her hand trembled slightly as she stared at her notebook, half from fatigue, half from nerves.

"Nothing," she muttered. "Trying to stay awake."

"You look like you're trying to disappear."

She stiffened. "I'm fine."

But she wasn't. She'd just pulled a double shift, burned her tongue on gas station chai, and this morning, someone had used the last clean towel. Her student loan notice had arrived in the mail that morning: some new balance she didn't understand, some warning about administrative holds.

"I heard you're doing something for winter break, you and those tech guys over there. All of your voices carry. It's true," she said, redirecting the conversation. "What is it, some big-deal tech retreat?"

Miles lit up. "Xanadu."

"Come again? Like that cheesy Olivia Newton-John movie?"

"That's what they're calling it. It's a weeklong intensive for emerging developers. Sponsored by four companies, Microsoft and Apple, and I think one from Sweden."

"Never heard of them. Sorry. Who names a company after fruit?"

Miles kept going. "There's even a software company that's offering internships to participants."

Harriet raised an eyebrow, pretending to have a clue about what he had said. "Sounds like nerd Disneyland."

He laughed. "Exactly. I'm pumped."

". . . and that brings us back to elastic potential energy," the professor was saying. His elbow knocked the catapult slightly as he turned toward the class. "Before we launch our volunteer here across the room . . ."

Muted laughter.

". . . I do want to note that the tutoring center has a few new names added to the roster. If you're struggling, and most of you are, you should take advantage. One of our new peer tutors is . . . let me see . . ." He squinted down at a clipboard and across the display table, almost making eye contact.

Harriet tried not to groan. Her neck ached. Her eyes were sandpaper.

"Ah, yes. Miles Hopper."

She froze. Maybe he wasn't looking directly at her.

A murmur passed through the rows. Several students looked around. And then he stood up. A quick nod and half wave as he quickly returned to his seat.

She looked at him. Really looked. He was already there, wherever "there" was. Already moving through doors she didn't know how to find, let alone open. He had direction. Belief in whatever would come next. Meanwhile, she was clinging to her Pell Grant by a thread and using cafeteria condiments as part of her meal planning strategy.

"I'm happy for you," she said, though her voice sounded far away. The kind of disconnect she found when she looked in the mirror each morning.

Miles seemed to pick up on it. He tilted his head. "You okay?"

"I just . . ." she trailed off, eyes flicking back to the chalkboard where the stuffed bear had been launched and was now lying face down on the tile. "I think I chose the wrong timeline."

"What?"

"Nothing." She waved it off. "Just tired. I worked another double at Club Pub last night."

He didn't push. That was one of his qualities she had appreciated, if she had thought about it at all. That he had the ability to throw her off and make her think. His ability to notice her without demanding, to make space for her without calling attention to it.

The professor's voice grew louder again, drawing formulas in the air like spells. Miles took notes. Harriet stared at her blank page and thought about disappearing. Like standing up and walking up the steps of shame, out the lecture hall door. Not in a dramatic way. Just quietly. In a way no one would notice.

She used to believe college was the place where everything would start. Now it felt like a waiting room filled with people who already had maps. And she'd misplaced hers months ago.

She pulled her sleeve down over her wrist and tried to focus.

THE LIGHT DRAINED AGAIN. The chalkboard, the stuffed bear mascot, the crowded lecture hall, all of it dissolved into static like a VCR tape hitting blank space.

Harriet felt as if she floated in the dark. Her fingers twitched, reaching instinctively for the strap of her college backpack, but of course it wasn't there. Just the smooth, senseless void of the Experience chamber, humming faintly like a refrigerator compressor working overtime.

She exhaled. Her breath sounded small. Defeated.

"Miles Hopper," she said aloud, testing the name like it might echo.

The Guide didn't answer.

Of all the possible memories, that's what the machine had dragged up? Not a beach weekend or a late-night diner run with friends. Not something warm, playful, or even helpful. No. It had given her Physics 101.

Her pulse was still elevated.

He hadn't even looked at her. Or maybe he had. She couldn't be sure. She couldn't trust what was memory anymore and what was this awful . . . playacting. Some alternate life vacation. The promises were fake. The line had blurred miles ago.

Back then, in real life, she'd been folding bar towels and wondering if her degree would ever matter while he had been collecting recommendation letters and shaking hands with advisers in zip-up fleeces. He had had a plan. He had probably had savings. She was still trying to figure out how to afford gas money. Even though it was well below a dollar a gallon in those good ol' days, Grown Harriet remembered the financial struggle was more than real.

In the quiet of the chamber, Harriet let her hand rest on her knee. She could still smell the pub's signature shrimp cocktail sauce on her fingers. She could still feel that awful, dislocated sensation of being in a room full of people and feeling like no one actually saw her.

"You could have picked something better," she muttered toward the air. "Why are you rubbing my face in this memory?"

Her phone beeped, and she dug it out from deep in her purse. A blink of neon green shimmered at the edge of the dark, like a cursor waiting.

The frog finally appeared. The bubble read, *Memory integrity confirmed.*

From above, the guide announced, "Emotional coherence sustained. Loading next event."

"Of course it is," she said. "You built this damn thing to hurt. Not to help."

But the voice and the message on her phone were already gone. Like her confidence that anything good would ever come from being inside this Experience.

Chapter Twenty

The library smelled like old pages, stuffy suppositions, and student anxiety. Somewhere in the stacks, a laser printer kicked into gear with a whine and a mechanical clunk, spitting out a long, perforated paper version of someone's midterm paper.

Harriet's arms were full of textbooks she hadn't cracked open in weeks and a mostly empty coffee cup from the vending machine stacked precariously on top. She dropped everything into a study carrel with a thud and sighed. At least the coffee hadn't spilled. She took a small lukewarm sip.

It was supposed to be a quick stop: Pick up a reserve book, maybe skim the chapter she'd missed during last week's lecture before heading into another shift at Club Pub. Her legs already ached preemptively from the idea of lugging trays of mozzarella sticks to drunk poli-sci majors.

She turned the corner toward the front desk, and then she saw him. It almost made her duck into the nearest corner. But that would be too obvious.

Miles Hopper.

He was half-standing behind the library's public computer terminal, peering over a pair of wire-frame glasses that definitely hadn't been part of his high school look.

She hesitated, her stomach tightening.

The librarian at the counter pointed toward a small bulletin board beside the tech help desk. "If you're looking for the tutoring schedule, we just posted today's sign-ups."

"I'm all set," Miles said. Cheerful, polite.

He turned and saw her too. Too late to hide.

For a second, his expression didn't change. Then his eyebrows lifted slightly. Not surprised. Just . . . mildly curious, like seeing an old book out of place on a shelf.

"Hey," he said, voice low and casual.

Harriet managed a nod. "Hey."

He stepped aside so she could pass, but she didn't move. "I haven't seen you around lately."

"That's right. You're tutoring now . . ." she said, ignoring the statement for now, gesturing vaguely toward the bulletin board and trying not to sound too incredulous.

He shrugged. "Yeah. Physics, calc, anything first-year level. It's through the academic resource center."

"Of course it is," she said, almost to herself.

Miles tilted his head, studying her. Not unkindly. Just observant. "You're still in Phys 101, right?"

She shifted her weight. "Was. I dropped after midterms. Pub schedule got brutal."

He nodded slowly, as if that made sense. "You always had that job, didn't you? Club Pub?"

"Still do," she said, brushing a hand over her coat sleeve. "Still waiting tables. Still sloshing around pint glasses to drunk frat boys who think quoting Bukowski makes them deep."

He smiled at that. "Sounds like you're in your element. You like all that bookish stuff."

"There's nothing bookish about developing carpal tunnel," she said, half-laughing.

A beat passed.

Miles adjusted the strap of his bag and glanced at the desk terminal, where a screen saver had started bouncing across the CRT monitor. "I, uh, saw your name on a flyer last semester. For the campus writing contest?"

Her cheeks warmed. "I didn't win."

"Didn't say you had to," he said. "I just thought it was cool you entered."

She hadn't expected that. Not from him. Not from anyone.

For a moment, the library felt quieter.

They stood there awkwardly, college kids surrounded by shelves of information neither of them fully understood how to use yet. But he didn't seem to mind. He looked comfortable in his skin, in his space. Like his future had already started writing itself. Hers still felt like it was waiting for instructions.

"Anyway," she said, gesturing to the copy machine, "I should . . ."

"Yeah," he said. "Same."

He gave her a small smile. Nothing dramatic, just familiar. And then he walked away, bag swaying, sweater sleeves pushed up, disappearing into a row of nonfiction texts about emerging tech that hadn't even made it to the public yet.

Harriet turned back toward the counter and let out a long breath she hadn't realized she was holding.

Chapter Twenty-One

The computer lab hummed from machinery punctuated with the students' typing, *click-click-click*. Harriet sat stiffly at a terminal near the back, where the flickering fluorescent bulb needed to be changed. Her knees were crammed under a beige desk with a peeling label that read *Property of University AV*. The monitor in front of her buzzed faintly. Blue background. White text. No instructions. *Log in with your university ID and password*, the taped sign above the screen read, like that explained anything.

She didn't remember setting a password. She barely remembered signing up for this thing. Her basics-in-business professor had said he was going to online grading and that she'd need to check her intra-email for updates. As if it were that simple. As if she knew where emails came from, let alone where they went once they disappeared into the screen.

She typed her last name. The professor's name. No. Her name.

"Invalid credentials," the screen chirped.

She tried again, slower. Same result.

"This is useless," she muttered under her breath. The kid two seats down gave her a pitying glance, then returned to his Minesweeper game.

Somewhere on campus, Miles was probably checking his email with zero difficulty. Probably breezing through a DOS interface or telnet or whatever magic trick computer people did. He probably even enjoyed it.

She scowled at the screen. Checked her schedule for her student ID, the most probable thing as a password, typed it in, and unlocked her computer.

A blinking prompt appeared: *You have (1) new message.*

She squinted and looked closely. She clicked into the link. It opened.

Her heart kicked a little harder in her chest. A slight payoff for all her trouble.

FROM: *mhopper@u-portal.edu*
   Subject: Library run-in
   Date: Jan 29, 1996 11:04 AM

HEY–

Sorry if I was awkward earlier. Good to see you. You seemed like you were carrying a lot (books and otherwise).

If you ever want help with physics stuff, I'm around. Office hours don't mean much, but I'm usually in the math lab Monday/Wednesday nights. I'd love it if you would stop by my table.

You're still sharp as hell. Don't let the pub suck it all out of you.

—M

HARRIET STARED at it for a long time. She didn't know how to reply. Or if she should.

The screen flickered slightly. She reached for the keyboard, fingers hovering, uncertain.

Then she logged out.

Let him think the system had glitched.

Chapter Twenty-Two

"Where to next?" Harriet complained, the hollow sound of her voice deadened as the Experience altered into a new memory.

The walls dissolved into the interior of a plush SUV. Harriet blinked at the road ahead, surprised to find herself behind the wheel. She glanced at her reflection in the rearview mirror. A hard-brimmed taxi-driver hat shadowed her brow, and a dark-blue jacket completed the uniform. "This really isn't my look," she said with a scoff, watching a flock of sheep dash across the asphalt and into the misty, open fields. "And this really isn't one of my memories."

The SUV idled outside a terminal marked with two towering white sails and the words *City of Sails* running down their sides. *Auckland Airport* glared from the building's face in bold, capital letters.

Harriet narrowed her eyes. A newspaper beside her in the passenger seat hailed the news of some city council meeting and increases in police funding with the date: May 14, 1997. This definitely wasn't her memories. This Experience was really glitching it up now. Her driver self reached for the paper.

The side doors thudded open, and three passengers piled in: two business-class men and a slouching teenager, or a teenager by comparison to the businessmen accompanying him. The kid shoved in a trash bag and a weathered backpack before settling into the bench seat at the very back. His coat bunched at the shoulders, and the scuffed Converses were taped up with silver duct tape. He crossed a leg over one knee and bounced it with restless energy.

Harriet craned her neck, catching a glimpse of his face. Even with the obviously new sports coat he wore, she recognized him in the baggy cargo pants, the white T-shirt, the painter's cap.

"Miles Hopper?" she asked from the front of the SUV.

"Miles Hopper?" she hissed from the Experience pod.

"Yes, we got him. Thank you, miss," one of the men in the back replied breezily.

The man in the middle seat, with a balding crown and calm eyes, looked toward her. "Driver, we're ready to head to the hotel."

"On it." Harriet gripped the steering wheel, glancing around. "Sorry. Just checking the best route."

From the passenger seat, she pushed aside the paper with a name written on it in dark marker: *Hopper*.

Great.

"Sheep crossing the road," she offered to explain the delay, noting the small herd grazing near the ditch. On the map open on the seat, the town center was highlighted, a straight shot to the destination. She turned the key in the ignition and started off for the city center.

The man in the front—Nigel, he later introduced himself—chuckled. "They've got right of way here." He handed Miles a bottle of water and a snack bag. "Bit of a haul, eh? Want some crisps? Proper lunch once we get to the hotel."

"Sure, thanks." Miles rubbed his eyes. "Met a boxer in LA. He offered me a drink."

"And you didn't turn it down." Nigel smirked.

"It packed a punch."

Harriet watched him through the mirror. Puffy-eyed, slouching, tired. Yet beneath it, the flicker of a grin. Miles looked even younger to her in this light. Scruffy but determined. Still clinging to boyhood but lacking the young-person baby fat, yet with that twitchy spark of ambition always just under the surface.

The second businessman, John, was quieter, more measured. He handed Miles a letter printed from a dot-matrix printer on paper with the fringe still attached.

"You were highly recommended by ICS," John said. "Gene sent us your file. They claim you can identify software bugs and help get the new factory running."

"I know." Miles leaned forward, suddenly focused. "It wasn't a great time to leave school, but the challenge was worth it."

Harriet stiffened. Was he serious? He was getting the royal treatment and getting paid to fix someone's factory? He could do this?

John glanced at Nigel, then back to Miles. "You came highly recommended for someone still finishing finals. But this isn't a class project. We've got real deadlines."

Miles's confidence surged. "I can fix it. I saw the files. Your assembly loop's getting caught in a recursive failback. It's a simple redirect."

Harriet scrunched up her lips into a tight, scrutinizing pucker. That was the Miles she remembered. Bold. Certain. Still slightly arrogant. And still chasing a bigger version of himself, even if he had no idea what that looked like yet.

Nigel pointed out the window. "Enjoy the view. You're in the land of the kiwis now."

"I have a final due and a girlfriend waiting," Miles muttered. "Let's get this figured out."

The men exchanged looks.

"Young and intense," John muttered.

"A little short-sighted," Nigel added.

John leaned back and nodded. "You'll be paid, Miles. Flight, hotel, meals. Covered."

Miles slumped slightly, hands in his lap, shoulders tight beneath the awkward-fitting sports coat. "Just checking. I can't afford a vacation."

"Let us know what you need," Nigel said. "We've got dinners planned. Some sightseeing. Someone to show you the city."

Miles pulled his cap lower. "I'll fix the problem."

Harriet noted the deflection. The guardedness. The same flickers of bravado he had used in high school, now dressed up in corporate expectations. It was a performance. One she knew too well. One she could relate to.

"Boy's a piece of work," Nigel whispered.

John nodded, then grabbed the corded car phone from the front seat and made a lunch reservation.

Miles stared out the window, jaw set, fingers twitching over the diagrams John had handed him. Harriet glanced again in the mirror. His youth glared in contrast to his confidence: fragile but unshaken. A little scruff forming after what appeared to be a day-and-a-half of flight time.

She pulled into the parking lot of a fancy-looking bed-and-breakfast. The gravel from the side of the road crunched beneath the tires as she turned. She felt it then: the sound wave metaphor. Her life had bent inward, condensed. And here was Miles, already rising on a different frequency.

Harriet opened her mouth to say something clever; something bitter, maybe. Maybe she could keep driving, beeline to the beach or mountains from here. She willed herself to examine the map . . . but the world tilted. The windshield went dark.

She was gone again. Back to the sensory deprivation, the darkness of the Experience. But the sharp sting of the gap between her world and this world she had been thrust into remained.

A scene appeared: a blurred vision of an apartment. It became muffled and then static again. Beige walls. A fan whirred.

Miles dropped his keys into a dish on a side table as he walked into the door and set his luggage onto the floor.

A woman leaned in, kissed him, and vanished into another room as Miles dropped onto a well-used couch. He didn't flinch when she returned with a couple of letters in her hand and dropped them in his lap. He just stared straight ahead. "You got some mail," she sang cheerfully before heading to the other room.

And when the TV buzzed on and the woman's voice drifted in from the kitchen, "Did you take a look at the letter?" he said under his breath, "How about tomorrow . . ."

She didn't press, but added with a playful lilt in her voice, "I got one too." In one hand, she held a large roll of tape, in the other a flower vase that she set on the dining table on a bed of newspaper. "You might want to open it."

"Why are there boxes all over?"

"You'll see," the woman said.

Harriet watched it all, outside of this scene, a presence fading behind the walls of his new life. In this life, Miles was still learning to fill the space he had carved out. And somewhere in the center of that silence was the rhythm of a life that might have aligned with hers, if only. But this wasn't something she should have seen. It was private. It was none of her business.

The screen flickered. Then it all dissolved again, and Harriet sighed with relief. This was so not what she had signed up for. This was not her memory.

"What the heck? Why am I here?" Harriet straightened up. "Am I in someone else's memory? Hey, the machine is glitching again!"

The Experience buzzed with feedback, but returned to the previous memory, scratching like a visual needle and trying to find the right track on a long-play vinyl record. She checked the frog on her app. The grinning amphibian's text bubble read, *Find the clues.*

Harriet's Experience focused, and she found herself outside the second-floor apartment, staring through a patio door of the apartment she had just seen Miles sharing with someone else. Inside was a starter living room complete with scruffed-up coffee table, a stack of moving boxes, and the energy of optimism.

"What is this? Where am I?" Harriet demanded from the patio deck. "Stop! I'm in someone else's memory."

"Harriet, we are working on the bug. Hold on."

"I knew it was you, Ted," Harriet huffed. "Don't they train you how to use these things? And I was just about to find my way around New Zealand. You could've let me peek at something. A beach? A vineyard? At this point, I'd settle for the Illinois State Fair. Why am I on someone's apartment balcony?"

"We have a few more stops on this journey before your three futures. Be patient, Harriet."

She scowled and searched the phone. "Find the clues? This Experience needs to get a clue." Hoping Ted was still up there, she asked, "Thanks for skipping the dull parts of working at the factory, but did he even see anything in New Zealand outside the factory? Who goes across the world and doesn't take it in?"

"Shhh. You'll want to hear this part."

A breeze shifted the drapes. Inside, a tall woman entered with a moving box, a modest diamond sparkling on her finger. She paused to admire it under the dining room light.

"Great. Now I'm spying on a happy couple. Fabulous," Harriet muttered. "Your app is only marginally better than a root canal."

"Listen," Ted said.

Miles pushed aside the remote and put his hand on the mail in his lap. His face was drawn, eyes closing and mouth slightly open as if he were about to fall asleep.

The woman turned, waving a torn envelope. "See? Here's mine." She waved it under his nose. "Guess what it is? Guess! You'll never guess."

Miles barely lifted his head. "How was your trip to New Zealand, Miles? That's great, Miles. So glad you're back, Miles," he said in his best singsong deadpan.

"Oh, don't be grumpy." She beamed. "This is so much better."

"What?"

"I got the job!"

"The one in Arizona?" He looked around at the boxes and bubble wrap littering the room.

She nodded, bouncing as she waved the letter in front of him to read it. "And you got a letter too." She held up a second envelope. "Open it."

He took it, mumbled something about needing the bathroom, and wandered to another side room for a couple of minutes before returning, rubbing sleep from his eyes.

She was packing again, humming. Across from her at the table, he unfolded the letter she had handed him. Slowly.

She hovered, finished with the vase, waiting. "Well?" She tapped her foot, arms folded close to her middle.

He grinned. "You might want to stop packing. Unless you plan to move on without me."

"What?" Her face fell along with her arms to her sides. "But I'm sure they wanted you . . ."

He let it hang. Giving her an overly serious stare. Then, breaking into a smile, he said, "I got it. I got the job."

She squealed and ran into his arms. The letter crumpled between them.

From outside, Harriet pulled away from the window. She closed her eyes, blocking the scene from her mind. This was just not her memory to see.

"Oh my gawd. This has nothing to do with me." And she wondered which of her memories would end up in someone else's Experience.

The Guide's voice said, "The Experience will continue now. Sorry for the inconvenience."

The apartment faded. She was back in the sensory pod of the Experience.

Harriet stood in the dark, sour with the weight of what she'd seen. The happiness had felt private. And worse . . . it had highlighted everything missing in her own life.

She was speechless.

The scent of pineapple suntan lotion drifted in. She sniffed. "Oh no. If you believe you can fix this with a vacation scene now, you have another think coming. I swear . . ."

The phone's text bubble announced, *Enjoy your next Experience!*

She shook her phone. "Hey! This is broken. You've crossed wires, you idiots! This isn't my life!"

The Guide returned. "Your realities have overlapped with this one. It will soon become clear."

Harriet clenched her jaw. "And what's with the tropical smells? I better get a beach memory out of this."

The voice replied, cool and robotic, "You've been approved for a vacation to Hawaii. If selected."

Chapter Twenty-Three

Miles sat, one leg folded over a knee, on the guest bed of his San Francisco condo, an island of cluttered intent in a sea of ordered chaos. Around him sat stacks of manila folders, crates of obsolete tech, a lifetime of old hard drives blinking softly with dormant secrets. His ancient Canon scanner buzzed as it fed one document at a time through its cracked lid, methodical and slow. No wireless connections; no risk. That was the point.

The late-morning sun finally burned through the fog, casting warm rectangles across his floor. Outside, the scent of baking bread drifted up from the corner bakery and tangled with the faint ozone of electronics warming to life. On his desk, a small toy robotic cat paced lazily, flicking its mechanical tail. It purred and tapped at the space bar with a paw.

Miles jumped to feed a new stack of documents into the scanner. "Some people would call a psychic," he said to his own walls. "Others build their own oracle."

It had been a long night. A long week. He had barely slept since launching the data aggregation for his most ambitious idea yet: the Experience App. This wasn't just a startup or a product. It was his redemption.

With every scanned page—birth certificate, SAT printout, first résumés, childhood artwork, awkward teen poems, breakup letters— he constructed a portrait of his inner life. His entire emotional DNA rendered in code. Every file encrypted and siloed in a non-networked system. It was a guarantee for no leaks, no exposure, and no judgment. Except maybe his own. But he was sure the benefits, especially using himself as the product's test subject, outshone any slight stain on his conscience.

He smiled wryly, thinking of his ex, Claire. She'd said he was too intense. That he never looked up from his projects long enough to notice the people around him. That he created things not just for his business plan, but to escape real life bustling around him. She'd left in silence, ditching the Thai food date, and their—*no, his*—dreams, taking nothing but her dignity. Now she was sunning herself in Aruba with a tan realtor in matching board shorts.

Fine. Let her have her sun.

He had something better. A new kind of tech. Something that could capture a life and spin it into three vivid futures. A self-contained app, closed-loop, secure. Like a soul mirror crossed with a simulation engine.

He had finally won Adriana's approval when he had pitched it as a private memory mini-appliance that analyzed and optimized one's life. It was safe, he had assured her. It didn't access the cloud, he said with confidence. It didn't use scraping, he told her with adamance. It didn't include any algorithmic ads, he said before explaining how people would pay just about anything to have a better life. That this would be far less expensive over time than multiple series of therapy—not that it was considered an alternative.

At first, she wasn't convinced. He could tell she was taking the bait, but very, very reluctantly, from the way she paused when he described it. The way her fingers twitched near her bracelet. The way she mentioned legal liabilities without mentioning them at all.

Still, she let him build it. And now he was feeding it a lifetime of his memories.

In the galley kitchen, a burrito in the microwave hissed. Miles checked the time remaining and lined up hot sauces on the counter, soldiers ready to flavor whatever half meal this moment allowed. His coffee brewed on voice command, and he pulled a mug from the cupboard. He moved like a machine, motivated by routine and efficiency, detached from the world around him. Happy with the way things could go exactly as he had planned.

He pulled out the sizzling burrito with a swift motion and tossed it onto a plate. He grabbed as many hot sauce bottles as he could with one hand and marched back to the war room, as Adriana would call his space when he was thick into any project. No one would dare to approach, interrupt, or touch anything during the development process, at least not at this stage.

He ate while watching the scanner feed the app more of his past. The machine analyzed everything he had collected over his life. He had uploaded long lists of names, dates, locations, emotions. It graphed his psychological highs and collapses, plotted against career milestones and personal relationships. A slow, digital autopsy of his lived experience.

Miles chewed without tasting, pouring more sauce into the crevasses of his burrito, his focus locked on the expanding timelines. He flagged themes to track: resilience, fulfillment, actual happiness, matching them up with word databases that reflected each emotion. He divided the input into numeric records, anecdotal texts, and image archives. Then he set the system to find patterns.

Not just trends, but recurrences. Repetitions that meant something.

He adjusted the input weights, fine-tuning the heuristics to pick up softer cues, emotional inflection in text, facial micro-expressions in photos, tones in handwriting. It wasn't just the peaks and valleys that mattered. It was what persisted in the data.

But then he noticed something.

A girl at the edge of a fourth-grade field-trip photo.

A familiar name on a middle-school science fair list.

A candid from a high-school graduation party, her head turned just slightly from his, as if they were tuned to the same frequency but out of phase.

He hadn't been looking for her. Not at first. But the algorithm had caught the pattern before he had.

Somewhere between his childhood notes and first careers, the signal had emerged. A strange rhythmic overlap. A hum in the data that only became clear when filtered through her file.

And that's when the photos started surprising him.

The AI had done its job well. Well . . . mostly. A few childhood faces were misfiled. Some photos tagged as strangers were actually just different-aged versions of the same people. People he used to know. Overall, not a bad trial run for something this ambitious.

And one person stood out.

Harriet.

Again and again.

Grade-school group photos. That shared science project. Tennis camp snapshots. High-school plays where she stood in the wings. College libraries. Parties. The almost tutoring session. Always there.

He leaned forward, hands hovering over the keyboard. At first, he thought it was a glitch in the facial recognition. Maybe the algorithm had merged profiles by mistake. But the time stamps were different. The metadata held. Cross-referenced and consistent.

This wasn't overlap. This was pattern.

He tagged her across the datasets. Ran an identity validation sweep. Her name popped up, confirmed in student rosters, newspaper clippings, class projects, even his old email contacts.

Harriet Last. The girl from school. From across the street growing up. The one who had never quite left his peripherals. Easy to overlook.

He rubbed his jaw, more baffled than anything. Not emotionally rattled but unsettled by the math of it. This wasn't just anecdotal proximity: this was statistical proximity. She'd shown up in nearly every quadrant of his developmental years.

Thinking back to the compilers professor who had imparted more than computer wisdom to him, he mulled over the big constants in life: death, taxes, entropy. And apparently . . . Harriet?

He reached back into the data, rewinding the time arcs. Her presence didn't spike. It stayed steady. Subtle. Unassuming. Present.

Always just outside the spotlight. But always in the shot. Like in the children's book *Where's Waldo?*, Harriet was in the backdrop of many of his own memories but also busy in her own ways. Not exceptionally involved with what he was doing, but she was there, and he couldn't get over it. He took a closer look.

In one photo, she grinned with her eyes closed, braids tied with red ribbons. A class photo on the hill outside their elementary school. He remembered sledding down that hill. Sharing a big bag of popcorn in fourth grade during a science movie. The one tennis photo . . . he and Harriet surrounded by high-strung kiddo campers. Smiling. Real smiles.

He narrowed the search to shared proximity. The app drew out webs of connections. He asked for mutual acquaintances, similar course schedules, even overlapping Spotify histories from later-era social data pulls. The further he zoomed out, the clearer the picture became.

She had been there the whole time.

He leaned closer. How had he missed it?

She wasn't a constant. She was a through line. A waveform barely out of phase with his own.

He began manually merging her data. He dragged her presence into a folder labeled *Threads*. He looked up from the screen, blinking.

He leaned back, the chair creaking under his weight. The scanner hummed on, but he was far away now. In memory. In math. In theory.

What was she doing now?

And what would the app say if he input her name as a primary variable?

He didn't know.

But he was surely going to find out.

But how?

So he did what any logical human in the modern era would do and began a frenzy of high-level research. He dove into her social media, her public files, her current picture from her employer's website, and, eventually, added her insurance conference itinerary. Everything that wasn't locked down and floating in some ether space or cloud became data for the machine. The Experience connected the dots and filled in spaces using its hyper-realistic immersive interface.

And the search verified what he had suspected: the fact that he had missed something notable, a correlation sitting in plain sight. A common traveler in life that he knew well. An out-of-sync thread that should have been so obvious, it took a lifetime of living to figure out. This was more than a coincidence. This really was a connection.

He looked at the data, observing the simplicity of it. There was no evidence stating they needed to fix their past. They had each spent years building careers, following dreams, making friendships. Or so it seemed. He just needed to find out why it mattered.

Chapter Twenty-Four

"Say, Ted? Guide guy?" Harriet's voice rang out in the void. "This is more than a glitch. I am in someone else's memories now. I think you've got to fix this."

"It's a temporary problem. And I'm fixing the loop right now," Ted said into the Experience pod speaker. "We seem to have one of your past memories intertwining with another one."

"But that's the thing. I'm not in these memories," Harriet snapped. "Why am I stuck watching a highlights reel of Miles Hopper's life? We didn't even spend that much time together. Not enough to warrant a full docuseries."

"We understand this must be confusing, Harriet. But please trust the system," Ted's voice replied, calm and practiced.

She rolled her eyes. "This fever dream of a reality remix is a mistake."

The world around her began to melt into something new. The concrete of the apartment patio rippled and re-formed into aged wood. The railing, now hand-hewn, supported a rudimentary thatched roof, the slats shadowing the porch in long lines.

A light-blue adobe building came into focus behind her, its paint sun-bleached and flaking. Whitewashed fences framed the lush green courtyard that extended in all directions. Small, well-kept buildings clustered around the open space, each one basking in the drowsy gold of early-afternoon light. The air was rich with salt and mango, bright and welcoming. A row of mismatched chairs lined the deck where she now stood.

Ted's voice cut in again. "Ah. The loop is resolved. We should have you back into your scheduled program momentarily. Hang tight!"

Harriet stared at her phone. The frog was now dancing, hopping flipper to flipper. "I don't know if you noticed: I'm not able to go anywhere. Meanwhile, I'm standing here like a background character in someone else's comeback tour." She lowered the phone and waved her arms to the empty ceiling. "How is this app supposed to help me figure out anything except to point out all of my look-at-what-you-missed moments?"

The ceiling pulsed faintly with sound, then Ted spoke, his voice drifting away as her next memory sharpened into view. "Oh Harriet, you didn't miss out. You must remember . . . you wanted to get out of that town too."

Harriet blinked. The quiet breeze carried the warm thrum of laughter from somewhere nearby. The paint chips on the deck shifted in the light like memories threatening to solidify.

"Wait. What do you mean, 'You wanted to get out'?" she asked.

But the voice above had dissipated. She glanced at her phone, and the frog's text bubble scrolled through a message: *We are preparing your next immersive file. Please hold. The Experience required extensive rendering. Apologies for the delay.*

She sighed, folding her arms and surveying the view. Something in the air had changed. Something lighter. Something just around the corner.

She didn't know what memory was coming next, but for the first time in what was seeming like a long, long while, she hoped it might be one of the good ones.

The paint shimmered. The walls wavered. Once again, she waited.

∿

TED LEANED back from the tablet and watched the rendering sequence spool toward completion. The Honduras program was heavy. It was clean code, sure, but weighted with sensory files and memory threads. Harriet's data had taken longer to cross-reference—something about her emotional tags being more scattered than expected. It didn't help that her resistance levels kept spiking.

He rubbed his temples and checked the system clock. The rendering would hold her there for a few minutes. Enough time to think.

While working, he recalled his last call to Adriana, the one after he had confessed that some parts of the project had stalled out while he had beta-tested other volunteers for the Experience App. Some future outcomes were inconclusive or unrelated, not to mention unsatisfying for the user. And she was worried about how long the timeline was to produce The Experience.

"This machine. If our users don't like their outcomes…it could mean the same for our company, Miles."

"Elegant things take time to produce and to debug," he'd said. It had sounded more noble than desperate at the time.

"Yeah, no worries. I can hold down the business while you pursue this new hobby of yours," she said dryly.

"You're the best, Dria."

"Darling, I know. That was sarcasm. Whatever this is, I just hope you get it out of your system soon. London flats are expensive."

"This is going to be big. I can feel it."

"I feel the lawsuits. And bill collectors. But cheer up, pal. I won't let us sink the ship just yet."

"Thanks for the vote of confidence. Also a little bit of reciprocal sarcasm."

"Sure. Have fun finding the meaning of life." She leaned in to whisper-talk to the screen. "I've got to go live mine now."

She'd blipped off the screen with a casual wave, but even then, he'd heard it. That slight thread of concern woven under her breezy charm. Adriana was no fool. She'd known it wasn't just some whimsical tech side project. And she'd warned him the Honduras file might lead

Harriet somewhere good. Somewhere meaningful. And it was taking up an extraordinary amount of their resources to produce.

He looked up at the simulation metrics. The algorithm had been weaving their stories together from the beginning. Every missed connection, every overlap, it wasn't random. It was elegant. Purposeful. If he could make a difference, change his path, and hers, in theory other people could live their best life too.

But what if she didn't choose that path? What if Adriana was right?

What if the outcome she needed wasn't him or anything they might have become?

He closed the system log and leaned forward, hands hovering over the manual controls.

"Not some do-good doctor in a mountain village," he said quietly. "I have to trust the algorithm."

The Honduras file stabilized. Harriet's vitals adjusted to baseline. The memory thread held.

He forced a smile and sat back again, tapping the side of his mug with the stylus. "She's not going to fall for a mango-scented monologue," he told the screen, trying to sound certain.

But the screen said nothing in return.

And the simulation rolled on.

Chapter Twenty-Five

T he blackness didn't last but faded into a swirling mist around
her. The floor beneath Harriet's feet grew solid, sun-warmed,
and faintly sticky with tropical humidity. Birdsong erupted around her,
layered in counterpoint with the clink of metal instruments and the
low hum of distant conversation. A faint breeze lifted the hem of her
bohemian-style skirt, her boots and scrunched-down socks covering
her ankles. Mosquito bites dotted her knees like itchy punctuation. She
wore a tank top with a faded health organization logo barely visible on
the chest. If one looked closely enough, you could see the iodine stains
now disguised within the rest of the pattern.

She blinked hard and opened her eyes. Finally, the Experience was
making some kind of sense. Harriet sighed deeply and full of relief as
her avatar-like self walked through one of her fonder memories.

A small Honduran village lay sprawled before her, tucked into the
valley's green cradle. Faded blues, sun-baked yellows, and pinks clung
to chipped stucco walls. The Clínica San Pedro stood off to one side; in
the distance, its tin roof shimmered in the midmorning heat. Harriet
looked down as the memory filled her mind. Her arms were tan and
freckled, her palms cracked from scrubbing instruments and
unpacking medical supplies from cardboard boxes and crates. A cloth

bag swung at her hip, a bag of supplies donated by a school group back in the States.

The dirt path curved around a strand of banana trees, their waxy leaves rustling in the humid morning breeze. Harriet walked past the makeshift fencing along the edge of a home. She adjusted the strap of her canvas bag and tucked a strand of hair under the faded-blue bandana knotted at the nape of her neck. She could still hear the faint morning radio from a nearby house, full of static and a serious-sounding news broadcaster echoing off adobe walls.

Ahead, a small boy balanced a dented bucket on his head, water sloshing at each careful step of his blue flip-flops. He stopped when he saw her, eyes wide, a timid grin. Harriet smiled and raised a hand. "*¡Buenos días!*" she called, her accent careful but warm.

The boy hesitated, then dropped the pail to his waist to wave vigorously. "*¡Buenos días!*" He pivoted quickly and hurried up the path where his mother was waiting for the water.

Farther down, a woman greeted her from a wooden porch while rocking on a chair. She wore a bright apron over a faded-pink dress, her arms dusted in corn masa.

"*¿Va al consultorio?*" the woman asked, nodding toward Harriet's bag.

"*Sí, señora. Como todos los días,*" Harriet replied. "*¿Su nieta está mejor?*"

The woman's face softened. "*Un poco. Todavía con tos, pero duerme bien. Gracias a ustedes.*"

Harriet gave a polite nod, suppressing the awkwardness that always came when people thanked her like that. She hadn't done much. She was still just the student, and she had only signed up for this internship to complete her foreign language requirement in one semester. She was figuring it all out, and part of her didn't feel she deserved this level of attention. The other part secretly loved it.

Past the cantina, she stopped briefly to let a pair of donkeys pass, their hooves clopping against the packed dirt. The older man leading them gave her a curt nod. "*Buenos, señora,*" he said.

She almost corrected him, to say she wasn't married, but the moment passed. Other workers insisted that it was a term of respect, so she let it go.

When she arrived at the low, cinder-block clinic, Harriet paused to take it in. It stood at the center of the town with its peeling paint, the worn red cross over the door, and the growing line of people already forming outside. There was a rhythm to this place, and she was just starting to understand it. Everything was slower. Everything was louder. Everything was . . . a little more raw and dramatic.

She let out a long breath and kept walking past the patients waiting to be seen.

The cicadas screamed in the trees like electrical wires about to snap. Humidity clung to Harriet's skin, sticky and constant, as she pressed a cool flat palm against her forehead. A beaded necklace one patient had given her clinked gently against her chest with each step through the concrete breezeway of the rural clinic. The air inside was slightly cooler than outside but carried its own scent with a tinge of bleach, sweat, and the faint metallic tang of blood.

She was greeted by the orderly, Hank, and the only licensed nurse in the area, a woman named Marta who happened to be the doctor's sister. She and the doctor had grown up in a mountainous village and wanted to give back to the community.

"¡Mira quién llegó temprano por fin!" came a voice from the back hallway.

Marta stepped out from the back room that doubled as a lab and cafeteria, her braids tucked under a crisp white baseball cap. She carried a clipboard and a steel thermos, which she held up and shook slightly like a prize. Behind her, a beaker on a hot plate was slow-boiling the coffee that they shared.

Harriet laughed. "I was only late yesterday. And that was because Hank flagged me down outside and needed help moving a generator. That thing needs a little TLC." She switched to English to help Marta keep her language skills sharp as well. They were both practicing and improving, a great match linguistically.

Marta raised an eyebrow playfully. "So now you're a mechanic?"

"Apparently." Harriet shrugged and leaned on the counter. "He said it's making a noise like . . . a goat stuck in a fan."

"Ah. Then it's probably working fine," Marta said dryly, pouring coffee into a chipped mug and sliding it across to her. "Drink before someone's baby decides to arrive early."

Harriet took a grateful sip, blowing in brief puffs first to cool it. "Thanks. This is the only reason I'm still upright."

Marta glanced at her over the rim of her glasses. "You didn't sleep."

"Maybe it's the high-octane coffee you guys serve around here." Harriet forced a smile, then added, "There's just so much I don't know yet. I thought reading the med book would help me unwind a bit and help me be more useful around here. I read two chapters on dengue last night, and I still don't know if I'd recognize it in real life."

"Well, hopefully, you won't have to deal with that." Marta's tone was joking but kind. "Books don't teach you how to listen to the patient. Or how to stay by their side when things get hard. That part, you already have."

Harriet looked down, the compliment landing somewhere unexpected in her chest. "Thanks. I just don't want to mess up. Or to be misunderstood and do more harm than good. You know what I mean?"

"You're here. And your language is pretty good. That's already more than most." Marta tapped the clipboard, then motioned to the hallway. "Now come. The line's growing and someone's donkey is trampling my flowers."

She'd been volunteering here for nearly two months, living out of a rented room with a family who offered her rice, beans, and shy smiles. The work was demanding, the hours long, and the emotional drain was more than she could have imagined, but there was something centering about it. It was pure in its mission, and the connection to the community was direct. And as a major perk, she would finish her college internship with a minor in Spanish, which appealed to her I-finally-did-something-noble inner milieu.

The waiting area of the clinic pulsed with motion. Metal-bladed ceiling fans rotated lazily overhead as individuals fanned themselves. A small boy with an infected toe whimpered on his mother's lap, the woman stroking his curls. In the corner, an elderly man sat on an over-turned crate, head tilted, eyes closed in patient resignation. The mandatory radio crackled out a melancholy bolero, its volume barely above a whisper, but just loud enough to keep time with the fly buzzing near Harriet's ear.

And there he was. Gabriel Mendez. Her supervisor. Her colleague. Her . . . something. He moved through the cramped space with calm urgency, calling instructions in Spanish, his white coat tied at the waist, sleeves rolled high. Sweat glistened on his temple, but he never stopped moving. His voice had the staccato cadence of someone trying to hold the world together with words.

Harriet set her clipboard down beside the cot of a boy recovering from dehydration and smiled gently when his mother murmured, "*Gracias, doctora,*" even though Harriet wasn't a doctor. She just nodded, biting back the correction, an interloper in her own life. Labels didn't matter as much here, and there were far more important issues to pay attention to. What mattered was that the boy was awake, his lips no longer cracked and his breath stronger than yesterday.

Behind her, the voice of Gabriel, the broad-shouldered actual doctor from Tegucigalpa, rang out in warm, accented English. "You're going to ruin us, Harriet. They'll think we have angels on staff."

She rolled her eyes and tossed a glove at him, which he caught with a smirk. "Flattery is great, but it doesn't mean I'll do the malaria meds round in the next town with you," she said, brushing hair from her temple and reaching for the next patient's chart. "And no . . . I will not help pluck the chickens for dinner, no matter how much flattery you send my way. A girl has to have some limits."

He laughed as Hank looked on from the hallway. He gave a look and elbowed Marta, who had been updating the order in which patients would be seen. The look that said what no one wanted to say when the only doctor for hundreds of miles in this tiny mountainous area took a strong interest in someone. Someone who was not a local. Someone who was most likely going to go back to their native home in less than a month. Harriet was a perfect distraction for the workers serving the endless grind of patients utilizing this clinic. And she wasn't the first volunteer to romanticize a simpler life in the mountains. This was the look that said when the distraction moved on with the changing seasons, the clinic would once again suffer. Dr. Mendez was known to become mercurial and withdrawn after volunteers left for their homeland. He would complain about the lack of supplies in their tiny, understaffed clinic. He shared fantasies about seeing Broadway plays, taking vacations, or having a sports car while living in a big city. He talked about starting a family. Marta often talked him down on days like those, taking him dancing at the cantina, where he was treated like a rock star. But even she could see it wasn't enough.

Later that night, Harriet sat on the cracked rooftop with Gabriel, sharing a soda and telling stories beneath a velvet sky. Stars burst across the blackness in unfamiliar patterns, and down below, the jungle made itself known, with chirps, hoots, and a rustling nightlife. Harriet leaned her back against the second-story wall, the windows to the staff sleeping quarters behind them. Her shoulders and feet were sore, but her heart was oddly full.

"I'm not sure I'll ever go back," she said lightly, in the moment. "Do you think I'm cut out for this type of work?"

Gabriel didn't answer her immediately. He handed her a tiny, wrapped candy he'd brought from town. "Even angels need homes," he said quietly.

She didn't respond. She was watching the horizon, the dark outline of mountaintops barely visible where they met the sky, imagining what it might feel like to stay.

Grown Harriet watched the sky in the shadows, never fully in control of her movements, witnessing it unfold like a worn VCR tape as her memory skipped forward to a new day. She took in the scene as her younger self entered from the storeroom, her long braid frizzing loose down her back, arm hooked around a stack of folded linens.

"I'll grab more saline," she said, voice rough from dehydration, her Spanish functional but accented. Her distaste for the water, always boiled over a wood fire or infused with drops of iodine to ensure safe drinking, had started to take its toll on her body. It was hard to drink, even when she was constantly parched.

Gabriel glanced up from an elderly woman, frail and recovering from the flu. "We're nearly out of bismuth subsalicylate. Check the shelf above the gloves."

"On it!" she yelled from the supply closet, her boots scraping the tile. "Checking for more Pepto!"

Her shirt clung to her lower back. The fluorescent light above flickered once, then steadied. Rummaging, she dug behind a box of bottled vitamins, pushing her hand to the far back corner of the shelf. She started to relay the news that they were out of the liquid. "I don't know if I see—"

When it happened. Quick, like the snap of a rubber band.

The sting came fast. Like stepping into icy water, but electric, sending waves of pain through her whole body. Her arm recoiled instantly, sending the rolls of gauze tumbling and scattering across the floor. Her mouth opened to scream, but it came out as a strangled gasp.

"¡Ay! What the . . ."

She stumbled back, her legs losing strength beneath her. The light seemed to tilt. A flash of movement. Gabriel caught her before she hit the ground.

"¡Escorpión! ¡Alacrán! Necesito ayuda, ahora!" he shouted.

Someone yelled ice, but she knew they were out. Ice was as rare in this area as electricity. They might have a cooling pack, the kind you crack to activate. She tried to whisper to Gabriel, weakly pointing to the cupboards with a tentative flip of her wrist.

He called to Hank for the antivenom. An antivenom kit was even more rare than ice and electricity. He hoped there was at least one kit left.

Harriet felt weak as panic crackled through the space like dry branches catching fire. Like the fire that was spreading up her arm in stinging pulses. The younger version of herself lay limply on a woven cot, lips pale, fingers twitching. Marta flew into full emergency nurse mode, swabbing her arm and cracking smelling salts beneath her nose to keep her conscious. Gabriel's hands hovered over her chest, listening to her heart. Then her wrist. The pulse was faint.

Gabriel's jaw clenched. "Stay with me," he muttered, gripping her shoulder a bit too hard.

Grown Harriet inhaled sharply. She remembered the fear. Not just of dying, but of leaving the work undone. Of being erased before becoming anything.

Her body had rebelled. Every breath a war. Her chest tightened until the edges of the world blurred. And then it went quiet.

When she came to, a breeze lifted the edges of a mosquito net around her. The afternoon light was gauzy and golden, pouring through the slats in the windows.

She turned her head. Gabriel sat on a stool beside her, slumped forward with his elbows on his knees. His eyes were bloodshot. He looked like he hadn't slept.

"You scared me," he said, not bothering to sit up. He was too tired for pride.

She coughed, her throat dry and raw. "I scare a lot of people."

He gave a small laugh, but it didn't reach his eyes. "I didn't want you to leave."

"I didn't plan to."

The moment held. The kind of silence where everything else drops away and the truth sits between you, waiting.

The letter arrived two days later. Delivered by a local teenager who handed it to her like a sacred object. It was a short letter from her mother. Her grandfather was in the hospital. Dying. She had to come home.

And so she left.

Torn between the family request to come home early and her commitment to finishing her allotted time at the clinic, she knew she had to go. But this new fulfillment she had found by doing something meaningful would have to come home with her. Her life in Honduras had caused a shift in her outlook. She now believed in pursuing something more selfless and loved the satisfaction of being needed at that moment in her life. Her heart was full.

She jumped on a truck heading to Tegucigalpa, promising to come back the following summer. Promising to bring candies for the kids, medical supplies, and other donations. She traveled over the difficult and ill-maintained mountain roads, arrived at the capital city nearly a day later, jumped on a plane, and never returned.

The light in this memory began to fade, the warm shadows stretching thin like cloth pulled too tightly. The sounds muted. The memory drifted. She had jumped back into life as normal once she got home, taking an opening at a large insurance company, a great opportunity for someone eager to get out of her parents' basement and to start paying back her student debt. Always intending on pursuing her work with small rural clinics, somehow retooling her skillset to better serve them. As a result, she never took her career seriously, never pursued advancements at True Blue to save herself for better pursuits. But she never had the energy to start a degree in nursing either.

Harriet stood again at the clinic threshold, the scent of jasmine and antiseptic already beginning to dissipate.

"Welcome back," Ted's voice, soft and slow, echoed around her, ushering her into a hospital scenario. "This memory is marked with high emotional significance. It may represent a pivotal alternate outcome."

"I know what it represents," Harriet said, her voice quiet and shaped by grief. "It's the last time I was part of something that mattered. The last time I mattered. The last time I felt aligned and alive."

She touched her wrist. The faint memory of the sting lingered there, as real as the ache blooming in her chest.

The world dissolved away.

And Harriet fell into the plain walls of a hospital room.

Chapter Twenty-Six

The room where her grandfather was receiving end-of-life care had all the warmth of a walk-in freezer, save for the bright crocheted blanket tucked around his legs. Her grandmother had brought it from the davenport where he would watch baseball six nights a week if he could. The relic, homemade with orange and brown and avocado-green yarn, had been stubbornly out of fashion since 1973. Much like her grandfather. He sat upright in the hospital bed and, in a moment of lucidity, was holding court over the hospital staff.

Harriet stepped into the room just in time to hear her grandfather bellowing at the nurse. "Let a dying man eat real food!" he shouted. "I don't want another spoonful of those damned strained peas!"

The nurse bustled past Harriet in the doorway, muttering something under her breath.

Harriet smiled softly and approached the bed. The old man looked thinner, paler, but his voice still could fill the room like a trumpet.

"Hey, Grandpa."

"Hey, Peanut," he grunted, his face relaxing at the sight of her. "How was your time playing Jane Goodall?"

"It wasn't quite that impactful," she said, taking his hand and gently pressing it. "But it was good."

"I hope you've got a lot of good stories. There's nothing good on TV. The Cubs lost again." He groaned with a shake of his head.

"I was sure I'd see them win the World Series this year, Grandpa."

He shook his head in true disappointment as he clenched his lips together before changing the subject. "Got any chimps in that big bag of yours that followed you home?"

"No chimps. Just some sunburn and, yes, a lot of stories."

Grandpa grunted when Harriet's grandmother walked in. "Brought your needlework again, huh?"

Her grandmother sat beside the bed, the chair's vinyl squeaking beneath her. "It's technically cross-stitch," she said, leaning over and propping his pillow. "I hear you were trying to charm the nurses again," she added with sarcasm. "They're just trying to do their jobs. Maybe go a little easy on them?"

"That pudding they like to bring nearly murdered me." He shook his fist.

"They said they would stop bringing you the peas, dear. No need to get upset," her grandmother said, patting his lowered hand.

Harriet forced a smile. His voice was becoming thinner now, his once-booming laugh more of a wheeze. But his eyes sparkled the same way they had when she had been a kid and he'd give her a sneak-sip of his beer during televised baseball games.

"I'd feel better if I had a pack of smokes."

"You gave that up," her grandmother reminded him. "And it doesn't go well with the oxygen, darling."

"So a dying man doesn't get to smoke one last cigarette?"

"You seem pretty with it for a man on his deathbed." She studied the pattern and adjusted her needle.

Harriet chuckled. "And hey, maybe this will cheer you up, Grandpa: I brought you a present."

Harriet reached into her coat pocket and slid out a small, clear plastic bag. Inside were two cigars. Not that she had any idea of what he would like—he was once more of a pack-of-cigarettes-a-day kind of guy—but word on the street said these Honduran cigars were some of the best.

"I knew I raised a good one," he said, half-laughing, half-coughing.

"You'll get me kicked out of hospice care for sure." His grin faded slowly, replaced by something more thoughtful. "I was always proud of you, you know. Even when I didn't tell you it."

"You didn't say it too much," she said softly. "But you didn't need to. I knew you were."

"You were always busy being someone. Helping people wherever you were. Making a life I couldn't have even imagined."

She looked down at her hands, tracing the seam of her jeans with her thumb. "It hasn't always felt like I was helping in any important way."

"Well," he said, "that's why God invented cigars." He took one and bit off the end, smoking it without lighting it. "For intentional reflection opportunities. It's hard to savor a cigar and not reflect on the good things in life."

Harriet nodded in her own quiet reflection.

"And bad whiskey. That's why He invented whiskey too. You don't have any of that in your bag, do you?"

"Uh, nope. Sorry," Harriet said simply, answering her grandmother's glare.

His eyes lit up as he examined the end of the cigar. "Well, now. That's very thoughtful, granddaughter. You're back in the will."

"There's nothing to inherit," her grandmother said, very matter of fact, busying herself again in her needlework.

Just then Harriet's mother stepped in, arms crossed but smiling. Harriet stood to greet her, and her mother pulled her into a hug, purse on her shoulder, keys jingling. "I told you not to sneak cigars in here," she said, scolding her with the same tone she had used when Harriet had been eleven and been caught sneaking ice cream before dinner. Harriet pointed to her seat for her mother to take.

"Oh, I did bring one other surprise." Harriet grinned, bent down, and unzipped her carry-on. "I have one more thing to show you."

"You did bring me a chimp!"

"No. Not quite, but it's very handy in the jungle." She pulled out a sheathed machete and held it up. "It's what all the Hondurans wear. You can do anything with it—cut vines, farm, clear paths, fend off wild animals. Very practical."

Her grandfather whistled. "Now, that's a souvenir. Where's that nurse? Maybe I'll give her a demonstration."

"Grandpa!"

"Oh my God, Harriet!" Her grandmother's cross-stitch fell to her lap. "That's really a machete?"

"Don't worry. It's not sharpened," Harriet assured her. "Everybody relax. Can't anyone take a joke anymore?"

They all laughed, and for a moment, the room felt more like home than hospital.

LATER THAT NIGHT, Harriet sat on the edge of her old twin bed, the one with the wooden spindle headboard and worn quilt that still smelled faintly of cedar and mothballs. It had been moved to a repurposed area of the basement, now a version of a private bedroom that Harriet would have once done three weeks of someone's chores for the privacy. But privacy really wasn't what she wanted right now.

The old box TV sitting on the low dresser was on but muted, flickering shadows of a local news segment across her walls. Upstairs, her parents were arguing about whether the sump pump would hold. Something about sandbags. The steady hum of a good Midwestern soaker drummed against the window, heavy rain that slapped the siding and probably pooled at the edges of the back patio.

She hadn't unpacked. The machete was stored again, zipped inside her carry-on, after her grandmother had snuck it away from her grandfather and ran into the hall to track her down when she had left. "Please, just keep it with you for now?"

"Sure. I didn't mean to stress you out, Grandma." She apologized, taking the broad knife and stowing it in her bag.

"No, it was perfect, Harriet. You made him laugh and smile. And that means the world to me."

Her work boots were tossed near the bedroom door, tucked under the same red jacket she'd worn to the hospital. Her grandfather's laughter echoed in her ears, soft now, already part of the past.

The cigars had made him smile. That was something too. It hadn't felt like enough.

She stared at her reflection in the black screen of the TV. Her outline was faint and doubled, the kind of ghostly silhouette she used to imagine was another version of her, one that did all the fun things when she couldn't. But this one was older. Circles under her eyes. A different kind of ache crossed her face.

She was supposed to go out that night. She had told Trixie they'd get together when she got back home. She had even typed an email response in the draft folder, something rambling and half-funny about Spanish verbs and what Professor Coss would say about her language skills now. She hadn't sent it. She'd stared at the blinking cursor from an internet café and thought, *What's the point?*

While hanging out by herself at the café, she had thought about reaching out to her other classmates. Miles had been the first to show her how to use email, and something about Netscape, and how to search the whole world, practically, from one computer. "It's called the World Wide Web," he'd said like it was a secret map only he could read.

She'd pretended to care at that time, wondering what she would ever do with electronic stuff. It would only connect with some of her friends from college who also had email addresses. And at that time, she had preferred to just call them from her home phone. But now she did neither. Now she wasn't sure if she'd just been tired, or worried, or trying to hide her growing apathy.

She ruminated about where her standing in school was. Now that, technically, her internship had been cut short, she would have to complete more requirements. Her mind wandered as the rain pounded down in a proper thunderstorm fashion.

The thunder cracked low and long outside, like a train passing in the distance. A flash-flood warning scrolled silently across the bottom of the TV. Good for the crops, her father would say. Bad for basements.

She lay back on the bed, arms folded over her stomach, eyes fixed on the ceiling fan that spun like one blade was slower than the others.

She used to think that by this age she'd be somewhere else. Anywhere else. A different city. A real job. A version of herself who wasn't always catching up. Definitely not camping out in the spare room on her childhood bed.

The hospital visit reminded her that time was running out. And not just for her grandfather.

She curled slightly, listening to the rain pick up pace against the windowpane. Through the floorboards, the muffled sound of her mother's footsteps passed by the basement door.

"If this is the Experience," she whispered, "what exactly am I supposed to learn from it?"

There was no reply. Just the pulse of thunder and the faint electric smell of storm-charged air—the buzz of memory, waiting to pull her under again.

Chapter Twenty-Seven

The next memory jolted into place with a thump of bass and the sour tang of spilled beer. Harriet stood near the jukebox in the dim interior of the Rusty Wrench, a dive bar just off Main Street that still smelled faintly of the 1970s decades later. Neon beer signs buzzed above heavy wooden tables with thick varnish. The music was too loud for conversation but not loud enough to drown out her thoughts.

She looked down. Worn jeans. A well-loved 5K running tee that benefited some obscure nonprofit she had volunteered for during college. The rubber soles of her shoes squeaked slightly on the linoleum. The scent of onion rings clung to her like her regret for coming here tonight. She had just finished a shift at Club Pub, where tonight, the shrimp cocktail she had served had come with a side of existential crisis. But it was Juan Pablo's birthday celebration, and she had promised Trixie she would make an appearance.

She fed two quarters into the jukebox and began scrolling through albums. Zeppelin was always a safe bet. From the back of the bar, two guys hovered near the pool table.

"I'm telling you, I just need to sell that bike. I've got plans."

"How much?"

"Just enough to get a new one. Something sleeker."

"You're not going to get one of those cruising bikes, are you? You'll be out of the gang."

A laugh.

Then one of them said, "Isn't that girl from high school? The one who ran everything? What was her name?"

Harriet ignored the comments and stirred her seltzer and lime, looking for Trixie. She would chat for a few minutes, wish Juan Pablo a happy birthday, and then slip out the back.

"I'm surprised she's still hanging around here."

"I think that's her. Harriet something. Student council. Theater nerd. Bookish type."

Harriet rolled her eyes. Of course they remembered her for what she used to be. Back when she had had plans and AP classes and scholarship interviews. Before mosquito nets and machetes, before Club Pub and living at home with no central air. She selected a Zeppelin track and turned just as someone approached the jukebox.

"Might be cliché, but you can't go wrong with 'Ramble On.'"

She blinked at the voice. That familiar half-cocky, half-sincere tone.

"Miles?"

He smiled, his beard patchy, his hair longer than she remembered. Same duct-taped Converses. Same frayed jeans. A white T-shirt with some startup logo faded across the chest.

"Hey. Wow. Are you a runner now too?" He pointed to her shirt.

"Uh, this was a long time ago. It was at least clean." She laughed and said, pointing to his shirt, "What's that?"

"Some little company I'm starting."

"Some things never cease to amaze me." She scoffed and changed the subject, "You seem happy and healthy. I bet your parents are really proud of you."

He scoffed, dropping his head. "They are pretty happy about how things turned out. They just wish I would stick around longer." He paused, "You're looking good yourself. What have you been up to lately?"

"Well, I may have an interview next week. Some paper pushing thing." She let out a long breath followed by a weak smile.

"Really?" He leaned in, interested and trying to hear her over a friendly disagreement going down at the pool table."

"Yeah. If it doesn't work out, I may look into grad schools. Not sure what, but maybe nursing." She added, "You look like you're doing well. Say, I just came to wish Juan Pablo a happy birthday, then I've got to get home.

"Hey! I'll get that guy a beer!" he scanned the crowded bar for their old friends, spotting the noisy bunch at a high-top table in the back. "Are you sure you don't want to stay awhile?"

They stood in the neon haze for a moment, the memory of high school flickering somewhere between them. Their crossed paths at community college, the few classes they had had in common, but she could never bring herself to respond to his friendly attempts to hang out. What was the point when their ambitions—or her new lack of it— were leading them both elsewhere?

"Come on, Harriet. Hang with old crowd for a moment. Grace us with your presence."

"Fine. Fine. I can stay awake for a half hour more."

"So what else is going on with you? Someone told me you were saving babies in the jungle somewhere."

"What? Who? Trixie? I told her to say it was at an internship."

"Not Trixie. My mom or someone at church…I don't remember."

"I just got back from Central America," she said abruptly. "Built latrines. Distributed antibiotics. Nearly died from a scorpion sting."

"That's badass."

"But sadly, unpaid." She was nearly shouting to be heard over the song blaring next to them.

"Ouch." He raised his empty beer bottle in a mock salute. "I just came back from India. Tech consulting. And a lot of sweating."

"It's probably like this heat." She swiped away some condensation from the side of the glass.

"Yeah. Pretty close."

"So how was India?" She sipped her seltzer and lime.

"Interesting. I taught some coding. Fixed some software. Crashed a wedding. And maybe proposed by accident."

She laughed. It felt good to laugh.

He stepped closer. "You want another drink? Or maybe a round of pool?"

She glanced toward the table, where someone had just racked the balls again. "I think I'm more of a jukebox philosopher tonight."

"I respect that." He paused. "You seeing anyone?"

She shook her head, a little surprised by the question. "No. You?"

He scratched the back of his neck. "Divorced. A couple of years ago. Not proud of it. Got married young. She was smart, career-driven. Left for Ohio."

"Oh."

"Yeah. We weren't exactly built for the long haul. I was still building this," he said, gesturing vaguely at his chest. "The app, the company, the brand. The whole thing, whatever you want to call it."

She nodded. "Let me guess. You're selling your bike to fund the next prototype."

He raised an eyebrow. "I did, actually. *To that guy.*" He overspoke, catching the attention of his friend, who waved him off and set up his next shot in pool.

Outside, they heard a crash. Then shouting. People rushed to the front window for a better view of a growing kerfuffle forming in the street.

Miles winced. "That might be the new ex. Or the almost ex. It's complicated."

Harriet peeked through the window. A woman in a crop top and combat boots was throwing barstools into the street. One smashed into the row of motorcycles lined up at the curb. One tipped over and caused a domino effect.

"I see your taste in relationships is still chaotic. Good."

"I like to keep things interesting."

"You like to keep things burning down. Maybe a little out of control?" she said in a tiny, slightly mocking voice.

"Fair."

She picked up her seltzer. "Good to see you, Miles. Really."

"Same. Hey, if you're ever bored of saving the world one restroom at a time . . ."

She smirked. "I'll know who not to call."

They paused as they smiled. Then drifted in opposite directions. Not quite strangers. Not quite something else.

And the Experience kept going, but this time the frog appeared with a party hat and noisemaker. He blew and unrolled the party favor, and confetti rained down her screen.

"That's different," Harriet said, waiting for the darkness to settle after the Rusty Wrench.

"Memory sequence finalized. First future self coming up next."

"Well, it's about damn time," Harriet said. "I have no idea what to expect."

Chapter Twenty-Eight

Adriana sat across the conference room from Miles, watching as he fiddled with the microphone clipped to his shirt collar. The audio system, sleek and newly installed, popped once in protest, then settled into a low hum. She adjusted the volume levels on the laptop beside her and gave him a subtle thumbs-up.

The annual shareholders' meeting was in full swing at a downtown San Francisco boutique hotel. One where glass walls reflected morning sun across polished surfaces and sleek buffet carts glided between tables like props in a stage play. Servers cleared half-eaten omelets and artfully arranged fruit skewers on white-linen-covered tables while glasses of orange juice and steaming coffee cooled beneath the idle chatter of twenty guests.

Adriana watched them from her seat near the podium. They had all the markings of high-net-worth investors, investors they had carefully curated and kept in their fold. Sharp suits, designer blazers, minimalist jewelry, quiet wealth. They had come from all over: Zurich, Singapore, the Valley, each with their own foundation or family office, scouting the next innovation worth their stake. Most had been with the company since the early days, when the so-called HQ had been the cluttered basement of a rental Adriana had shared with three former dorm mates and a broken boiler. Back then, everything had felt scrappy and optimistic. Now it felt like high-stakes theater. And Miles, as usual, was center stage.

She glanced at him again—animated, electric, testing the mic like it was his sidekick. His enthusiasm hadn't dimmed since those early days, and for that, she was grateful. But she also worried. His latest idea veered into philosophical tech territory. It was more abstract than profitable, more vision than validation. She hoped to God it wouldn't spook the board. It was hard enough to keep attention in a saturated market. Harder still to keep the investors smiling while your product pipeline lagged one innovation cycle behind the Big Four.

Miles clapped his hands, signaling for attention. "Good morning!" he called, voice rising with practiced charisma. "I want to respect your time and get this presentation started."

The room softened. Conversations hushed. Forks clinked quietly against porcelain.

"We are truly excited to share the latest data with you today. The stats were uploaded to our site last week and emailed for your review, but today's about celebrating success. Yours and ours. Hard-earned, every cent. Our shared investment in people, ideas, and, frankly, problems worth solving."

The slideshow flicked to a simplified graph of quarterly growth. Then, just as quickly, to a collage of their less glamorous hits and misses.

"But let's not pretend we hit gold every time. Some of our products soared. Some . . . did not. Who remembers this little beauty?"

The screen flashed to a promotional ad for a game concept that had flopped: a virtual dog park simulator released during peak COVID-19 lockdown.

Chuckles rippled through the crowd.

"Yup," Miles said, smiling. "Launched the week shelter-in-place went into effect. Talk about timing. Build-a-dog, log-a-friend, stay six feet apart. Dogs too!"

A few investors laughed louder now. The next slide cued up.

"Then there was the doll combat game," he added as the video loaded. "Paintball princesses. Honestly, we had too much fun building it. The market? Less amused."

Laughter again. Good-natured but wary.

"We've had our missteps, but we learn fast. We pivot. And sometimes, you get a gem like Design Your Pet Rock!" A rock with googly eyes grinned on-screen, wearing a tiny digital cowboy hat.

Even Adriana chuckled despite herself.

"That one caught fire. We still don't know why. The point is, you can't always predict the hit. But you can control your resilience. You keep building. You stay curious." He nodded toward Adriana. "And with that, I'll turn it over to the real brains behind our operation. Please give a round of applause to our COO, Adriana Steel."

The audience clapped, some out of politeness, some with genuine respect, as Adriana walked to the podium. She smoothed her blazer, adjusted her mic, and took a steadying breath. The room felt warmer under the spotlight. She launched the next set of slides, her voice level, cool, British-tinged.

"Our legacy products continue to perform. The location-finding line remains our top performer—fifth consecutive quarter at number one. Our video filters maintain a strong foothold in the creator space. And yes, the pet rock is still selling."

Light laughter again. She clicked to a graph with tidy upward arcs.

"We've trimmed projects that underperformed and doubled down where the market speaks. We're stable. But we also know stability without vision leads to stagnation." She clicked to a final quote slide. White text on black: *"The future is not laid out on a track. It is something that we can decide, and to the extent that we do not violate any known laws of the universe, we can probably make it work the way that we want to." —Alan Kay, Inventing the Future*

She looked up. "And now, back to our fearless idea man, Mr. Miles Hopper."

Applause came easier this time. She smiled as she walked past him, muting her mic. "Go easy on them," she murmured, squeezing his shoulder. "Heavy on the charm, okay?"

He gave her a wink and reclaimed the podium as she sat down with a quiet sigh. She didn't know what he would say next. She never really did. But she had a folder of contingency plans and a text draft ready with her excuse to move up her flight if the room started to sour. At least she had the wine country tour lined up, a silver-lining consolation prize before flying back to England.

Tanya hadn't come—hadn't even pretended to want to. Even the promise of redwood groves and vineyard tasting flights wasn't enough to lure her away from the London rhythm she loved. Tanya was likely curled up at home with her script notes and a warm cup of chamomile, preparing for another night backstage at the Garrick, where she'd signed on to work makeup for the never-ending run of *Cats*. Theater, quiet evenings, the light commute. It was her kind of world. Not schmoozing. Not last-minute pitch decks and brand campaigns held together by grit and charisma. Adriana didn't blame her. But it did make this part lonelier.

She turned her focus back to the screen, where Miles was gesturing animatedly, the room hanging on his words. Whether it would all crash or catalyze into something real . . . she'd know in about fifteen minutes.

MILES RESTED his palms lightly on either side of the podium, fingers curled just over the edge. The room had warmed during Adriana's part of the presentation. They liked her. Her clarity, her polish, her numbers. She spoke in a language they trusted.

Now came the part they didn't expect.

He cleared his throat and tapped the screen remote. "Let's talk about what's next."

The projector flickered, shifting from the quote to a single word in bold white font:

EXPERIENCE

A FEW BROWS FURROWED. One man with a luxury watch adjusted his cuff, half-interested. Miles let the silence hang just long enough before continuing.

"You've all backed us for years. Through location apps. Games. Tracking tools. Some of it practical. Some of it . . . let's call it 'whimsical.'"

Light laughter. Good start.

"But all of it centered on the same question: What problem are we solving?" He clicked again. The screen now showed a looping video montage: people on subways, in airports, checking their phones, swiping without joy.

"I believe we've entered a new era of disconnection. Not from each other, but from ourselves. From meaning. From emotional clarity."

More silence. A few leaned forward.

"We're introducing a product that doesn't just manage data. It helps users understand the patterns in their decisions. It pulls from memory-linked behaviors, correlates emotional tags, and yes, it generates simulated outcomes."

He waited for the shift. The moment someone in the back raised an eyebrow.

"Simulated . . . ?"

"Yes. Carefully. Ethically. We're not talking about brain-jacking or replacing real life. It's not VR," Miles added quickly, sensing Adriana's tension from the front row. "This is a tool. Think: personal insight engine. Think: cognitive mapping for the every person. What if you could see how a choice in college rippled into your midlife? What if that knowledge helped you pivot?"

The room had gone very still.

Miles leaned forward, lowering his voice like he was letting them in on a secret. "We're calling it the Experience. And it doesn't sell a product . . . it offers people a better version of themselves."

One woman blinked rapidly. Another man scratched a note on his legal pad.

"The prototype is already showing promise in early testing," he said. "We're not here to manipulate people. We're here to show them the shape of their choices. Imagine the value in that."

He let the last slide fade in: an image of a branching tree, its trunk rooted in binary code, its branches forming a human brain. Then he paused. No closing joke. No "Thank you for your time." Just stood there, letting the idea settle.

Applause came slowly at first. Then a swell. Stronger than polite. Curious. Maybe even impressed.

Adriana rose beside the table, mouth pressed into a line of restraint that Miles knew far too well. He walked back to her, passing a server replenishing coffee.

"I told you they'd go for it," he murmured, that lopsided grin already forming.

She shot him a sharp look. "You were two slides away from a TED Talk hosted by Tony Robbins."

"And yet," he said, flicking an invisible speck from his lapel, "I landed it."

"Barely."

"Gracefully."

"Delusionally."

He winked. "You love me when I'm delusional."

She sighed, the corners of her mouth betraying the faintest smile. "Remind me next time to hire a lion tamer. It might be easier than working with you."

"And yet, here we are. Still funded. Still fabulous."

Adriana rolled her eyes but offered her water glass for a quiet toast. "To not crashing the ship, Captain Ahab."

Miles clinked his glass against hers. "And to dreaming big, even when you almost get thrown overboard."

LATER THAT EVENING, Miles sat on the rooftop deck of their San Francisco headquarters, his suit jacket slung over the back of a metal chair still radiating heat from the afternoon sun. Below, Market Street buzzed with the end-of-day shuffle. Horns, buses, footsteps, and voices overlapped in familiar chaos.

He held a tablet in one hand, the other stirring the ice in a glass of something that pretended to be whiskey. The shareholders' meeting had gone better than expected. Adriana had smoothed over the rough edges with a perfectly timed quote and enough charisma to sell sand in a desert. Still, the question circled: What exactly were they building?

Miles stared past the glass railing, eyes unfocused. He had always thought in terms of sound. Vibration. Rhythm. Feedback loops. But this? This wasn't sound.

Not anymore.

He pulled out the newest of his tiny notebooks, the vegan leather worn smooth from back-pocket use, and scribbled in tight, efficient loops:

✓   ELECTROMAGNETIC WAVES.
- ✓   *Oscillating electric + magnetic fields.*
- ✓   *Travel without a medium.*
- ✓   *Perpendicular. Perpetual.*
- ✓   *Invisible. Powerful.*
- ✓   *Not sound. Not music.*
- ✓   *Not parallel lines—crossing without ever touching.*
- ✓   *But light. Always light.*

HE TAPPED the pen once against the margin, then added:

Some people connect by sound. Others, by signal. The best ones, you never see coming. But they can change your whole spectrum.

His first test of the Experience had shown him three possible lives. All viable. All compelling in their own way. One involved a cabin in the Sierras, a golden retriever, and a partnership built on quiet mornings and shared code. Another had him backpacking for years, free and untethered, a digital nomad with no legacy but a thousand microblog entries.

But the third . . . Harriet was in the third.

And not just present. She was thriving. Still snarky. Still skeptical. Still the one person who could slice through his logic and find the soft, dumb truth underneath. In that life, they hadn't rewritten the past.

They'd simply . . . started sooner. Or noticed what had been there all along.

He didn't want to believe the system could manipulate outcomes. That it had shown him what he wanted to see. But when he traced the algorithm's trajectory, he saw the weight of patterns, the hinge points, the quiet yeses that could've changed everything. He saw it.

A different kind of wave. Not measured by amplitude or decibel, but by resonance. Repeating, always perpendicular. Always orbiting.

He stood, slid the notebook back into his coat, and glanced at his reflection in the glass. His hair was messier than usual. His tie was slightly askew. But there was something in his expression he hadn't seen in a while.

Not guilt. Not pressure.

Hope.

The door creaked open behind him. Adriana stepped out, heels clicking against the deck as she held up a bottle of kombucha like it was contraband. "You looked too contemplative up here. Figured I should check you hadn't thrown yourself off the deep end, metaphorically or otherwise."

Miles smirked. "I was just thinking."

"Oh God," she said, walking over and plopping into the chair across from his. "You're doing that again."

"I may need to change the whole metaphor. It's not sound anymore. It's light. Electromagnetic resonance."

Adriana took a sip of the kombucha and grimaced. "Of course it is. Next, you'll tell me you're made of stardust and trauma."

He let out a soft laugh. "No, just regret and machine learning."

She leaned back, shielding her eyes from the sun with one hand. "You know what I regret? Letting you name the app. 'Experience' sounds like an online spa retreat."

He didn't answer, but the smile stayed. For once, he wasn't defensive. Just . . . steady.

Adriana watched him for a moment, then said, "Well, as long as you're not about to rebrand it as LightWave or SoulSignal or some sci-fi nonsense."

"No promises."

She stood, brushing invisible lint from her skirt. "Fine. But if you start quoting Nikola Tesla again, I'm calling your therapist."

He laughed and turned back toward the stairwell, the hum of the city swelling behind him. Inside, the simulation console was waiting. And so was she.

PART III
Light (Electromagnetic Waves)

Chapter Twenty-Nine

The automatic doors whooshed open, and a gust of artificially chilled air smacked Harriet full in the face like a passive-aggressive slap from the universe. She winced, blinking as the fluorescent lights of the co-op grocery flickered overhead. Her cart's front wheel immediately betrayed her, thunking against the worn entry mat and dragging to the right like a car with bad alignment.

She leaned into it, correcting course with the half-defeated posture of a woman who'd been up since dawn, wrangling a preschooler who had just discovered the power of using crayons on the wall.

A gleeful shriek echoed through the front lobby. Somebody's kid was making a heck of a lot of noise.

Hers? A feeling of being watched crept over her and settled into her gut.

The shrieking child, attired in navy track pants with a white stripe and matching sweatbands, bounded his way back to the cart. He bounced as he vied for her attention. "Mom. Mom. Mom. Mom."

Definitely hers. Definitely needed some energy to manage this one. Energy she would have to use sparingly if she were to get through this shopping adventure with her sanity intact.

Mac, eight and forever in motion, broke into a sprint as he came from the bakery. "Can I get a cookie?" he asked, lifting a sample from under the protective dome, his wrist sweatband shaking as much as his body.

"No," Harriet said, already regretting the trip. "Wait, maybe. If we survive produce."

She sighed and shifted her bulky canvas tote higher on her shoulder. It had been a promotional item from the wellness conference she didn't remember signing up for but somehow still received emails from. Her shirt was an oatmeal-colored oversize henley now slightly crusted with toddler breakfast. It clung to her under the arms from both exertion and the weight of motherhood. Leggings, because jeans felt like too much work. A pair of knockoff Birkenstocks completed the look, spotless only because she'd cleaned them with a baby wipe on the way out the door.

She noticed her reflection in the glass of an endcap cooler case. She was happy to see her curls were mostly tamed today, pulled back into a scrunchie she was pretty sure had originally belonged to her daughter. A fine sheen of tired glowed on her forehead. She told herself, *I'm dewy, not sweaty.*

It was only as she finally gained traction with the rogue cart wheel that she glanced up and Harriet realized where she was from inside the Experience. Taking it in that despite having very little contact with kids in her actual life, she was in the mindset of this mother self.

She took in the surrounding gentrified neighborhood with lush lawns and artsy gardens. This grocery store was not just a co-op, but one that had moved into the old Piggly Wiggly, just blocks from her elementary school years home. Also a block away from Miles Hopper's place. Of course it had evolved into something with kombucha on tap and organic guava jerky.

Chip, apparently her youngest, kicked his light-up sneakers against the cart seat and yelled, "Food party!"

"Yeah!" Mom Harriet said with a plastered-on smile. She drew in a deep breath and plunged into the store, past the automatic produce spritzers and right into the thrum of Saturday-morning chaos. Somewhere, her daughter squealed again, like a happy hamster. Harriet followed the sound.

Dot, age nine and on a self-declared vegan campaign, walked ahead of her with her arms spread out, holding the store flyer. She browsed the store sales. "If you get the nonorganic grapes, you'll save a dollar thirty-two."

"Thank you, sweetie. We'll invest it in your college fund."

"I'll go check out the rest of the sales in the fruit section," she said before Mom Harriet could ask her to wait.

Chip was now singing a made-up jingle about grapes in a bowl while Harriet tried to steer toward the bananas. Mac moved on from the cookie discussion and darted into a cereal aisle with the agility of a martial artist.

Harriet tried not to panic. This was their Saturday routine. How did four kids have this much energy?

Harriet grabbed a bunch of bananas and continued on to find Dot in the bulk foods area. She was leaning into a bin of dried mango slices, one small hand buried up to the wrist in the scoopable drawer. Cache, age five, was whining beside his sister, begging for her to share a treat with him.

"Why don't I get to eat some?" he wailed. Harriet produced a stick of gum from her purse and split it in half, giving part to the dejected child and shoving the other piece in her mouth. "Dot." She said her name in that low, pointed tone that communicated the holy trifecta of motherhood: embarrassment, warning, and resignation. "We don't snack from the bins."

Dot looked up with wide, innocent eyes and mango stuck to her bottom lip like lip gloss. She held up a slice, showing off her discovery. "It's chewy and vegan!" she declared, delighted. "Besides, it's just a sample."

Harriet sighed and reached down, plucking the sticky strip from Dot's hand and dropping it into the compostable bag swinging from the side of the cart. "We're buying that now. Along with your germs. No more samples."

Behind her, Chip hiccupped from the cart seat, where he had managed to remove one sock and had begun chewing it. His curls stuck out at all angles, giving him the look of a very satisfied mad scientist. Harriet reflexively adjusted the strap on his overalls, which had somehow twisted itself halfway around his torso despite her having fixed it fifteen minutes earlier.

"Hey, Harriet?"

She turned, instantly clocking the voice as one of the semi-familiar playground parents. One of those people you'd shared six months of potluck signup sheets with but couldn't remember if they were team gluten-free or team non-GMO.

It was Janelle. Mom of twins. Always in floaty cardigans and high-functioning yoga pants. Today, she wore a rose-colored headband and carried a mason jar filled with something green and ominous. A sprig of mint bobbed near the surface. Possibly parsley. Possibly built under a spell.

"Oh hey," Harriet said, summoning a smile from somewhere behind her sleep-deprived eyeballs. "You survived the second-grade field trip?"

"Barely," Janelle said with mock horror. "We lost a kid for six minutes. Not mine, thank God. But still."

Their laughter came easily, the communal kind that lived in captivity between sports bleachers and preschool parking lots.

"Oh my gosh, Janelle. That's crazy. Know what else is crazy? Swim lesson signup. I swear all the mini-me classes were taken before they opened it up. I stood in line for an hour with these monkeys trying to get them all in on a Tuesday slot. Now we're hustling over to the pool three times a week."

"Ugh. At least my Camille got in the ten a.m. spot. I don't have to get up early now! Hey, did you hear about the art teacher's sudden sabbatical?" She looked around to see who could hear them. "I heard there was more going on in the supply closet than cleaning up supplies, if you know what I mean?"

"Oh, I think so." Harriet swiped a piece of renegade hair back over her ear. "Where did you hear that?"

"PTA. Which, by the way, the elections are early this year. And I would so love to have you on the board with me. We have an opening for secretary that I think you would be just perfect for. Tell me you will let me help you get elected?"

"Uh, I'll have to see about that. I think with the pet store and

Miles's work, I may not have time to do that."

"But it would be so much fun!" She jumped a little, nodding excitedly, as if taking on the job of secretary pro bono was the dream destiny of every toddler mom. Dot, now swaying back and forth in her sandals and sundress, began eyeing the bins of chocolate-covered pretzels with predatory interest. Chip let out a growl from his seat, then immediately began gnawing on the side of the cart.

"Well, see ya, sweetie. Maybe at book club?"

"Yeah!" Harriet said as Janelle moved along with her minty elixir and murmured goodbye.

Harriet lingered a moment longer by the bulk bins, nudging the cart forward. It was surreal, raising her kids here. In the same gentrified pocket of town where she'd grown up, just down the street from Angelo's and her old high school stomping grounds. She could still picture the Hopper house before the whole neighborhood had seemed to get a facelift. Beat-up siding from where balls, bikes, and frisbees had made their marks; a basketball hoop rusted above the garage; and Miles hopping the fence with an armload of fireworks or whatever terrible mischief he and the gang were cooking up that week. Now the old corner store where they used to shop after school for Fritos and store-brand soda had gone granola-style grocery store with a freshly ground peanut butter station and produce bins labeled in chalk handwriting. *Curated imperfect kumquats.* What did that even mean?

The neighborhood had grown up, apparently. Just like her.

And yet. As she adjusted Chip's sock and steered Dot away from a sample tray of sips of wine, it felt a little like she was crashing a life someone else had organized properly. Like she was playacting stability with a cartful of crusty wipes, a slew of snack-demanding tyrants, and the shadow of her grade-school self hovering somewhere near the organic paper towels.

She caught sight of Mac moments later, crouched by the magazines and giggling at a glossy cover featuring tanned models in beachwear. "It says hot beach bods!" he whispered, like he'd uncovered a crime.

She nudged him out with her foot. "We'll talk about objectification later. Now march."

They made it to the cereal aisle. Amazingly, all four kids were within arm's reach. And a fresh war began.

Harriet was holding two bags of granola in her hands, trying to decide which label looked less suspicious. She examined the grams of sugar with the scrutiny she used to reserve for deciding which cassette tape had been more deserving of her hard-earned mall money. That's when Dot and Mac approached her like two lawyers ready to fight it out in her court.

"Frosted Flakes!" Mac yelled. "She got to pick the cereal last week!"

"Granola," Dot countered. "It's much healthier."

Harriet sighed and put both granolas back on the shelf.

"Marshmallows!" screamed Chip, squishing the bag with glee.

A tiny hand tugged at her leggings, and she turned to her second-youngest child. "Mom," Cache whined, holding up a crushed box of Sugar Teddies. The cartoon bear on the front flashed a manic grin and two thumbs-up. "Can we get this one?"

"Honey, I don't think so."

He went into full pout mode. Pools started to form around the edges of his eyes, and his bottom lip started to tremble.

From behind them came a crash. Dot and Mac were nowhere to be seen. Clearly a sign they had something to do with this.

"Put it back, please." Harriet glanced at the heap of cereal boxes she had intentionally decided someone else must have knocked over at the end of the aisle. Probably (not) her kids.

Harriet steered the cart away from the fallen cereal boxes and scanned for her two oldest kids. The pair appeared busy at the other end of the aisle. Dot studied a jar of pickles, and Mac tapped a foot on the floor as he counted ceiling tiles.

"Mom! Did you see that?" Mac shouted in fake surprise.

Harriet pressed her fingers to her temples. "Quiet game," she said sharply. "Whoever's quiet the longest picks the music on the way home."

A small miracle occurred: silence.

Harriet grabbed a box of Cheerios from the shelf and tossed in onto the heap of food in the cart. Everybody groaned, whining like air escaping a balloon.

"What? You can put a spoonful of sugar on them. Head to the checkout, please."

The kids protested further, shouting out to support their own case.

"Let's go. Oh, and I guess I win that round. Everyone gets to listen to my music."

More groaning as the three non-cart kids slumped toward the front of the store.

From the observation chamber, the real Harriet blinked, lips twitching in stunned amusement. She had no memory of this reality because it wasn't hers. But the moment was so vivid she could practically smell the spicy-sweet mangos Dot was chewing. Dot's commanding, mini-adult voice that reminded her of her own. Chip's chubby little fist grabbing at marshmallows and squishing them through the bag as he giggled. Her own adult voice barking out commands in a cereal aisle like she was strategizing for a war. The chaos was overwhelming and kind of . . . brilliant. Like how blaring horns, pounding percussion, and vibrating strings somehow all come together to form a symphony.

It was amazing. These kids looked like her and also not like her. They had varied temperaments that she could relate to. Each kid had imprinted on her heart in these few moments she had witnessed them. And she knew already that Chip must be her favorite. If parents are allowed to have a favorite child.

Her simulation continued with the dreaded purgatory for all parents: the checkout line. Filled with goodies, toys, magazines, and gum, which was destined to become glued to one of their heads of hair. The checkout line was the perfect spot for capitalizing children to sneak a few extras into the cart without getting noticed. Add in the energy crash after the excitement of the outing wearing off and the disappointment of not getting what they wanted beginning to set in.

Harriet closed her eyes and exhaled through her nose. "Just . . . leave it. Mac, take Cache up front and wait for me. We're checking out."

Mac had opened a bag of cheese balls and was casually eating them with sticky hands. He glanced back at her, insolent. "What? I'm hungry."

"Now!"

"Jeez, someone didn't get enough coffee this morning," he whispered to his little brother. He took Cache's hand obediently, covering it in a cheesy mess, and pulled him toward the front of the store.

To Harriet's dismay, the checkout lines were packed three carts deep across the row of registers. When they finally reached the conveyor belt, she was completely exhausted, but luckily, Dot—and Chip—began unloading groceries like contestants on a timed game show.

"Good work, guys," Harriet said, carefully rescuing the eggs from the chaos and placing them somewhere they wouldn't be immediately pulverized. The children "helped," which both kept them busy and technically counted as teaching them responsibility. She could complain about the apples rolling around the grime-coated cart like old-timey train hobos, but she'd have to wash everything anyway. Maybe including the kids.

The fortunate cashier to get her brood looked like she'd aged five years during her shift, and she wasn't getting any younger trying to understand the circus Harriet had around her. Chip tried to hand the woman a crayon in exchange for the marshmallows he was holding. She took it and looked at it, puzzled.

The half-eaten cheese balls crossed over the conveyor belt. "I've got this, Mom," he said, stepping back into line and handing the mittful of money to the lady. The cashier studied the change in her hand.

Harriet motioned to the checkout lady to hand it back to her. She took the insufficient funds and squished them into her front pocket. "Honey, thank you, but you have to clear that purchase with the boss first next time."

He pouted, a deep frown, and shoved his hand into the open cheese ball bag to defiantly fill his mouth with the dry, powdery snacks.

At the cart, Dot played with Chip while Cache eyed the shelves of candy bars. His gaze locked onto the cover of *Sports Illustrated*, where a model stretched across the hood of a sports car.

"Seriously? Just stand up there by your brother." Harriet rotated the magazine backward and motioned to the far end of the cart where a bored teen loaded their goods into paper bags.

"I wasn't looking at anything," Cache muttered, eyes darting away and eyeing up the row of chocolates. Mac had gravitated back to her, sensing an opportunity, and grabbed a nougat-filled chocolate bar. He held it up right in Harriet's face while she leaned over the cart for bags of frozen peas.

"Stop!" She swatted the candy bar away, "You picked cheese balls. That's your treat."

"This one's on sale," Mac sang, holding up the candy bar.

"Get four and one is free!" Dot chimed in.

"Then get three more, make it four. Make sure one is a Charleston Chew."

Dot rolled her eyes. "Charleston Chews stick in my teeth. No fair."

Mac shushed her and immediately smiled as innocently as he could. "I know you like the strawberry ones."

"I want gum," Dot added. "Bubblelicious. That one."

Harriet nodded. "Fine. But only if—"

"I want gum too," Cache said, looking up with the soulful eyes of an abandoned puppy.

Harriet looked over the growing stack of candy bars now sitting on the conveyor belt, the line growing impatient behind them. "Too late. No gum. No candy. You already have cheese balls." She yanked an extra tub of peanut butter from the cart and set it aside. "Dot, take the keys. Get everyone in the car."

As she turned back to the register, Harriet blinked, half-stunned. They'd done it. They'd swarmed her with snack logic, double-teamed her with sale math, and now four candy bars were sliding across the scanner as if she'd wanted them all along.

She used to judge parents like this. The ones who caved. The ones who couldn't hold the line at checkout. Now she understood: that line didn't hold. Not under the full-court press of negotiations from three snack-fueled bandits with sticky fingers and weaponized charm. This required some pro-level parenting.

The real Harriet, still inside the Experience machine, exhaled a slow breath. She hadn't known any of this. The way a child's voice could tilt the air in their favor, melting your heart. The strange triumph of calling it a personal win just because no one had cried. It wasn't polished. It sure wasn't peaceful. But it was hers to shape and cultivate. Or could have been. A life measured out in not-smashed-eggs victories, in tantrums and minimal toddler teeth marks, in quiet cart rescues no one ever noticed. She hadn't expected it to be so draining. She definitely hadn't expected it to feel this . . . full.

She handed Dot the keys. Too tired to override this premonition of doom based on the lack of good judgment, welcoming the slim chance of her being able to pay for the groceries in peace.

"Can I drive?" Mac asked, eyes glinting with mischief.

"Try it and die," she shot back. The cashier stopped, dropping the boxes of mac-and-cheese carelessly into the paper bag as she locked eyes with Harriet.

She turned to the cashier and forced a smile. "You get it, right?"

She did not. The cashier, a woman with permed white hair and a name tag that read *Edith*, didn't make eye contact, suddenly consumed as she scanned a carton of juice boxes. "Never had kids. Allergic."

"Same," she said sarcastically, mostly to see the woman's reaction. She was a stone.

"One hundred thirteen and sixteen."

Harriet blinked. "Seriously?"

"You've got like, sixteen bags, lady," Edith wheezed as if she would die without a cigarette at that very moment.

"Right. Lots of mouths to feed." She shifted into her brightest smile she reserved for public moments like this and handed over two fifties and a twenty, watching her cash disappear with the swipe of a weathered hand.

Outside, the minivan honked. Then someone laid on the horn with the urgency of a four-bell fire alarm. Moments later, Dot burst through the doors, panting. "Mac tried to start the car! Cache's buckled in and the whole car's rolling!"

Harriet looked up. The minivan was drifting slowly across the lane, bumping toward a light post.

"Shit."

She tossed her receipt at Edith and sprinted outside, pulling out

Chip from the cart and running after Dot. She bolted through the sliding door and across the parking lot. At the driver's side door, she passed the toddler off to Dot and yanked the door open. Harriet slammed the barely rolling minivan into park, jolting the whole thing to a sudden stop.

"You. Are. Grounded," she growled at Mac, "Seat belt. Now." She pointed to the back seat next to Cache, who was clapping with excitement.

"Do it again!" Cache said as Mac moped through the center of the vehicle and fell into his spot in the van. Harriet popped open the back door.

The bagger had followed her out with the well-loaded cart, unmoved by the events. A bored teen with braces and earbuds, he listened to his iPod nano while unloading the groceries into the back. "Thanks for shopping The Corner Collective," he mumbled.

Harriet shoved two quarters at him from the dash. "Thanks. Seriously."

Inside the car, Dot was buckling Chip into his car seat while Mac muttered something indecipherable.

"Play the silent game," Harriet ordered. "First one to talk loses a cookie."

"Tattletale," Cache whispered at Dot, who was sitting in a captain's chair.

"Mom! He talked!" she reported instantly.

"You talked too!"

Harriet turned up the radio, drowning them out with a throwback pop song. Somewhere between the bass drop and a chorus about beach hair and bad choices, she imagined herself on a quiet shore with zero children and one large cocktail.

"No cookies for anyone."

The crying came instantly. Synchronized sobs. Full drama.

She didn't flinch. "Not until you learn how to play the quiet game." She smiled, lost in a Caribbean daydream the whole three blocks home.

Chapter Thirty

He looked down at the name tag on his company shirt, the one that read, *TED—Experience Guide*. The one that clearly wasn't his own.

The real Ted was an intern who worked on product demos. He was one of the guys they usually sent to university fairs and trade shows to wheel the console in and show off the novelty features. To show an audience the generic simulations and such that made the machine a fun, hyperrealistic movie—a little trippy, but hardly accurate.

In reality, when one stepped into the Experience, it was more like shaking a Magic 8 Ball and getting some kind of suggested outcomes based on a few basic demographic questions that a participant answered before entering.

The real Ted had a big college test to study for. Miles didn't mind borrowing his shirt, and it somehow seemed more legit since Miles rarely handled these events. But watching her now, stumbling through memories she hadn't touched in decades, he felt like a coward. The name on his chest meant nothing. Not compared with the one she still didn't know was watching her from behind the curtain.

Miles leaned forward over the tablet, standing vigilantly outside the Experience pod, his eyes flicking across the panel of real-time biometric readouts. Harriet's vitals had spiked just a little right after the runaway car moment. He dragged a finger along the waveform graph, then paused to zoom in on her neural activity overlay.

A microburst of confusion. Frustration. Then . . . was that warmth?

He blinked, then let the data rerun, but slower this time. Huh. There it was again. The kind of uptick that wasn't usually created by embarrassment or stress. It looked suspiciously like . . . bonding.

He shook his head and pushed back slightly from the high table where he was monitoring Harriet's progress. "Well, I'll be damned," he murmured to no one.

The kids had worn her down. Not just the simulation version, but her. The real Harriet was warming up to this pack of wild children that she had been duped into believing were her own. She had stepped in as a surrogate with seamless efficacy. Fascinating.

Harriet was the one they'd hoped was the key to making this technology plausible and demonstrative of its power to change people's lives in significant and informed ways. She had not disappointed, but he hadn't anticipated this particular simulation to offer much insight from his career-driven friend from his past.

This simulation was the domestic one, the stroller-pushing Harriet with snack-bar negotiations and diaper-bag improvisation. But the machine had mapped her better than he ever could have manually. Even if he had bothered to try a bit harder to figure her out in person, he couldn't have guessed this about her. He had had enough time to try.

And she was responding. It was wild. Discovering the many sides of Harriet was almost as much fun as figuring out the math that made this machine do its magic.

He glanced over at the display tablet. In the corner, a video feed looped silently: Harriet had a suspicious look to her, brushing a chocolate stain from her sweater, then glancing toward the cart where Chip sucked his thumb. Then a warm look of contentment radiated from her, almost sheepish, like she wasn't sure how she had gotten there.

He could've told her, prepped her better, before she had entered the machine.

"That was a big detour, huh?" he said softly, momentarily out of sync with his Ted-the-guide ruse. "You're doing fine."

Then, catching himself, he cleared his throat and stood straighter, glancing around the hall. Adriana would roll her eyes if she caught him getting sentimental over brain wave data. Still, he didn't pull back the feed. He watched the rest of the checkout sequence, tapping the edge of the screen in sync with the heartbeat sensor like it was a rhythm he suddenly wanted to memorize.

HARRIET PULLED into the driveway of their two-story craftsman, gravel crunching beneath the tires. The side of the house was lined with tidy lilies and overgrown hostas. She turned off the ignition, and the car exhaled its final sigh. In the back seat, the boys began to stir, unbuckling and piling out of the side door. Grown Harriet recognized the house, but it had been repainted a forest green with tan trim and red accents. The new version of her childhood home across the street was painted cheerful blue, with white trim and a well-kept yard. "Everybody grab something," she ordered, a futile request.

Dot reached for Chip and hefted him out of the seat. She carried him to their mother, the toddler's feet thumping against her thighs. Cache bolted to the tree house, sniffling just enough to ensure everyone noticed. Mac had dashed from the car before it had fully stopped and found a hiding spot behind the garage.

Miles stood by the hedge with a hose in one hand and a beer in the other. He passed the bottle to their neighbor, Milt, whose porch candy bowl served as an unofficial flag of friendliness. The neighborhood honorary grandpa to the kids waved to Harriet as she walked up, Chip on her hip and frustration from the morning excursion radiating from her.

"Take him?" she asked. "Is your mom home? Maybe we could drop the kids off for a few minutes. Time with Gramma H."

Miles didn't hesitate. He took the baby with practiced ease, settling Chip into the crook of one arm.

Harriet blinked, caught slightly off guard. The backyard smelled like sun-warmed plastic toys, charcoal starter that had spilled a bit the night before, and overripe strawberries Dot had smashed earlier on the patio. She noticed the ants were already forming a swarm, overtaking the sweet surprise. Somewhere behind the fence, someone's radio was playing classic rock, and the rhythmic thud-thud-thud of kids taking turns on a trampoline provided the percussion.

"Nope. It's bowling tournament weekend," Miles said.

"That's right." Harriet lifted her hand to her forehead and sighed deeply. "We have got to get another babysitter. We just do."

"Even with the best ones next door?" He winked. "Grandma and Grandpa love watching the kids."

"I can't keep up with their social schedule. Hell, I can't keep up with my schedule."

Chip snuggled into Miles's chin as if it had been just yesterday that he had held him in the hospital. Harriet brushed her hair behind one ear, feeling the stickiness of sunscreen she had applied that morning and graham cracker crumbs clinging to her skin. Her shirt was slightly wrinkled from pressing too many paper bags to her chest. Popsicles were now melting with the other freezer foods in the back of the minivan and dribbled down her front. She had had it. But somehow, the morning had folded in on itself, the better side of this life making itself apparent. And here she was, patiently soaking in the moment, watching Miles cradle the baby of the family like it was nothing.

"What's the story with Mac?" he asked, bouncing Chip, who tried to put his fingers in his father's mouth. He bit back playfully, and Chip giggled, full-throated and utterly delighted. "Dot was storming around, shouting about some car drama at the store?"

Harriet looked over her shoulder. Mac had eased out of his hiding place and was now nicely playing with Dot on the swings Miles had built them years ago. A rare moment of confluence between the siblings. Mac pushed her on the spinning swing, gently, and seemed like a sensible human. So different from the highly fueled rampage she had just witnessed at the grocery store. "He knocked over a cereal display, tried to buy candy he hates, and rolled the car into a light pole while I was paying." She exhaled in a flat sigh that was supposed to be humorous but came out closer to defeat.

Miles didn't laugh. He just nodded, like this was part of the job. Like any parent worth their grilling tongs who had seen worse before noon.

She looked at Chip's face tucked under Miles's jawline, and something shifted. This version of life that was foreign to her, the kind with car seat buckles and checkout chaos and pop-up BBQ invites wasn't polished, but it had its own gravity. And Miles fit into it a little too easily.

She hadn't realized how much she'd been holding. Holding in this version of her life, but also in her life in general, until someone else had reached out and taken the weight, even for a minute.

And then the bubble of the moment burst when Mac pushed Dot a little too hard and she fell off the swing. Crying, she chased him down for redemption. He turned and threw a soccer ball at her face, and she erupted into loud bawling.

Miles winced and shook his head. "Classic."

"Don't even start to tell me how he's just a boy getting out the wiggles. I saw how bad that was."

"I won't. I'll talk to him."

"Thanks."

Miles carried Chip to the backyard, where Dot had reclaimed the swing beneath the treehouse. He took on the dad duty and settled Mac in the quiet corner for a five-minute reset. She looked angrily at her brother from the swing. Miles walked toward her and checked her face for damage.

"How's my favorite girl?" Miles wiped at the tears dripping from her chin. "All better?"

"I'm your only girl, Dad," Dot said through sniffling, wiping her nose on the back of her hand.

"Not true. What about your mom?"

"You said she's a grown-up."

"Then you're my favorite non-grown-up girl."

She giggled a tiny bit and leaned back in the swing, eyes following a trail of ants navigating the strawberries on the porch.

Miles set Chip down in a smaller fenced-in play area and wandered around the car to inspect the bumper. "That'll buff out," he muttered in front of Milt, who was now trimming hedges. Milt just chuckled and continued cutting away.

"He almost killed us!" Dot shouted, now hanging upside down from the swing like a bat.

Miles looked up. "You seem pretty alive."

"You should ground him forever," she said vindictively.

Mac turned toward her and stuck out his tongue. Once he saw his father looking sternly at him, he tucked his head back under his hands at the kid's picnic table where he sat.

"Got it. I'll take it under advisement."

Harriet stood at the back of the van that was open like a canopy, pulling out grocery bags loaded to their limits. Paper handles cut into her fingers already damp from condensation, threatening to break with the slightest bump. Miles appeared at her side without a word, grabbing the heavier ones like it was second nature. She gave him a quick glance of gratitude that dissolved all the chaos from the morning. She started toward the house and opened the screen door with her free hand.

They moved through the kitchen in quiet rhythm, setting bags onto the counters and brushing away the slick moisture from the frozen waffles and stick packs of yogurt. Harriet peeled open a bag of grapes and handed a few to Dot, who had appeared briefly in the doorway with an urgent report: "Chip is eating dirt."

"Good for his immunity," Miles said automatically, waving her off. Harriet added while piling buns and bread on the counter, "Just keep him away from the squished strawberries, please? I don't want to have to deal with those stains."

The window above the sink framed the backyard like a slightly disheveled family portrait. Dot had returned to the swing and twirled with abandon. Cache dug happily in the sandbox with his trucks, free from any competition from his energetic siblings. Chip toddled in a curious disarray across the patchy grass. All the while, Mac sulked with theatrical flair at the picnic table like a prince in exile.

Harriet let out a breath. Not quite a sigh. Not quite peace either. But something close.

Then Miles stepped behind her, arms wrapping around her waist with an easy confidence that made her shoulders tense. Then drop. The tension released when he rested his chin gently against the top of her head.

"How's my actual favorite girl?"

She rolled her eyes but didn't move. The weight of him behind her was surprisingly reassuring, like being bracketed in place during turbulence. "Still not interested in your favorite line."

Miles chuckled against her hair. "You used to be."

"I also used to think Charleston Chews were a gourmet dessert," she replied, reaching blindly into a bag and pulling out with deliberate care a carton of eggs that were miraculously not cracked.

He didn't answer right away. Just stayed where he was, arms still loose around her middle. She could feel the warmth of him even through the tired haze of the morning and the cold sweat from the milk jug dripping down her arm. And for a moment, just a moment, she let herself lean back into it.

He kissed the back of her neck. "You're exhausted."

"You noticed."

"I took the morning off from the repair shop. The lawn needed some work, and I figured we could tag-team this."

"I was going to take them to the pet store this afternoon. Agnes canceled again. Sick. Someone has to cover her shift."

"Maybe we need someone new."

"Maybe. It's hard to hire someone reliable. They all think it will be great to work with all the animals until they understand how many cages they have to clean every day."

"I can take Mac and Cache with me to work. They can wind up cables and rewind VCR reels. You and Dot can go get some spa time."

"She'd love that."

"Would you love it?"

"Honestly, I would just love to take an uninterrupted nap."

He reached for a package of shredded cheese. "I was thinking . . . when you take Dot for a spa trip, maybe Kyle can run the register at the pet shop for the afternoon. I've have the boys at the shop. We can clean the cages later or maybe before opening tomorrow morning."

"So, about the spa day . . . can we afford that right now? I'm not sure the store is going to make its budget this quarter."

"The budget is fine. Have you seen how many exotic fish were sold last week? Besides, you deserve it. The repair shop had a good week. And I've already booked it. Pedis for my favorite girls. No arguing."

She turned toward him. "That's the best thing I've heard all day." She melted into a Miles bear hug.

"Better than a Charleston Chew?"

"Better than four Charleston Chews. Which are in one of these bags, somewhere. I actually like them, you know. Mac has no idea what he's missing."

Miles started stowing milk and butter in the fridge. "Got another repair today on the answering machine. VCR again. Some woman refuses to upgrade to DVDs."

Harriet huffed, lining up cans of beans in the built-in pantry, rotating stock. "That lady isn't wrong. VHS has soul. Our kids live on those tapes. You have to admit it."

"Yes. And Monty Python. *Young Frankenstein. Godzilla.*"

"True enough. Those movies shaped me. And possibly warped me."

"Explains your sense of humor."

Harriet smiled and leaned against the counter. "You're not complaining."

"Never."

"I'll order pizza tonight too. Let's feed the monsters, put them to bed early, and reclaim the night."

"And watch some terrible TV?"

"Mandatory."

"Sleep?"

"Optional."

They finished the groceries in silence, the kind that had become their shared language over the years. Their shoulder-to-shoulder effort was interrupted only by the occasional child shriek outside. When the last bag was emptied, Harriet reached up to brush a stray curl behind Miles's ear.

"I still don't know how this became our life," she said.

He shrugged. "Chaos has a way of choosing us."

She nodded. "Yeah. But I wouldn't trade it."

Miles leaned slightly, shifting his weight so Harriet could keep unpacking without losing the shape of the moment.

"You know," he said quietly, "this whole thing you and I've got going here . . . it's good. Feels real."

Harriet paused, one hand still in the grocery bag, fingers grazing the cardboard box of granola bars. She didn't look at him. "Real doesn't mean easy."

"I didn't say easy." His voice was low, steady. "But I used to picture you somewhere else. In an office tower downtown. Some place with bad coffee but great views. A sleek desk with minimal decor. Or maybe no desk at all like a foreign correspondent, catching the news from some dramatic war-torn area of the world."

Harriet snorted. "Yeah, that sounds about right. I was different back then."

"You're different here." He hesitated, just long enough for her to notice. "Maybe happier?"

She turned toward him then, just enough to catch the edge of his expression. Maybe even a little hopeful.

Before she could answer, a soft thwack echoed from the backyard, followed by a high-pitched scream, more territorial than of pain—theatrical outrage.

Harriet froze. "Dot."

She darted to the window. Dot was standing in the middle of the yard, arms crossed, glaring daggers at Mac, who was gleefully brandishing a soggy water balloon like a trophy.

"I thought he was in a time-out," Miles said, studying the backyard.

"Not it," Harriet muttered, grabbing a dish towel and handing it to Miles.

"Already on it," Miles said, cracking the sliding glass open to holler out the window, "Mac! Time out! Now." Then: "Parenting," he said with a grin, accepting the towel. "The slowest interrupted conversation in human history."

"That's deep." Harriet laughed in spite of herself. "Let's see if I make it to the end of one sentence before another mini-crisis happens."

～

FROM THE QUIET of the monitoring station, Miles watched as a younger adult version of himself bolted through the back door, dish towel in hand, and Harriet yelled something to the kids about manners from the kitchen window. The tablet didn't have the surround-sound quality in this mode. His tiny earbud speaker was just enough to enhance the live visual render and synched biometric markers, but he didn't need the audio much. Her body language, her dramatic expressions, her reactions to each child's drama told the whole story.

She was trying not to laugh. She was pretending to scold. And she was doing it perfectly as if she had practiced this mock sternness daily as a mother for a decade.

He zoomed out slightly to capture the full scene. Dot was making her case to her father—him—appealing to his soft side with tears and dramatic hand gestures, assumedly like her mother would. Chip now army-crawled gleefully through a sprinkler-turned-mud-patch, taking the unsupervised moment to indulge in forbidden play. Cache dangled from the bottom step of the tree house ladder, pouting like a brooding gargoyle that had his birthday taken away.

Miles stepped back from the tablet and stood straight in the exhibit hall. This was remarkable.

The data was one thing: her elevated heart rate, an apparent flush of cortisol, along with a flood of oxytocin. But none of it explained the way he felt watching this simulated reality unfold. There was no graph line for measuring her regret. No time stamp for understanding the complexity of what she had been longing for. Just the tight ache of wanting something you'd convinced yourself you were better off without. And from what he could deduce, she was very good at this version of herself.

He hadn't built the simulation to make her feel like this. Not specifically. It had been meant to expand her thinking, to give her access to alternate outcomes, to help her see how far her choices could stretch.

And maybe she could see how much of an impact she was capable of making on others.

He felt off about how easily she was doing just that. She was giving him a lot by experiencing these simulations. She was proving that the machine could immerse a person into a life they wouldn't dream of, one they would have been successful at. But at what cost? And what purpose?

He had his reasons. Reasons she would probably hate and, with luck, she could possibly overlook. If she made it to the end. And his sleight of hand hope to get her to try it on her own worked. That was something the machine had predicted. But did she really know what she was signing on for? Do the means really justify the ends? It was a gray area.

But now, watching her leave the kitchen to join the ruckus in the backyard, him steadying the clean towel over one shoulder, Miles was beginning to doubt his motivation for showing her this. The machine was skillfully handing her the life she could have lived. And it would take it away too. He watched Harriet's simulation finish as she mediated a sibling dispute with ease and a gentle smile, and it didn't feel hypothetical anymore.

This was real. At least to her. And there would be consequences to deal with. Adriana was right. She was always right.

Maybe it was becoming real to him, as he noticed an unfamiliar ache below his rib cage. And Adriana was maybe right about that too.

He tapped the side of the tablet as Harriet reached for an old juice box someone had tossed toward the bushes and held it up like the white flag of peace. "Who wants a juice?" she sang out, and the whole crew rushed into the kitchen.

"Yeah," he murmured to himself. "You'd have been really good at this." Then, after a beat, "You *are* good at this."

And for the first time since booting up Harriet into the system, Miles wasn't sure whom her simulation was really for.

Chapter Thirty-One

T he lights dimmed. The scent of dish soap and dryer sheets faded into nothing. The scene of the kitchen, the rustle of paper grocery bags being crammed under the sink dissipated. The kids giggling around her as they helped once again with stacking the remaining cans in the pantry melted into the background, along with the vision of these little versions she could have hypothetically created. With him. And the noise vanished into an astounding unnatural hush.

Harriet stood in the void once more.

She didn't move. All her energy was spinning through her mind, replaying this maternal version of herself. She didn't speak. Her voice was gone with this concocted idea of motherhood. She just stood, blinking into the pitch-black space, the afterimage of her minivan still burned behind her eyelids.

A breath. Then another.

What the hell was that?

"No."

Her voice cracked, echoing back at her, small and strange in the dark.

"No, no, no."

The floor beneath her was no longer the restored wooden planks of their remodeled kitchen. The kitchen and home she apparently lived in with Miles *fricken* Hopper. And was raising a family?

The air didn't move, but somehow, it pressed against her skin like a thick silicon suit. She rubbed her face, half-expecting the scent of Dot's hair detangler to still be there. But it was just a vision of a person, a situation, a family that didn't exist.

"That was not what I signed up for," she said, louder this time. "What the hell was that, Ted?"

The digitized, emotionally cautious version of Ted responded, "We hoped the domestic scenario would offer clarity. Many users express regret or curiosity around child-rearing and partnership roles they chose not to pursue."

"I never wanted four kids," Harriet snapped. "Four kids? A car crash? Charleston Chews?"

A long pause. Harriet waited.

"Dot was charming," the voice offered.

"She was fine. They were all . . . fine. But that version of me . . . she was a machine. I could smell myself as the stress oozed off me. I was barely functioning, held together with sensible clothes and caffeine. And bribery. That works, amazingly, by the way. A completely under-rated strategy."

"You managed. You adapted."

"I survived. That's not the same thing as thriving." She was panting, spitting out the words, not sure why, now that she was out of the chaotic simulation, the chaos inside her had increased.

Harriet paced now, or tried to. The floor of the Experience pod gave just enough to make her feel off-balance. Her hands flailed in front of her, testing the invisible parameters of the space. She had to do something to alleviate this stress.

"Let me guess: Next I get to see myself as a pageant mom or a homeschooling minimalist running a goat farm in Oregon?"

"No," Ted said. "That file has been archived."

"You mean that was a possibility? Ted! I was kidding!"

"We are preparing a different alternate reality for your review. One that aligns with your stated interest in job fulfillment, creative output, and warm weather."

Harriet stopped pacing and said with continued sarcasm, "Finally. Something I actually asked for." She looked around the dark room for a glimpse of the hidden cameras, anything. "Wait a minute . . . warm weather, creative outlets. Am I going to be some kind of crystal-wearing maven in Sedona, Arizona?"

The silence was telling. Or just another instance of some glitch in waiting. The next faulty remix of her life. It was probably a bit more engaging than the positivity seminar she was supposed to attend for work. If she was still employed whenever she got out of this simulation.

"Well, this should be interesting," she groaned, but lightly, as if finally getting into the spirit of this Experience thing. "If I see one dream catcher, you'll be cruisin' for a bruisin'." She snorted. "Did you catch that? Ted? That was supposed to be funny. In a throw-back Thursday kind of way."

A faint shimmer of light formed at the edges of the pod. The sound of a door chime echoed from nowhere, the scent of paint and pine cones slowly unfurling in the air.

Please enjoy your next Experience, the frog's text bubble announced.

And just like that, Harriet was witnessing another part of the lives she had never lived.

Chapter Thirty-Two

Miles leaned closer to his screen, the flicker of Harriet's simulation thread sharpening into focus. The title bar loaded first: *Alternate Life 3—Chicago Conference Sequence—Subject: Mendez, Gabriel.*

He froze. "Ah, shit," he muttered. "That's not supposed to come yet.

His fingers hovered over the interface like he might stop the simulation, and he fumbled through the menus to cue up the Arizona scene. The one she was hoping for: warm weather, laid-back job, cool guy to hang out with.

The machine hummed, indifferent. The projection glowed with its usual serene confidence.

Adriana's face popped into the corner of his screen, and her voice floated into his earbud. He had patched her in, needing her support after that last scenario. He had no idea how much impact this next one was going to have on him too.

"You checking on the next batch?" she asked, the glow of Harriet's biometric readings reflecting off the lenses of her glasses in red-and-blue zigzags.

Miles didn't answer right away. He zoomed in on the pre-sequence metadata: medical conference, family-unit modifiers enabled, reunion sentiment triggers high. All the familiar flags he told himself not to worry about. All the crap Adriana had assured him was necessary for an authentic reading. An authentic outcome. She had told him to stop being jealous of the machine and its possible outcomes. More than once.

He cleared his throat. "Yeah. Just making sure the runtime's not overloaded."

"Is that the Honduras guy?" Adriana asked casually. "The one with the soulful eyebrows and refugee camp fan club?"

Miles exhaled through his nose. "It's the guy from San Pedro, yes."

"Relax," she said, grinning as she checked her screen. "It's not a telenovela."

The image on the tablet sharpened. Gabriel stood at a podium in a crisp dark suit, smiling as he set a laptop into place. Behind him, two kids scrambled to pick up spilled Doritos and a woman called for them in Spanish. She was elegant and adorable, wearing the equivalent of an early-era Hollywood dress—red with white polka dots—perfectly matching heels, and hair up in an effortlessly placed red headband. Harriet's avatar hadn't entered yet, but her digital signature hovered just off frame.

Miles swallowed the knot rising in his throat, bracing himself and repeating in his mind that this was just a simulation. And a simulation was not real, right? That suit. That perfect, helpful, obedient family. Gabriel probably did sunrise yoga and made pancakes from scratch while his wife read leisurely each morning in bed.

He stepped back from the tablet and the Experience pod, pacing the edge of the exhibit. "It's too much. Too polished," he said into his earpiece to Adriana.

"You're jealous of a pediatrician with a too-fancy necktie from Doctors Without Borders."

"I'm jealous of how easy he makes it look." Miles ran a hand through his hair, then muttered, "No. Actually, I'm not. I just think it's going to overwhelm her. You saw how the last one impacted her."

"Or," Adriana replied dryly, "it'll remind her she made a difference once. Even if she didn't marry the guy. And by the way, you don't have to make yourself the star in each one of her simulations, buddy. I think she's starting to make the connections all on her own."

He paused before his answer. The machine had already begun its sequence prep. "I guess we'll see, won't we? I just want her to find a path that makes her happy."

"I hope she sees it that way, Miles. For your sake, I truly do."

But from here on out, it was up to her. They both understood that.

Chapter Thirty-Three

The shift into the Experience was clean this time. No lurching fade, no sudden dark void. The atmosphere was almost as if she were back in the exhibit hall of the convention center. But smaller and darker, with ornate wood flooring, and a floral scent of the arrangement that adorned the alcove in a sleek vase.

Harriet blinked and found herself standing in the hallway of a boutique hotel, an older one with the embedded rich character of old money and dark wooden doors leading to conference rooms and dining halls. Behind her was a row of tables with finger foods and a water station with trays of fruit to garnish one's drinks. The other side of the hall was lined with tall, backlit signage indicating the agenda of the medical nonprofit seminar. Looking down to the lanyard hanging around her neck, her badge read, *Volunteer Coordinator: Harriet Last.* The clipboard in her hand felt familiar, catching slightly on her shoulder bag. Comforting, even.

Voices buzzed from open doors in the nearby rooms. The presentations, keynote panels, the distant sound of someone laughing too loudly floated into her ears. She knew this place at her core, even though she'd never actually been here before. That was how this machine seemed to work. It built what should have been.

But it didn't exclude the very real parts of her that she found less promising and even more of a hindrance to her at times. A familiar tug of anxiety danced just beneath her ribs. Something important was about to happen in this simulation, like smelling the charged air of lightning before it actually struck.

She scanned the hallway, unsure of whether to go left or right, when a child's voice rang out, high and impatient, followed by a patient, low-toned reply in Spanish. Her body recognized it before her mind did: a jolt of energy, an alertness. She reflexively straightened.

Gabriel.

She turned to watch, amazed at how well he had cleaned up from the days of washing down in the grubby waiting area and triaging the limited supplies they had had at the clinic.

He was older now. Deeper lines in his face, a few grays at his temples. Still smiling like the sun shone from inside him. Perhaps even a little brighter than she remembered.

Harriet felt her breath catch, but like the memory of her real experience, it lasted for only for a second. Then she exhaled and adjusted her clipboard. He had gotten his wish in this simulation too—to come to Chicago and with his own family, which was genuinely satisfying for her as well.

Of course, this machine would take her to yet another fake reality where she was not the star of her own movie. The simulation had brought her here for a reason, she could only assume. That reason had a name, a family, and a 1:00 p.m. keynote address in the Redbud Room.

She gave a polite smile as Gabriel's eyes found hers. Would he even recognize this version of herself? The last time they had met in real life, she had been just twenty. He hadn't been more than seven or eight years older than her.

She examined the feelings circulating through her as he walked closer, his smile broadening. She was certain that she wasn't in love with him. Not ever anything more than a flirty, immature infatuation, a crush with a common goal of helping others and the flattery of having his undivided attention. But she had once admired him and his selfless desire to improve the lives of others, so fully that the echo of it still warmed her in unexpected ways.

She stepped forward to greet him. And her second alternate life.

HARRIET SMOOTHED the front of her blazer, the sharp edge of her clipboard tucked into her elbow. The hotel conference corridor buzzed as attendees filtered into the main conference room. They were chatting as they selected their seats and poured coffees while holding muted conversations in a dozen accents. She glanced down at the welcome packets in her arms and took a breath.

"Ms. Last?" He held out a hand, bending slightly to look her more in the eye.

She turned and reached out to match his gesture, shaking his hand. It was warm, a warmth that connected to her whole body.

Gabriel stood before her in a trim charcoal suit, his conference lanyard with a banner attached underneath that read *Speaker* slung around his neck. A boy, maybe ten years old, hovered behind him tugging at the strap of a Nintendo Switch case, while a younger girl peered up at Harriet from beneath a pair of oversize sunglasses. His wife approached seconds later, balancing a cup of tea and scanning the signage overhead.

"Dr. Mendez," Harriet said with a smile that surprised her. It had been nearly a year since their last email. An impersonal note about clinic updates, funding status, and a quick reference to an inside joke about a runaway goat. In this simulation, it could have been at least a decade or two since they'd shared a sweaty, work-packed summer in Honduras. "Welcome back," she heard this version of her simulated life say.

"You look well," he said. His accent was lighter now, his English more fluent, but still rich with the punctuated rhythm she remembered from the old clinic days.

"Doing my best," she replied. "You've got a full house today." She pointed to the rows of padded burgundy-colored seats, quickly filling as the MC approached the stage and announced that the program would begin soon.

"I'm used to having a line of people waiting to see me," he said, laughing, but his eyes carried the serious weight of his work. "But I have to admit this is a big house!"

Harriet returned the smile, this time embracing the memory of the clinic—always full, always busy. "It's a bit bigger than San Pedro."

Gabriel turned and gestured to his family, beaming. "This is my wife, Alma. And these are our kids: Mateo and Sofia."

Harriet crouched a little, giving Sofia a playful wink. "Nice to meet you both."

Alma nodded just slightly, her hand extended, her smile a practiced blend of warmth and schedule awareness. "Gabriel mentioned you help coordinate these conferences. Thank you for helping our little clinic to keep running. The chicken incubator . . . it is a blessing. There are eggs every day now." Her English was smooth but simple. She turned and whispered something to the boy in Spanish, and he put down his Nintendo and frowned.

"I'm glad that project worked out and that we got the extra generators. The only thing I wish would be that they also had a chicken-plucking machine." She laughed, a little too loudly.

Alma looked at her, confused. Gabriel nodded, even though he must not have remembered the joke from that summer. She was going to have to pluck a chicken at some time during her internship. But then the scorpion bite. And her early departure. And now this ill-placed reference to her summer as a volunteer. One of many rotating volunteers that they now matched to the clinic each month.

"Actually, I work with a global aid group now that coordinates with several smaller organizations, like the one I worked with when I first went to Honduras. We help them recruit skilled volunteers and organize supply chains for clinics like San Pedro," Harriet explained. "This conference is more of a satellite meetup, with a focus on the supporters."

Gabriel tipped his head in thought and thanked Harriet. "The support has changed the clinic in so many ways. The extra medics are making sure the clinic is staffed every day now. Even at night." Was he referring to the time he had had stay up all night? The time she had nearly died from the sting?

"I'm glad you're speaking today. It's a big deal, and it should bring in a lot of support. They will love to see how their donations are being used, which builds their trust and encourages them to give more." Her tone was practiced and professional. "I know I loved my time there and the incredible work everyone did. And look, I'm still doing this work." Harriet swept her arm in a general movement across the lobby. "Well, helping in a slightly different way now."

"We're grateful to be here too," Gabriel said.

His wife motioned to the hall and ushered the kids to the front where seats had been reserved for them.

"They'd love the science center," Harriet offered to her. "It's three blocks west—hands-on exhibits, a butterfly house. And they have astronaut ice cream."

Both kids perked up. "Cool, Mom. Can we go?"

Alma nodded. "That might be a good idea. Thank you, Ms. Last," she said as they worked their way into the door.

As his family wandered toward their seats, Gabriel lingered, his expression shifting from what he would say in his presentation to something more reflective. "I still think about those days at the clinic. You brought a lot of order. And grit."

Harriet smiled, then shrugged. "It was mutual. We were both just trying to keep wounds dressed, inoculate the masses, and keep the clinic from falling apart."

He hesitated, then added, "I sometimes wondered . . . if you'd ever considered staying longer. I mean, you were good at it."

"Sometimes I wonder that too," she said quietly, then she heard herself share, "But I love my life here, connecting with clinics like yours around the world. It multiplies what I could have done if I had stayed." He folded his arms, deep in thought as Harriet continued. "I believe it was a special summer. It planted this seed to connect supporters here in Chicago to the clinics where they are needed the most."

A pause. Then a subtle smile flickered at the edge of his mouth. "Well, the clinic's still standing. And I'm happy to hear you are well."

Harriet watched his family sit as the lights flickered, signaling the beginning of the program. She nodded once. "I am."

"We both have a job to do, then. It was a pleasure to see you again, old friend."

"Yes, I completely agree," she said as he put a hand one her shoulder with a strong pat. Then someone started talking into the microphone, and he turned toward the Redbud Room.

After he'd gone, entering through the front entrance farther down the hall, her eyes skimmed her clipboard, scanning the schedule. But her thoughts drifted—past Gabriel, past Honduras, to a question she hadn't let herself voice aloud.

What if I'd taken a chance? On anyone. On anything.

The hall erupted into an energetic show of applause lasting for a minute as the president of their organization took the stage to thank the supporters. Harriet shut the doors to the hall, closing it up as the final stragglers entered to find their seats. A little hole started to open in her heart and nagged at her. It wasn't grief, exactly. It was more like the awareness of something she'd set on a shelf and forgotten, only to rediscover years later with the dust still clinging to it. Not regret. Just recognition of what she had once been able to do.

And perhaps do once again.

AFTER THE INTRODUCTIONS were over and Gabriel and his family had been seated, Harriet found herself alone near the tall windows of the adjoining mezzanine lounge, taking a sip of coffee before sneaking into the back during his speech. In the distance, she saw the park next to the children's museum she had recommended. Farther behind it was the Ferris wheel circling proudly over Navy Pier.

She stood at the edge of the glass, coffee cup cooling in her hand, and let her eyes follow the line of skyscrapers that reached like ancient pillars of industry into the early-afternoon sky. Lake Michigan shimmered, a slate-blue expanse cut by sailboats and distant ferries. The wind here was sharp even in spring, carving its way between the buildings and sending flags flapping against their poles.

Chicago. She had dreamed of living in the city. Having no need for a car. Having an endless list of social events and entertainment venues to attend.

And to organize volunteers. Something that made a difference in so many ways. This work suited her, and she was telling herself the truth. She loved this life and her small studio apartment that overlooked the less pretty side of Chicago. But she was here, and in the Experience, she was living this life.

In her real life, Harriet had never lived there. Never worked an exclusive conference in a boutique hotel catering to wealthy patrons. But everything felt exceptionally real. Her badge. The scent of paper on her program and the nearby buttery pastries. The way the light filtered through the glass, catching on dust she couldn't quite see.

What she could see was in this version of her life, she was viable, with a possibility that called to her. One where she stayed tethered to people who needed her instead of a remote office cubicle where she pushed paper around year after year. Where her solitude wasn't a void but a choice.

The ache that filled her chest wasn't painful, exactly. More like the slow throb of something unspoken, something knocking, patiently, waiting for her to pay attention. Not quite longing. Not quite regret. Something more significant, but just out of reach. Just the faint sense that she'd paused too long at a fork in the road and now better understood the direction she'd missed.

The clouds shifted above the lake. A gleam of sunlight stretched across the water like a path.

And then it all began to fade. The glass melted into darkness. The air stilled. The light around her collapsed inward, not suddenly, but like the softness of curtain folds being drawn at the end of a long, strange play.

She closed her eyes.

When she opened them again, the windows were gone. But the feelings remained. The room around her was sterile and humming and quietly void.

She exhaled slowly.

Another life and another vision of what could have been. Not exactly something she would have chosen. Having been given a choice. This Experience had promised her three alternate endings. It had one more chance to make her . . . happy? What exactly was it that she wanted from this process? She had entered it like a photo booth, expecting to leave with three tiny mug shots stacked on a small black-and-white strip.

Still, she waited a moment before speaking. Let the feeling wash through her one more time. Let it go.

What do I want?

The question wandered about aimlessly in her mind with an irritating lack of clarity. There was a lot that she had done in her life. And although her job wasn't exactly rewarding, she had Lilli. And the clients she worked with at the insurance company got the lives back together after a disaster happened. What was so bad about her job and being forced to attend a little positivity session? The conference was a break from the regular grind.

"Ted? Are you up there?" she asked finally. "I'm ready for my last Experience when you are."

The computer guide was silent.

She checked her phone. The frog was driving some kind of sports car and now had hair that was blowing back. He was smiling behind dark glasses. *Prepare for your third Experience!* the message bubble said before the car zoomed off her screen.

The floor around her turned to a dusty light brown, and she felt the prickly air as sand slowly pelted at her in small windy gusts. She looked down at her sandaled feet, flattered that her toes popped with the color of a desert rose as they poked out from under a same-colored crepe skirt. A linen shirt was tucked into the waist, and she noticed she was wearing several silver-and-turquoise rings and bracelets below her rolled-up sleeves. Her hair was tucked under a large-brimmed hat that shaded her from the dessert sun.

In one hand, she held a folded red apron. In the other, the shoulder strap of a large leather purse that matched the sandals and skirt. She walked to a Jeep parked in front of a low, adobe-style home and climbed in. She started it and heard a familiar song playing on the radio. The music piped into her Experience as she felt the lightness from the optical illusions of blurred images swirling around the seamless walls. The song from Eagles became more crisp as the lyrics played and she drove on to the dusty road humming about Winslow Arizona.

And as Harriet fell into the next Experience, the Jeep disappeared into a puff of dessert road dust.

Chapter Thirty-Four

"Nice touch," she said quietly. "Can I assume that song was an indication of what to expect?" She scanned the scene for clues about her next life of possible adventures, curious about what her third vision of her future would reveal.

She had enjoyed a joy ride on the desert road and had arrived at a shopping center. The Jeep was now parked a few rows back in the parking lot, and she approached the front of a large craft store, where she pulled the red apron over her wind-blown hair. She looked at herself in her reflection in the storefront window and noticed that her hat had been removed and her hair was now tucked up in a messy bun and held back with ornate combs.

The music shifted into standard piped-in store music when she entered the sliding doors. Harriet noticed the potent smell of paints, the dusty scents of dried flowers, and the earthy undertones of naked wood products. She walked to the back room and checked in using a computerized system.

This version of her life took over, and Harriet relaxed into this last vision provided by the Experience. How bad could this final one be? It wasn't likely to show her anything that valuable. Harriet accepted viewing this version of her life, certain it would all soon be over, and let the simulation overtake her senses.

She walked to the front of the store and took her place behind a register, carrying a large water thermos with a long straw out of the top. A worker from another register placed a large box at the end of the checkout counter for her to unpack when the lines died down. There were not many customers when she worked those early-afternoon hours, and she opened the box to find kids' painting sets. When finished, she rested her palm on a register. A few customers wandered the aisles of craft supplies.

Not the most exciting job. Casual, but interesting. Her other hand covered her phone in her red apron pocket, the standard uniform for this craft store. Then she looked at both of her hands, worked and thin, boney. There were stains and rough patches that felt dry and brittle. A coworker with the name tag *Yesenia* passed the counter, a box full of smaller boxes to be shelved weighing down her arms. "Harriet, the new glazes you ordered are in the back."

Apparently, this Harriet did pottery. And somewhere in Arizona. At least she didn't seem to be wearing any crystals—yet.

"They finally came in!" Her new version of Harriet checked her watch: 2:09. "I've got a break coming up."

"I thought you would want to know."

"Thanks." Harriet looked at her phone and tucked it back into her front apron pocket. She scanned a customer's bundle of raffia pumpkins, the kind that looked like they belonged on a Vermont porch, not outside a stucco duplex in the middle of Phoenix. The register beeped in approval. She dropped the pumpkins into a paper bag, resisting the urge to make a crack as the customer left about how they'd probably combust if left outside for more than ten minutes.

"Yesenia!" Harriet called as her coworker zipped past with a box of wire wreath forms. "Do people really put pumpkins on their porches here?"

Yesenia snorted. "In ninety-degree heat? Only if they want them to cook into soup on the concrete."

"I thought so. We should sell warning stickers—'Not intended for outdoor use in actual fall weather.'"

"Fall weather?" Yesenia swept a hand dramatically toward the sun-baked window display. "It's summer here until Thanksgiving and then boom! Everyone has windbreakers and light sweaters."

Harriet raised an eyebrow. "That desert air can chill once that sun is gone."

"Yes, a break from the heat." She plopped the wreath forms on the floor and pulled a garland of artificial maple leaves from the box. "These? Total lies. We don't have trees that do this. People just pretend."

Harriet picked up a pumpkin-shaped soap dispenser from another box she was unpacking at her stand and examined its gold-leaf detail. "Is it weird I kind of like it? This whole . . . desert-fall decor?"

"No. It's weird that you still act surprised. You've lived here how long now?"

"Long enough to know that October smells like sunscreen and cinnamon pine cones." She dropped the dispenser into a basket. "But not long enough to stop missing real fall."

Yesenia smirked. "It's a mystery, right? We just fake it better each year."

Behind them, the automatic doors whooshed open, letting in a blast of dry air and a woman in yoga pants carrying a reusable tote and a mission. Harriet sighed and straightened her apron.

"Brace yourself," Yesenia said under her breath. "Pumpkin candle season has officially begun."

Harriet smiled. "Here come the gourds."

The front door reopened, and another customer came in, a guy in his fifties with graying curly hair that was high and tight above a close-shaved beard.

Harriet said a standard greeting, "Welcome in."

"What?"

"Welcome in." she repeated. "Can I help you find something?"

"No. I've got it" He looked at her, puzzled, then continued. "Yes. I'm looking for model paint. Something weatherproof."

"Huh. I'm not sure about weatherproof, but we do have small pots of paint in the dollhouse and diorama section. Try aisle twenty-six on the right of the center walkway. Back of the yarns section."

He smiled and sauntered down the aisle, scanning as he quickly walked with the gait of a man who doesn't want to be bothered with all the trite and mediocre details of pedestrian living. He disappeared past the yarn display, and Harriet took care of another customer. A mother set three picture frames on the counter and a small drawing kit for the daughter at her side. The child grinned, a mouth missing its two middle teeth.

"Do you take the paper coupons still?"

"Sure. Try the app, though. It has extra discounts." Harriet scanned a barcode. "Here's one for an extra ten percent off your purchase today." She could see the stress lessen for the woman just a tiny bit as Harriet took her payment and placed the receipt into the bag with the frames. The little girl snatched the drawing kit and danced her way out of the store.

The man looking for model paint was walking briskly to the front of the store, taking big steps and scrutinizing the small glass bottles in his hand as he walked up to her line-less register. "I thought this stuff was only a dollar a bottle."

Harriet scoffed, "Like, when?"

"Hmm?" The man looked up as he set down the paints and reached into his back pants pocket for his phone. "What did you say?"

"These paints are top of the line. If you want them for a little less, I recommend that you come back next month. There's a yearly craft paint sale that would be a better time to stock up." She picked up the nearest jar to scan it.

He nodded thoughtfully. "Did you grow up here? You have an accent."

"What?" she asked and scanned another jar of paint.

He tipped his head back and rubbed the back of his neck. "That was rude. What I mean is, something in your voice sounds like where I grew up. In the Midwest."

"Yeah, actually. I haven't been here for long. I grew up near Chicago."

"I thought you looked familiar. Clementine High? Maybe?"

"Yeah. And you?" Harriet paused, taking a closer look at the man.

"Yeah." He swiped an arm from his shoulder to his hip and

mimicked the roar of the high-school Wildcat mascot. He coughed a bit. "It's been a while since I've had any team spirit. I hate sports, actually."

"Okay." Harriet checked to see who else was watching this awkward little reunion. Yesenia would have a field day with this. "Were you there when we won the state football championship?"

"That was probably the last time I paid attention to anything with nets and balls."

"So, 1987?"

"Gawd, that makes me feel so old, but it was a good year."

"Miles?" She leaned back to take him in, setting the last jar into a small paper bag. "We are probably on the same page of the yearbook."

"And you lived across the street."

"For a long time. Well, you're far from home now too. How long have you been living here?"

"I'm only here for the winter months. Normally, I live near the city." He looked around and when she didn't react, he said, "San Francisco."

"Oh." Harriet typed away at the register, aware of the divide between where her life had taken her compared with the apparent ease of his life. Who could casually spend fifteen dollars per ounce of model paint and ignore the multipacks for the same price? "A snowbird. How nice for you . . ."

"I guess so. And you? What are you doing in the middle of the desert?"

"Getting away from the snow, I guess." She tore the receipt from the machine and handed it to him. "It's nice to see an old classmate."

"It's great to see a friendly face." He took the receipt and, without a glance, shoved it in the bag.

"We have art classes if you're into that sort of thing. I teach one on pottery on Tuesdays."

"Pottery. I didn't know you were into that. I remember you being more of a student council- and theater-type kid." He checked a notification on his phone and dismissed it.

"Well, the whole world is a stage." Harriet started to ring up the next customer who had joined her line and looked for the barcode on a small bunch of dried flowers they had placed on the counter.

Miles started to walk away, but turned back. "Hey, would you have a drink with me sometime?"

Harriet smiled as the woman placed a small spool of ribbon next to her flowers. "Um, I'm pretty busy right now." She placed the flowers and ribbon in a bag. "That's five ninety-three, please." As the customer left, Harriet turned to Miles. "Are you asking me out?"

"Like coffee or a burger and a Coke." He rocked back on his heels. "It would be fun to catch up about the good ol' days."

"Maybe? Come to my class. We can catch up then."

"Pottery . . ." He picked up a flyer with the class schedule. "I could use another hobby."

"Uh-huh."

"I'm serious. How do I sign up?"

"I think there's a QR code on the flyer. I'm sure there's room for one more."

He pulled out his phone and snapped a photo of the flyer before putting it back on the counter. "See you Tuesday!"

"Okay, sure. See you then."

Harriet waved at Miles, who left through the automated glass door, then asked a lady at the counter, "Hi, did you find everything you needed?" But her mind was on Miles and how unlikely it was that she would ever see him again.

Chapter Thirty-Five

Harriet bit into a piece of ham sandwich in the break room; it had toasted bread, a slice of cheese, and stone-ground mustard that dribbled out of the side when she squished it. Her friend Lilli faced her from a video call on her phone that was propped up by a cluster of unglazed pots on the least dusty table in the craft classroom. A row of circular tables used for spinning pots and a sealed barrel of clay filled the half of the classroom where she sat.

"I'm telling you, Harriet. You've got to meet my Tio Jorge. He has a coffee shop, like in the bougie downtown part of town. You could display your art there like a real artist, *mi amiga*."

"Yeah, maybe. I'm kind of busy."

"Doing what? Teaching those classes? Eating that sandwich? I don't see nobody in there."

"Class starts in a half hour. It's lunchtime. What are you doing? Aren't you supposed to be working?"

"Yeah, yeah. I've got a big presentation later. And I needed to calm down a bit, so I thought about my friend and wanted to check in on her."

"That's actually . . . kind of sweet."

"And I'm coming back home this Christmas, and if you don't come and make tamales with my grandmother, she will never speak to you again."

"I'll put it on my calendar."

"You better." Lilli looked over her shoulder to signal to someone that she was busy. "I better go soon, but I have enough time to find out how it's going with that Miles guy."

"Miles? He's a friend, Lilli. Someone I went to school with as a kid. He just happened to stop in the store last week."

"How romantic."

"Not really. We were never romantic."

"Use your imagination, Harriet. You wouldn't know a good thing if it were handed to you with a bow on top."

"He's probably coming to my class today."

Lilli closed her eyes, smacked her lips together, and hummed, swaying side to side as if to imaginary dance music. "Can you feel that?" She opened her eyes. "That's love calling out to you."

"I don't think so."

"Alright, *chicacita*, I've got to go break some glass ceilings."

"I know you will. Talk to you tomorrow?"

"Of course. It's a lunch date." Lilli blew the phone a kiss. "*Ciao ciao.*"

"Bye." And the phone blipped into darkness.

Harriet went to a cupboard and began pulling large bottles of glaze from a gray metallic shelf. She stacked small bowls next to the paints and lined up various brushes. Her notes on painting techniques were queued up on the presentation screen, ready for the next class to begin.

A tap on the door startled her. When she looked at the glass, she saw Miles holding two coffees, one in each hand. Grinning, he motioned to the door handle. Harriet walked to the door to open it.

"Am I too early?"

"Class doesn't start for twenty minutes."

He handed her a coffee and set the other on an open table. "Oh, that's a bit too hot. Careful when you sip it."

"Thank you?"

"It's not terrible that I want to butter up the teacher a little, is it?"

"That depends on what you mean."

"Not literally, of course."

She shot him a slightly concerned look, followed by a deep breath. "Of course not. You can have your pick of spots. Just avoid the front right table. That's Josie's spot. She just might fight you if you sit there. Trust me, it's not worth the drama."

"Josie?"

"A retired mechanic with a biting sense of humor and a knack for crafting interesting body parts."

"Fascinating." He chuckled and sat atop the nearest table. "What rating does this class have?"

"It's all PG. We don't have nude models or anything. There are a couple of kids who come once in a while too." She pulled out a selection of brushes and placed them near the glaze bowls.

"Am I stopping you from getting ready?"

"Amazingly, I have it all set up." She leaned against the podium and played with the cardboard sleeve around the coffee cup. "I have to admit that I'm a little surprised to see you here. I didn't think you would be back."

"I'm taking some personal time. Work-life balance is important, you know?" He took the cover off his coffee to let it cool.

"Alright. So, some of these students are more advanced, but I'll review the basics once I get them started. Sound okay?"

"Sure, sure. We have a couple of minutes before class starts?"

"Yeah, a couple."

"So let's start with Arizona. How did you get here?"

"Well, I was working at True Blue Insurance since a couple of years after college. I worked in underwriting."

"That's cool. When did you stop working there?"

"A couple of years ago."

"Retirement?"

"I wish." She spun the coffee sleeve slowly. "There were cuts. I was laid off. And was lucky enough to get a small severance package. It was enough to move to a warmer state with better taxes. But retirement? Naw. I'll be working until I'm ninety."

"How did you get into pottery?"

"I took classes here. Studied up. Learned on the job." She leaned into the podium. "It's a lot less stressful now. And I get a lot more vitamin D as a perk. How about you?"

"I've never taken pottery before. It seems like something fun to try."

She scoffed. "No. I meant, are you retired? Working?"

He laughed. "Coin laundry."

"Excuse me?"

"Coin laundry. It's just something I do. Like when I take something everyone knows isn't literal, but I can only see it as the literal thing."

"I'm not following."

"Like coin laundry. It's a place where you can wash your clothes. Back in the day, you would put real coins into slots to make the washer and dryer work."

"Yeah. I'm familiar with how those things work." She smiled, her eyebrows twisting as he wove his point.

"I once asked my friend Ben . . ."

"Ben Petersen?"

"Yeah, him. We hung out a lot."

"We had like five classes together."

"That makes sense. He was the smart one in our group."

"I think that's a compliment. So, coin laundry? I still don't get that."

"Coin laundry . . . we were driving around one night, like we did all the time back then, when we drove past the laundromat next to the pet store."

"The grungy one with wooden floors? I loved that store. It smelled like pine needles and fur."

"Yeah. You know the one. So we drove past it. And I told Ben that I didn't know why they have a store just for washing coins. Like the coins that went into the machines also had to be clean? It made no sense."

"Coin laundry." She scoffed lightly. "I believe I do that more than I let on. That's a good one."

"I obviously get it now. But it comes in handy when these things happen. And they happen way more than I want most people to know."

"I suppose it could be awkward."

"Everyone at my company knows I have those moments. 'Coin laundry' is the way we explain it."

"Hmm. I may have to be extra careful when explaining techniques maybe?" She leaned against the table, taking a sip of her drink.

"Take it easy on me, ok?" He grinned.

"And what are you doing when you are not adding more hobbies to your busy schedule?"

"Me and a business partner have a startup. I'm pretty excited about this new tech we're creating. It's life-changing even."

A set of fraternal twin boys walked in and went to the supplies table to grab brushes. They argued over who could use the fanned brush with the green handle before taking seats in the back of the room.

"Hi, boys. Grab your art from the back table. Today, we're going to go over new glazing techniques."

One punched the other before sprinting to the table of fragile clay pots.

"Fight nice or not at all, please . . . Life-changing? Like what?"

"We're working on some heuristic algorithms that can offer people insights into their lives."

"Like magic therapy?"

"More like ways to analyze your life for its best outcome."

"That sounds like cheating. Why would someone want to do that? I mean, this isn't what I expected for my life. But it isn't terrible."

"Right. It's also like a vacation. Take a break from your reality to see an alternate life? I mean, people could find that cathartic."

"Or creepy."

The door opened, and three more students walked in: two chatting women and an elderly man.

"I've got to get the class started soon."

"That's alright. I have a plane to catch."

"You're not staying for the class?"

"Maybe next time."

She set her cup down. "Lilli told me you might just be looking for a good time. Maybe just someone to pal around with when you're in town."

"What does that mean? Who's Lilli?"

"My friend. From True Blue, actually. But that's not my point. What do you honestly want?"

"I'm just interested in seeing how your life turned out, Harriet. We've known each other since we were three."

"And we rarely spent time together outside of school. I don't think you ever called me. Even once. It's like we lived in our own lane and stayed there."

"Maybe that was a mistake."

"You're acting weird, Miles. I have a class to teach."

"See you next time?" he asked, pausing. "I mean it. Work-life balance is a big challenge for me. Same time next Tuesday? My doctor would say it's good for my stress."

"Tuesday."

"I already paid for the class. I'll be here. And do homework if needed."

"Ok. See you Tuesday."

Harriet grabbed the slides clicker and began her presentation in front of the class while some students set up clay on the throwing tables, working independently. The boys and the two women sat with their brushes, waiting for the presentations on painting glaze. Josie was already painting away on her foot project when Miles walked out the door. "That's a mighty fine foot!" he said and cheerfully waved goodbye.

Harriet tipped her head back in response and helped one man pour glazes onto his bowl.

Chapter Thirty-Six

The transition hit like a breeze through her doorless Jeep when driving to her job in this life-version. It was small at first, then fully pulling her in. Harriet blinked into the light, finding herself once again at the clunky beige register. It hummed beneath her palm, its keys worn to a soft shine. The skylights above cast a light effervescence over the aisles, and somewhere in the distance, a child coughed near the yarn section. The scent of glues and cheap cinnamon-scented candles from the centerpiece-making class this morning wafted around her in layers.

Today, she wore the red apron over a long sleeveless dress belted with a broad leather belt and matching sandals. The vinyl tag on her chest had her name; painted flowers lined it as if they were an intentional part of the design.

The phone in her pocket buzzed with an unread notification. It was 1:25 p.m. Had the Experience taken a turn into the hellish repetition of the *Groundhog Day* movie? If so, it was a trip that she watched with guarded curiosity, knowing full well what this clunky Experience was capable of putting her through. But this, this was chill and comforting. She relaxed, hearing her new version exhale with a luxurious stretch.

Yesenia hustled past her, boxed votive holders stacked in her arms.

"Here you go, Harriet. Let me know what you think of this new 'spooky scent.' Even though the name is kind of stupid, I might like it."

Her other self dug into the wrapped candles and pulled one out. "Spooky scent . . ." She sniffed vigorously as Yesenia watched from the corner of her eye, stacking paper products in the impulse buy area. "Oh my gawd, that's . . . No. Just no. That reeks!" Harriet coughed and set the candle and the remaining box on the far end of the counter. "I'm leaving that for Rex. He loves that kind of stuff, all gory and whatnot."

"Fair enough." Yesenia giggled and leaned over the bins to whisper to Harriet. Harriet laughed along with her, tucking a perpetual stray hair behind her ear. This life didn't feel unnatural. In fact, it felt suspiciously satisfying.

The glass doors slid open with a chime, and Miles entered: less hurried, more polished. And walking toward her.

"I'm off in ten minutes," she heard herself say. "And I'm hungry."

"Well, I hope you don't mind that I picked out a place for us."

"You're kind of the guest in this area. It makes sense."

"Are you okay trying this rib joint up the road? It has great reviews."

This was probably the time to share that she had been a vegetarian for the last six months, but instead she heard herself agree. "Sure, I haven't tried it yet. But on one condition—I get to drive." She took off her apron and stepped out from behind the counter.

"Deal," he said.

"I'll clock out." Harriet draped the apron over her arm. "I'll be right back." She left for the break room as Miles sorted through some fidget toys, clicking away and spinning the gadgets like a grade-school boy.

THEY FOUND a table beneath a faded awning outside The Rib Crib. The roadside building opened into a courtyard with umbrellas and cornhole games. It was painted with desert colors and a pop of lime green. The sign above the door was a cartoon-styled pig wearing a napkin and donning a knife and fork grinned maniacally over a plate of ribs. The parking lot was packed with SUVs, sunburned out-of-towners, and locals in Cubs and Giants hats. Flat-screened TVs bolted above the window played games at full volume, complete with crackling commentary and the occasional reaction as the Cubs stole a base or cracked a line drive.

"Didn't realize there would be so much baseball," Miles said, scanning the jerseys. "It did say online it was popular with the tourists. I was hoping for a little hometown nostalgia. And well, just some great Arizona BBQ."

"It's possible that half the Midwest migrates here this time of year."

"I get it. You don't have to deal with fifty-below temps here. But I didn't know it was so baseball-oriented."

"The Cubs are in the finals. The regular season is done. This is a big deal," Harriet replied. "Almost as big a deal as spring training. Up in Cooperstown, all baseball fans drop in to see the new talent hopefuls each season. They come for the baseball but leave with the heat."

"I didn't know you liked baseball so much."

"Yeah. I don't go out of my way to watch, but I enjoy it."

Their trays arrived. Meat piled high, fries spilling over the paper baskets, pickles sweating in the heat. Harriet picked up a rib and eyed it. "Wow, this smells fabulous. Dig in! So much for dignity."

Miles wiped his hands on a paper towel. "Dignity is for restaurants with forks."

Harriet methodically unwrapped her utensils, spread her napkin across her lap, and dabbed the corners of her mouth after each delicate bite. Miles, meanwhile, was already halfway through his first rib. "This is ridiculous," he said around a mouthful. "I might die happy right here."

She eyed him over her unsweeted tea. "You've got sauce on your temple." She laughed.

He wiped at his forehead with the back of his hand, missed entirely, and kept chewing.

Harriet delicately pulled apart a rib with a plastic knife and fork, her expression a quiet mix of enjoyment and culinary caution.

"You eat ribs like they're surgical procedures," he observed.

"And you eat like someone dared you," she shot back.

He grinned, licking barbecue off his thumb. "Still judging, huh?"

She smiled faintly. "Not judging. Savoring."

He dipped a fry in sauce and held it up. "Want one?"

"I value my dress. And being able to fit in it," she said dryly, but took the fry he handed her and tried it anyway. "Not bad. What exactly is fry sauce?"

"The secret nectar of the gods."

"I see."

She was neat, cautious, composed. He was still the opposite: a one-man demolition team of meat and napkins. And yet, the rhythm of their conversation, the ping-pong of memory and wit, felt almost . . . natural.

"This reminds me of Angelo's," she said, wiping her fingers with a fresh towelette. "Remember that pizza dive by the school?"

"The one with the busted jukebox?"

"And fans that only worked in winter."

"I used to swear their pepperoni slices had magic in them," he said.

"They had grease. That's all."

"But those garlic knots!" He leaned back, chuckling. "You would try to get some of the toppings on the side. I remember the waitress put the kibosh on that."

"And you got two large slices and tennis inspiration," she shot back with a smirk.

"I totally remember that. We planned a very successful attack that evening."

Their laughter carried for a beat longer than either expected. Harriet set down her red acrylic cup, her fingers still resting on the cool condensation forming on the sides. "You were funny back then," she said softly. "And clever."

He glanced sideways. "And you were going to take over the world. Still are."

The compliment landed somewhere between them. She waved it off but not unnoticed. "I suppose, if you consider my world. Perhaps my propensity for peddling craft supplies and teaching pottery," she said between bites of another fry.

A gust of desert wind swept through the lot. Napkins fluttered, dust kicked up, and the Cubs lost a fly ball on-screen. Miles stood and brushed crumbs from his shirt, oblivious that the dejected fans around him were leaving in droves and hastily discarding their trays in the bussing area. The restaurant seemed to let out a long, slow exhale of disappointment as the people left. Another year without the World Series.

"I should probably let you get back to real life."

"Same," she said, rising with more poise, picking up scattered napkins from their table.

At the edge of the table, he paused. "So . . . see you Tuesday?"

Harriet pulled out her sunglasses from her purse and pushed them up over her nose. "Are you in town?"

"Yeah. Sure." He typed on his phone. "I've got to grab an Uber and get to the airport. But I have a couple of days off next week. And I'd like to actually make something in class this time."

"Alright. We'll see what artistic talent you throw on the pottery wheel." She lifted her purse to her shoulder as he quickly paid the bill, tapping his phone to the automated payment terminal at their table.

"I got this. Thanks for the ride, Harriet. See you soon." He gave her a two-finger wave and disappeared into the sun-washed crowd of tourists and baseball fans.

She stayed a moment longer, watching the TV out of habit. The commentary about the Cubs' loss was droning on. The day had a taste of something old, something unfinished. She wiped one last smudge from her palm and turned away to find her Jeep.

BY MONDAY EVENING, Harriet had convinced herself he wouldn't come.

She folded her laundry, scrubbed her kitchen counters, and let a barrage of messages from Lilli go unanswered. She kept her hands busy, her mind too. But every time her phone buzzed, her eyes darted toward it with something like hope that was dismissed quickly as silliness. It was fine. Really. It had just been lunch. And ribs. And memories dipped in sauce and swallowed with familiar comfort.

By Tuesday morning, she was back in her work rhythm. She wore breezy cotton overalls, oversize compared with the tank top she had on. Her hair was pulled back into a twisted cloth headband. She drove the shortcut to town that day, opting for the rough roads over the more civilized highway.

In the store, she opened the classroom studio windows to let in the desert breeze and set out the beginners' clay. Ten students were on the list. Ten spaces were prepped. No empty chairs. No expectations.

The studio smelled like drying clay and juniper coming from the essential-oils diffuser near the door. She arranged the aprons on their hooks, double-checked the glaze samples, and turned on the soft-indie playlist that played quietly through the old Bluetooth speaker on the window ledge.

She recognized most of the students who had signed up—two retirees, a pair of young moms who had come together, Josie the foot-casting mechanic, a college kid in a hoodie, a few other random souls, and the man in a pale button-down shirt standing awkwardly near the supply sink.

"Holy crap."

He was here. He looked relieved that she had acknowledged him.

"You did come to Arizona. Please tell me you had something else to do here."

"Work-life balance is important, Harriet."

"Well, I am pleasantly surprised. I would have lost that bet that you were going to show for this."

"You bet against me?" he said with mocking rejection.

He hadn't shaved that morning. His hair was wind-tousled and damp at the temples, like he'd come straight from a walk. Not the San Francisco startup version of him she'd remembered after chowing down on barbecue. Just khakis, a well-worn watch, and a ceramic tool kit in a plastic bag she recognized from the shelves, price tag still dangling.

"You came," she said, setting down a stack of sponges. "And I saved a spot for you. Right here." She pointed to a table in the back left. "It's close to the computer I use to project my slides."

"I told you I would."

"I figured you'd be busy."

"Supposed to be," he said. "Flights were a little tricky, so I drove. I couldn't sleep anyway, so I got in the car and drove."

Harriet nodded slowly. "So . . . you're dedicated to this pottery journey."

He smiled. "Yup."

"You want some coffee? You could make a cup." She gestured toward the single-serve pod machine on the other side of the room. "And we're doing hand-thrown bowls today."

"Sounds a bit dirty. I still can't believe you have no problem being elbow-deep in this," he said mock suspiciously, poking a finger in the lump of clay at his station. "But you turn up your nose at a plate of ribs as too messy."

"I'm a complicated woman."

He laughed under his breath and headed to his station. "I like that."

"You're a complicated guy."

"I don't disagree." He sat and opened his bag of tools. "Am I going to need any of this today?'

"Probably not. I can issue you a refund." She laughed, pointing to the table of tools at the front of the room.

"I didn't want you to think I would come to class unprepared."

Class began the way it always did. Harriet ran through the basics, first with the slides and then with her giving a demonstration in the front of the room—wedging clay, centering—all while discussing the stubborn rules of symmetry. She showed them how to use the bat and foot pedal, how to coax the shape with both firmness and grace. Before long, the room was filled with the soft, rhythmic hum of wheels and the occasional slap of a misfired lump hitting the table.

Harriet dropped in on students, checking their work and offering tips. Josie proudly displayed a bowl, flat as a pancake, that she was now fashioning into a hand. The moms chatted, sipping from their "water" bottles, while the hoodie guy meticulously shaped his bowl with a tool. She worked her way to the back of the room, ready for Miles's project. Miles wasn't a natural.

"Why is it so lopsided?"

"Ah, let's slow down the speed a bit. Go slow."

His first attempt deflated into itself. The second was taller but leaned like the Tower of Pisa.

"Be honest," he said as she circled to his side. "Is this the ugliest cup you've ever seen?"

"It's not a cup. It's a metaphor," she replied.

"For what?"

"Your work-life balance." She smiled, tight and teasing.

That got a chuckle from the woman to his left. But when Harriet leaned closer, brushing a hand along the edge of his clay to guide his pressure, she felt him still slightly under her touch. Not uncomfortably. Just . . . aware.

"You're strong with your right hand," she noted.

"Used to draw with it all the time."

"I don't remember that."

His eyes flicked up to hers. "Fourth-period study hall. I showed you my sketch of that grumpy vice principal with the mole."

"And got a detention for it." Harriet shook her head, remembering, "Man, that substitute teacher was a crab."

"When that substitute took it away, I said it was my property and he couldn't have it. You told them it was an artistic protest." He smiled. "And it was."

"Well, the only thing protesting right now is that lump of clay. Why don't you give it another try?" She moved on to the next student, pulse ticking slightly faster than before.

The rest of the class went smoothly. No kilns exploded. Nobody cried over a ruined glaze. Miles kept trying, though his third bowl looked vaguely like a melting volcano.

"Thanks for not being too hard on my creative efforts," he said. "You make the class a lot of fun. I'm actually learning quite a lot about symmetry."

"Thanks. I like teaching," she replied. "It's quiet. Focused. Nobody asks for quarterly projections. Or demands that we somehow lower our liabilities."

"My doctor would approve of this class." He leaned against the edge of the worktable. "I think I needed this. The slow circle of movement. The mess."

She nodded. "Most people appreciate that once they get over the sloppiness of the craft."

"I'm flying back tomorrow," he added, glancing toward the studio door. "It was totally worth the drive through the desert to get here. Even if my bowl looks like it survived a natural disaster."

"It has character." She folded her arms. "What are you doing this afternoon? Want some tea? I could show you my studio. It's not much, but it too has character."

He looked down, hesitant. "I would really like that. You drive?"

Harriet considered it. "Absolutely." Her instinct flared to deflect, to joke. But something steadied her instead. "Okay," she said. "One condition."

"Sure."

"You have to come back next week to finish the bowl."

He grinned. "Done."

THE PROMISE HUNG in the air longer than intended. He looked at her, something caught behind his smile, like he wanted to say more.

Then his brow pinched.

He swayed.

"Miles?" Harriet reached forward to steady his arm. "Are you okay?"

He grabbed the edge of the worktable. His other hand shot to his chest. "Wait—"

The sound he made wasn't a groan. It was a rupture of pain. His knees buckled, and he slumped to the floor, panting and clutching at his heart.

"Miles!" Harriet was at his side before he hit the floor. "Get help!" she shouted.

The class froze, and every table whirred to a stop. A bowl shattered on the tile behind them. Josie cursed and pulled out her phone, calling for an ambulance. Someone bolted for the front desk, slamming the door open behind them.

"I think—I was supposed to show you—" he gasped, eyes wide, fingers fumbling in his jacket pocket. "What I found out. About my alternate life. What we—what we missed."

"Don't move," Harriet said, lowering him gently onto her lap. Her hands cupped the back of his head. "Just stay with me. Josie's calling 911."

He blinked hard, his breath growing ragged. "Harriet . . . listen."

"No, you don't get to . . . Don't say goodbye, Miles. Don't you dare." She gripped him and gently readjusted his head. "What can I do to help? Where does it hurt?" she asked, rapid-fire.

"There's no time." He gritted his teeth against the pressure in his chest. "You . . . you always could change your life . . . even when I didn't. That's what I wanted you to see."

"What are you talking about?" She instinctively pushed the curls back from his forehead, a comforting gesture. She glanced at the clock. How long would it take to get someone here?

"I kept rerunning the data. It kept leading here. To this. To you."

She clutched his shirt. "Stay awake." She listened for the sound of an ambulance, straining to hear what couldn't manifest soon enough.

"Promise me . . ." His voice cracked. "You'll make a change for you."

"What are you talking about? Hey, stay with me. We have plans, bud. You don't get off that easy," she bargained, hoping her playful joke would rouse him back to vitality.

Then his hand slipped from hers. His eyes fluttered shut. The tension in his body went slack, terrifying in its weight.

"Miles!"

The siren hadn't arrived. The class was still frozen.

"Miles, stay with me," she whimpered, shaking him slightly as his head fell to one side and his arm slid to the floor with a soft thud.

But the room was already dimming. The edges flickered, the floor fuzzed, the air thickened like glue. She could still feel his heartbeat, or maybe it was hers, pounding into nothing.

Everything went black.

Chapter Thirty-Seven

The tile floor dissolved beneath her.

One moment, Harriet was cradling Miles's head on her lap, shouting for someone to call emergency services. The next, she was weightless, unmoored, drifting through a world of colorless static. The same void of the Experience, vibration and heat and the acrid bite of glaze dust still in her lungs.

Stunned by the revelation she had just seen. No . . . lived. No . . . experienced.

She stood, somehow still upright, in the center of the space. The void pressed in around her, seamless and blank.

"No," she whispered. Her voice didn't echo. It simply existed. Then vanished.

She remembered when her grandfather passed away and how she made him laugh. Grabbing at her emotions, bruised, confused. She had no reference point for something like this.

"No, no, no, no, no."

Her hands moved in front of her, searching for corners or seams of the pod again. She knew the pattern by now. Blankness. Crazy transitions loaded with metaphors and enigmatic music. Emotional ambushes.

But this time, something was off. The usual shimmer of light, the sound cue, even the frog app, were gone.

The machine had failed. Or she had failed the machine. It was ridiculous to think that she had broken the machine. That her life was going to be a problematic one to analyze. Hadn't she joked that would happen?

She clenched her fists and spun in place. "This isn't the deal. You don't just . . . kill someone off without a reason."

Still nothing.

Her mind was reeling with a new reality: being stuck in the simulation—indefinitely. If he was in almost every one of her memories and futures—and died—couldn't she die too? Her breath stuttered.

The darkness pressed tighter, a vacuum she couldn't quite scream into. Her pulse pounded in her ears. There must be a key. An obvious one.

"Miles," she asked into the silence, "what were you trying to show me?"

The image of him flashed again, but only in her mind. His face pale, eyes locked on hers with something desperate and unfinished. He'd been in pain, but also . . . sure. Like he knew it was the only way.

She dropped to her knees to the floor. Her fingers curled around nothing. The walls revealed . . . nothing.

"You said I could make a change." Her voice cracked. "What the hell was that supposed to mean?" she shouted to the air above her.

Still the same blank, persistent, and relentless pressure of nothing.

"What change, exactly, am I going to make when I am trapped inside this machine?"

Then, finally, a glitch: a flicker. A smear of red-and-white static across the edge of her vision. Perhaps the machine had been released from its last broken moment. Perhaps it would finally stop toying with her life. Perhaps she had stumbled upon the key.

She felt her heartbeat echo once, syncopated and raw. The pounding repeating in her ears as she looked for signs of change. Looked for a way out of this technological nightmare.

A voice emerged, barely audible, caught in digital distortion.

"Harriet . . . your next Experience . . . is . . . load . . . ing . . ."

"No," she said sharply. "Not until you tell me if he's okay."

Silence.

"Not until I know what that was. That wasn't a simulation. That was real." She pressed her hands to her head, fingers digging into her scalp. "I don't want another made-up pottery scene. Or a mountain-life fantasy. Or even a perfectly planned beach vacation. I want out. I want answers."

Another flicker.

A twinkling of a music box, distant and faint, filtered into her space. Warbling as the lighting flickered—reds, pinks, and smeared streaks of black crossed the field of her vision in time to the familiar childhood tune.

Soft. Familiar. An acoustic guitar riff, worn with repetition and dust. It looped gently, a sound that somehow hurt to hear.

The void wavered, its edges bending.

She stood slowly, heart still hammering. "This better be worth it," she whispered, jaw tight. "One. Last. Time."

A breeze brushed against her cheek. Her knees trembled. Her mouth was dry, her lungs filled with the memory of clay dust and panic. But she moved forward. Because she always did.

Because maybe now, finally, she was starting to understand that she could make changes in her life and she always could.

MILES SLUMPED against a side wall of an wall in a bathroom as he contemplated taking action to really push the limits of the Experience. He desperately needed to know what happened in there. The hum of industrial air vents overhead did nothing to cool the sweat clinging to the back of his neck.

He'd pulled off the Experience headset barely three minutes ago, stumbled past the curtained booth area, and told the intern that he needed five minutes alone to supposedly make a phone call. "Just watch the feed and call Adriana if you need any help."

"Yes, Mr. Miles," was all the overly polite intern had said.

Now he crouched over a sink, taking handfuls of water to his face. "What am I doing?" he asked the mirror with sudden conviction. "I don't know her like that, or any of my trial participants, very well." He looked up with horror at the face in front of him. "This machine. This machine made me do it."

The video call crackled once before Adriana's voice snapped into his ear. "Do you think that will hold up in court?"

"Dria! Thank God." He adjusted the phone set in his ear and opened the video feed on his phone. She was sitting at her flat in London, still in her robe, eyeliner already smudged.

"You're late checking in," she said. "So I assume either you passed out or she got out and punched you."

"I missed it," Miles said without looking up.

Adriana frowned. "Missed what?"

"Her reaction. The part where she sees me collapse in the simulation. The screen blacked out . . . well, ejected me, I guess. Right before." He pressed the heel of his hand to his brow. "I don't know if it landed. I don't know if it made sense. I don't know exactly what she saw."

"Miles—"

"I didn't hear her. Didn't see her face. I could've been another narrative blip, for all she knows. Another fake love interest the machine threw in for tension."

"You were never that."

"And now I feel like a jerk. How didn't I see this coming, Dria? Is this really going to help her? Why don't' I think these things through more?"

Her face was sour, like she had told him several times. "You made the machine to improve a person's ability to reflect upon and to make positive changes in their lives." She softened her comment with a sigh. "Like you are doing right now."

"But she doesn't know that!" His voice cracked in the back of his throat. "I tried to show her something real. Not some polished better-life scenario. Something fragile. Human. Me. And then the system cut out."

Adriana stayed quiet for a moment. The sound of a siren passed outside her window.

"You're outside the exhibit now," she said finally. "She's not. Maybe get back on the feed and finish this thing. We'll have a lot of debriefing to do after this one."

He nodded slowly, fingers curling around the phone. "And I have no way of knowing what she saw next."

"You know her. Better than anyone at this point, maybe even herself. Don't quit just because something hurts."

He gave a dry laugh. "She might quit because it hurts. Wouldn't you?"

"If you remember, I was the one who vowed to *never* try out this machine of yours."

"Many times."

"Then maybe this is the part where you stop controlling the variables and let her decide."

He leaned back against the wall, throat tight. The convention noise muffled through layers of drywall and carpeting. Somewhere, a microphone was tapped into life, then announced a raffle prize over the intercom. He rose from the sink and walked back to the exhibition with Adriana's silent support still in his ear.

But inside that machine, they knew that Harriet was still sitting with the aftermath. Still processing what she had seen—or hadn't.

And for the first time since he'd built this entire system, Miles felt like a passenger in his own story.

He closed his eyes.

"Let's keep her in it a little longer," he said quietly. "Let her go where it takes her."

Adriana's voice was softer now. "We'll keep the signal clean."

He nodded. "I'll check in once she's done." He ended the call.

Then he returned to the booth and found a chair. He sat back, legs stretched out in front of him, eyes on the ceiling tiles, and waited for the machine to decide what came next.

Or maybe . . . just maybe, there was one other way to find out her reaction.

He ripped off the headset and called over the intern. "Karen?" He handed her a second tablet. "Can you drive this for a while?"

"Sure?" she said with a faint smile.

"Great," he said definitively. He put a helmet-like portable prototype on his head and stepped behind the machine to boot it up. "I'm counting on you."

Karen slowly lifted a thumbs-up and glanced at the tablet, uncertain.

Chapter Thirty-Eight

Harriet stood in a silence so loud it shook her. The pounding of her heart pulsed rapidly: tub, thump-thump-thump-thump. The red hues around her pulsed in sync with her body's function. Maybe it was a sign that the Experience had finally gone offline? Maybe she was now the one in control of her own Experience. Again and again, it pulsed, slowing with her heart as she calmed down. And anger set in.

What *had* just happened? The vision had ended like an old-school film that had broken and was now clanking with rude aggression against the metal spool that was supposed to have guarded it. What had she just witnessed? Why was this a part of her alternate life? And . . . was she really the last person Miles saw?

Would see, she reminded herself. If this one vision of gazillions of possibilities, if this one version of his life, interwoven with her life for some insane reason, were to come true.

Her pulse was regulating itself at a less frenzied pace, and the new anger surfaced again. But this time, it felt powerful. This time, it had purpose and direction. This time, she stomped toward the blankness, arms braced in front of herself, groping in the inky dark to find her way out.

This machine was a farce, and she wasn't going to escape it on some salesperson's timeline. It reminded her of a timeshare pitch she had once sat in on. She did get a short cruise in the Bahamas where she stayed in a dungeon of a cabin and sipped drinks with tiny umbrellas. It had hardly been worth it then, and whatever this Experience was worth, she would never go through this again.

This was not a vacation. It was not worth a vacation later. She had just watched a person die. The idea of living one's best life had nothing to do with any of this weird app and its sensory-depressed sweatbox.

She found an edge, rough, for as slick as the interior seemed. Perhaps one of those new dark paints that absorb all the light, creating an inexplicable darkness unknown on the surface of the planet. She gently followed the wall, hand over hand, lightly placing them on the surface until she found the accordion door.

Groping, she tried for a handle or a lock, but couldn't find one. Harriet pushed her fingers into the side crack and jimmied at the space to make it wider. Forcing it, she pulled until the muscles in her forearms ached and her shoulders shook. She grunted and gave a primal-sounding yogi breath, and it popped open with a final solid yank.

The lights were overwhelming and at first blinded her vision with a ring of whiteness that followed everywhere she tried to focus. She could make out the distant booths of the convention hall. Her nose returned to full function as bitter coffee and some strong food odor overtook her sense of smell. The combination of bright lights and scents made her eyes water and nose drip.

A man in a red shirt became bigger, his outline lost its blurriness, and she saw he was holding out a tissue for her to take.

"I'm not crying, Ted." She grabbed it and blew her nose without a smidge of grace. "If that's who you really are!" She was not sad or overcome with any emotion except anger. She had plenty of that.

"Who's Ted?"

Her eyes came into focus. The woman in front of her was not much taller than Lilli, but unlike her work friend, she was blonde and didn't seem to smile much. "Ted was my guide."

"Oh, it happened again," the young woman said quietly but with urgency.

"I'm sorry? It what?"

"We have to get you back inside now."

"Absolutely not. There is no way I am setting one toenail in that crazy box."

"Then you may never know what your best life is."

"I do! I do already! I get it. I have a good life. I should be happy about it. My friends. My job. I don't know why this machine was playing back all my memories and that last scene. The one with Miles *fricken* Hopper . . . That just doesn't make sense."

"Sorry, lady, but I have to do this. Your memories have run the rails. If you don't get back in, you may not only never know what your best life was, you may never see it again."

"I am so taking this to court."

"Let's fix this, shall we?" And Karen opened the door and shoved Harriet back in.

Harriet stumbled backward over the doorframe base and tumbled back into the Experience chamber. She fell but didn't hit the floor. Her falling continued as the wind picked up from her impossibly long fall. Tumbling like Alice down the trunk of a tree into Wonderland where nothing made sense at all.

Chapter Thirty-Nine

M iles stood alone at the edge of the exhibition floor, tucked behind a decorative wall of retractable banners promoting *Smarter Living. Better Outcomes.* The fake ficus nearby had more color in its leaves than he did in his face.

His red polo shirt had come untucked. His badge hung crookedly. His watch buzzed. He ignored it. He was booting up the Experience for him to enter.

A video call came through. Adriana's face blinked to life, projected just above the camera with her usual sharpness, but her tone was unusually quiet. "I see you have taken the Experience to a new territory? I really wish you would have let me know."

"She's still in," he said. "I needed to know."

Adriana let out a long, knowing sigh. "I thought you could still use the support."

Miles didn't move, but let the sensory helmet take over his senses, listening to Adriana as his guide.

"We traced her fall back through the alternate loop. The sensory crash didn't knock her offline, but the machine rerouted her to something . . . different. Stable, for now."

He leaned back against the wall. "She's not supposed to still be in. That should've been the end point."

Adriana's eyes narrowed. "Then why did you keep going?"

He let out a breath. Not a dramatic sigh. Just tired. "Because I was trying to tip the scales."

"And now you're pushing the code to the limit?"

"She most likely thinks I died. I didn't get to see her face. I didn't even get to finish the sentence."

Miles shook his head slowly, eyes fixed on the gleaming floor where the Experience began to sharpen into a scene around him. Harriet's scene. A bonus scene. She was still showing in his screen as a small lit avatar.

"I pushed too far. The machine has a standard default: a quick check-in on the person followed by three enjoyable life scenarios. But not this time. We went all out and used every ounce of this machine's capabilities to aggregate her life into three very refined outcomes. And for what? She's going to destroy me. And I don't blame her.

"You have to let her process it, Miles. And to accept the outcomes. That is truly what the machine was designed to do. Not for us to curate outcomes we think we need."

"I had no idea how hard this would be."

The scene around him formed into lush vegetation; overgrown flowering bushes surrounded the porch of a single-story home—blurry at first, sharpening at a snail's pace.

"Right, ol' chap. You're doing great. And that may be the least of our problems, if I'm being honest." Adriana tilted her head. "So what happens if she walks?"

"She walks."

"And if she sues?"

"I show up. I back her."

"And if she never talks to you again?"

He hesitated, then looked down at his shoes. "Then she made the right call."

Adriana's tone softened. "I've never seen you let go of a project before."

"It's not a project anymore," he said. "It's a person."

She nodded. "Miles, let's go over it later. Right now, we still have a job to finish."

He gave the faintest smile. "Yeah, and it may be our last."

From the main floor, the ambient music of another vendor's demo played through a speaker, something smooth and artificial trying to sound real. It felt dead to his ears as he scanned her biometrics.

Miles rubbed his hand over his face. "Whatever comes next . . . it's hers."

Adriana tapped a key off-screen. "We'll monitor from here. She's safe for now, and you, you know better. She's almost finished."

He gave a quiet nod.

Then he turned, walked toward the porch as Adriana's voice subsided, and didn't stop to smell the roses.

Chapter Forty

When the world resolved into a new Experience scenario, an additional one she had not expected, it came without fanfare. Knowing she still had more to endure, she would have typically been furious, but the quiet peace of this scene was a bit unnerving, demanding that she pay attention.

The wind moved through the porch screens in a lazy ripple, lifting the edge of the linen curtain. Somewhere beyond the front yard, a dog barked once and then stopped. It was a familiar sound, part of the rhythm in this new place filled with light breezes, modest houses spaced at a distance, cicada calls cutting through the humidity.

Harriet sat in a wicker chair, a wide mug in her hands, the tea long cooled.

Her porch was deep, shaded by an awning with morning glories curling along its frame. A hummingbird feeder dangled from the eaves, catching sunlight in quiet flashes. On the rail beside her, a cardigan lay folded, pale blue and worn at the cuffs.

The wooden planks beneath her bare feet were warm from the morning sun. She wiggled her toes without thinking.

It was all so . . . peaceful. She rose, cup in hand, and retrieved the mail from the metal box attached to the post near the steps. Paging through the ads for window installation and lawn care, she checked her address on a utility bill and apparently now lived in Georgia. She paused at a letter labeled *To: Grandma*, complete with hand-drawn flowers around the edges.

Taking her mail and her cup, she turned to the front door. The screen door squeaked softly when the wind shifted, and she found it comforting. Inside, the little wood-frame house was cool and dim. The walls were thick and whitewashed, with shelves built into the far wall holding candles, shallow bowls, and smooth river stones. A fan clicked lazily above her as she set the mail on the table.

There were books on the shelf she hadn't finished, a bowl of oranges, and a tasseled bookmark snuggled inside a book on the coffee table. Everything was neat and in its place. A faint smell of cinnamon and toast wafted from the kitchen, and when she passed through it, two coffee mugs sat drying on a folded tea towel. The second cup made her pause.

And she didn't seem to be waiting on anyone. This Harriet lived a simple life. A very quiet life.

This version of her life felt crafted by someone who understood what she'd always claimed to want: solitude. Cleanliness. Predictability. A warm beverage, a stack of books, and no interruptions.

And yet . . .

She picked up the photo on the small side table. The frame was light wood, glazed in cheerful colors. Inside was an image of herself, smiling with a man who sat beside her. His arm was draped around her shoulder as she warmly leaned into him. Their faces were lit with contentment.

Miles. *Fricken.* Hopper.

She stared at the photo. The longer she looked, the less real it felt. Not false exactly, but faint. As if printed from a first-generation photo printer that faded after a year. In this version, he looked older, more gray, deep wrinkles set at the corners of his eyes.

She set it down, walked to the back door, and glanced up and down the driveway, where it curved out of view of the street to a large shed behind the house. A bush at the edge of the lawn rustled beneath a magnolia tree, the blooming white flowers interspersed between its wide, waxy leaves. She didn't brace herself, when movement along the bushes intensified, and she heard growling.

Instead, she stood, curious, and opened the back porch door. The air was still thick with quiet. She stepped slowly, pressing her palm to the small of her back, her joints unfamiliar in their cracking and aches. This was not the younger version of herself she had seen in other scenarios. She wore cropped linen pants and a faded shirt that bore the ghost of a handprint design that was printed on the front, possibly from a summer art camp. Her hair was streaked with silver and pulled back in a loose, frizzy bun. Sunspots marked her forearms.

A small charcoal-gray dog bolted from beneath the bush, a frog stuck helplessly in its mouth. The dog ran to her playfully, crouching down in a dare-like stance as she tried to take the live frog away. "Put it down!" she heard the more tired version of herself say. Her slow grab resulted in the dog running down a stone path to another part of the backyard.

A studio window along the side of the shed came into view. A low cinder-block-and-cedar combo with a metal roof, open on one side like a carport. And a man sat out there, hunched over a wheel. For a moment, she assumed it was a student taking in some studio time until he turned slightly. Even from the distance, she recognized the posture. The arms. The dogged concentration.

It was Miles. *Fricken.* Hopper.

He looked older. Not just aged but settled. His hair was nearly all white, his face thinner. He wore thicker glasses now and a yellow bandana at his neck. His hands moved deftly, coaxing the clay into shape. She could see his mouth moving, talking to someone out of view, then smiling faintly at their reply.

"Hi there, handsome," she heard this version of herself say. He blew her a kiss before diving back into his project.

She entered the wooden studio, large windows looking over a hedge of lilacs in the back. In the main room, shelves held coils of pottery, glazed mugs, planters, and oddly shaped vases. A table was strewn with brushes, clay shavings, and a stack of signup forms for upcoming classes at the community center. Harriet picked one up, squinting at the handwriting. Her own name was printed at the top as the instructor, and the rest of the form listed the workshop title: *Finding Form in Function. Monday and Thursday evenings. Seniors welcome.* She let the flyer drift back to the table.

Harriet picked up another photograph. This one was of them standing together in front of this studio that was slightly shinier with no paint flecking off the windowpanes. They weren't smiling or posing. Just existing in the same moment. Side by side. Parallel.

She stared at it, unsettled by how real it looked. The kind of photo you forget someone took. The kind that only exists if the moment happened.

And she wasn't sure this one had. She wasn't sure this moment hadn't.

She traced the edge of the photo, then placed it back where she had found it.

The breeze returned, warm and dry. The wind chimes stirred. Then, like a tide receding, the porch, the light, and the quiet world of adobe and clay began to fade.

She had followed with her simulated self up to this point, awake and aware, but not fully in control. This time, the Experience wasn't guiding her. It was offering her something.

And she could feel it.

There were no oddly placed encrypted messages for her to discover. No voice saying her best life was still unfolding. Just wind chimes, wooden floors, and the rhythmic rotation of the potter's wheel clicking away in the background. Her bare feet on the planks. Her pulse, calm for once.

Then, behind her, a faint creak of a step. The potter's wheel had stopped, creating a sound vacuum that pressed against her eardrums.

She didn't turn.

She didn't have to. And she felt the quick embrace from behind warm her shoulders. He turned her and held her at an arm's length, his face somber as if he had to deliver bad news.

"I didn't come to sell you anything," Miles said.

"What?" Harriet studied his aged face. "Are you real right now? Am I?"

"This conversation is." He looked to his feet. "Everything else is made up. The Experience pulled elements from some of your subconscious vibes that fit well with your optimal life. I'm an interloper here, but I needed a moment to talk to you. To explain. To let you see what I saw in here."

She looked out toward the lilac hedges, silent, their scent softly filling the area, and she glanced to the flowering bushes guarding the other side of the lawn. "Go on. Explain. I have nothing else to do but to listen."

"Alright, I'll start with the facts." He walked around the table, leaned on it like he belonged there but didn't presume to. "I mean, we are here in the convention hall, Harriet. But I'm not really a salesman. I did start this company. And I really created the Experience. But I want you to know that I found all these versions of you by mistake."

Harriet froze. Her feet felt nailed to the spot where she stood. A lightness swirled in her chest and head, making her wonder if this version of her was capable of passing out. Taken in by the simulation of their older lives. Together. His older appearance and hers. His confession.

"I didn't program this one," he said. "Not fully. The system pulled from your untagged data. Fragments. Hopes. Sketches you never spoke aloud."

She gave him a sidelong glance. "This scenario feels different."

"It is." He paused. "You're lucid now, aren't you?"

She nodded. "I think I have been on and off. I could manipulate a few things in some of these scenarios."

"I wondered how much you would be able to do. I wasn't sure how much of it you'd remember later. I needed to come ask you . . . if this was worth finding out."

"I remember it all." Her voice didn't crack, but it carried weight. "The pottery class. My time in Honduras, the pink bedroom, the Gatsby party. And you. And your heart attack."

He turned toward her slowly. "I knew that you would need to have space. Real space to see what I saw. Not one I controlled. I had found so many ways our lives ran along, side by side, I wondered if our paths would ever truly cross." He paused, but she didn't react, deep in thoughts that he really, really wanted to know. "It seems that even in a controlled sim, people still had autonomy. And that at its core is what makes us human. I wanted you to see what could have been between us. Or with someone else. I wanted to show you other ways your life could be. Because you didn't seem happy the last time we met."

"Which was like, college?"

"I think right after. Juan Pablo's birthday party."

"The Rusty Wrench... yeah, yeah."

"And the Experience led me to...investigate what you were up to now."

"Investigate, by that you mean...stalking?"

"Ok, ok. Light stalking is a bit extreme, but I did do my research."

She looked at him fully now. "So what is this? The one we are in right now. How is it that we are doing this in real time?"

"A future the machine projected . . . about twenty years from now. Your inputs, your decisions. And . . . the probability of me showing up."

"As myself?" she asked. "And you . . . as you?"

He nodded. "No disguises. No salesman voice. No hidden algorithm."

Harriet leaned back in her chair. "So we're both awake in a memory we've never had."

"Exactly."

They sat with that.

She picked up a mug, fingers tracing the ceramic rim. "You scared me. And you put me through a lot."

"I know. It was a risk, and I . . . I just couldn't see it any other way." He shoved his hands in his front pockets. "I completely understand if you run right out the Experience pod and never speak to me again."

"You could've just emailed me." She leaned into her hands on the table and stared him in the eye.

He laughed. Not loudly. But the real kind. At least she was still talking to him. "Would you have replied? It seems like you would have written me off as crazy. You never were a big risk-taker, Harriet."

She backed away, taken aback by how realistic the wood, the dust on it, the smell of the paints were to her. "You have a point."

"I wanted to build something better than an apology," he said.

"So you did all this work." She swept her arm across the simulated room and met his eyes. "And now what? What happens when I leave the Experience?"

"I just want to be in the room. With you."

She took a deep breath. "I don't know what I want yet. And that is a whole lot to take in."

"That's okay. Take your time. You have plenty of time in here."

"I don't know what *this* is. And I've seen way too much of my life today. I probably should just get back to work, if I'm being honest. The real me has real bills to pay."

"To be honest, the real me has a lot to think through too."

"And I might wake up tomorrow and forget we ever talked." Harriet walked toward his side of the table, sculpting tools in between them under the light.

He looked out toward the trees. "Then I'll remind you."

Silence again, but not empty. Full.

"I mean, what do people remember when they get out of this Experience?"

"It varies. In some test runs, the subject fully remembered everything. Other times, they felt like they had had a long nap that made them more tired than before."

Harriet reached for the photo on the table. "Is this us in the future?"

"It's a simulated version of us. We can never tell what could happen in our real lives."

But in this version, both of them looked older. Still smiling. Still there. "This is fake," she agreed. "But could we come back here if we wanted?"

He took in a deep breath. "Again. It's unclear if the Experience would re-create this scenario exactly. And the bigger consideration you may want to think about is this: what choices will you make when your Experience is done?"

And the studio room began to fade. Tools and trial lives lingering with the lilac bloom breezes between them. Still choosing.

Chapter Forty-One

Miles leaned against the side of the Experience exhibit's control booth, half-sitting on the edge of a folding table littered with wires, tablets, and a lukewarm bottle of conference water. Karen had returned and was beginning to pack up their supplies into plastic totes.

Technically, this convention hadn't even been on their rollout calendar. No one except Adriana and himself knew about testing the newest patch in a public setting. But Harriet was their perfect match for the system, and she was going to be there. He had run the predictive data three different ways. If she didn't show—who knows, got sick or something—it would only matter to him.

And if she recognized him? Well, that had been part of the problem Adriana had insisted he address. They hadn't seen each other, hadn't spoken, written, texted, or participated in any class reunions over the last twenty years. He had bet that the unlikelihood of her recognizing him would just have to be enough. And if she spotted him and called him out, he would have pitched the idea to her anyway. And probably in the exact same way. Someone had to let her know. He couldn't sit on this secret much longer.

Luckily, Ted the intern had a name that sounded like a salesman. Like a TED Talk. He was also busy this week, and it was easy for Miles to step in and borrow his shirt, like a costume. It was harmless and a bit forgettable. Something that would get her in the door without suspicion, he had hoped. But watching her now in the Experience, stumbling through memories she hadn't touched in decades, he felt like a coward. The fake name on his chest, the CEO on his real business card—both meant nothing.

On the tablet propped up in front of him, Adriana's face blinked into view, her computer screen glowing on her face, her London flat in the background. Her brow was furrowed.

"You're not pulling her out?" she asked, voice low.

"No," Miles said. "Not yet."

"It's been thirty-two minutes, give or take."

"I know." Miles sighed. "I went in and it went well. It was time to let her decide what this all means now."

Adriana tapped something off-screen. "Vitals are stable. Respiration's evened out. Brain wave pattern's shifted. Calmer than it's been the whole session."

Miles exhaled. "She doesn't need my interference. Not anymore."

Adriana hesitated. "We played this closer to the edge than I'm comfortable with."

He nodded. "Same."

"We misused the interface. Let emotion override protocol."

"Completely."

"We introduced live variables into an exploratory sim."

"And pushed someone in the middle of a burnout spiral through her own reflection on second chances."

Adriana tilted her head. "So we agree: ethically speaking, we're trash."

"I think we're human," he said quietly.

"It's still shitty, and we're going to have to live with this." She paused. "Still. If she walks out and sues us . . ."

"She signed wavers. We'll agree to compensation and avoid the courts and the bad publicity."

"What if she walks out and never talks to you again?"

Miles looked down at the Experience booth: flat black paint, crude design, hardly anything more than a prototype. Her pulse line ran steadily in the lower corner of the tablet's screen.

"Then I deserve that." Miles took a clearing breath. "That truly was the goal, and even if I strayed too much during this implementation, how the Experience is interpreted by the user is completely up to them. I will have to accept that."

Adriana studied him for a long beat. "You're not pacing."

"No."

"You always pace."

"I think I'm . . . done interfering."

Silence stretched between them. Convention noise buzzed faintly in the background. People were returning to the hall after finished sessions, talking loudly, sipping coffee.

"What do we do now?" Adriana asked.

Miles looked back at the pod, his own reflection faint in the tablet's screen. "Now?"

He took a slow breath.

"Now it's up to her. Then we pack it up. We start over."

Chapter Forty-Two

The door creaked open in front of her, and she pushed the accordion door to the side. It responded not with a crisp ceremony of finishing an accomplishment, but with the reluctant groan of something overused and unremarkable. Harriet stepped out into the overwhelming brightness of fluorescent lighting. Her eyes narrowed. Her breath came in shallow sips that evened out as her surroundings became more familiar, defined by what she remembered, real.

The convention hall spread before her. A person wearing a red polo walked toward her, holding a fishbowl of vacation raffle entries in one hand and a bottle of water in the other. "Would you like to take a seat?"

Harriet should have been excited by seeing only a handful of entries in the small bowl. Her muscles ached like she'd been holding tension for a lifetime. Her feet were heavy. Her heart? Too fast, too unsure of all the scenes she had experienced. What she really wanted now was a nap to recuperate.

Behind her, the machine stood silently open. No lights, no ambient hum. Just matte black casing and the memories of what she would decide happened next.

The person in the red shirt and a nametag saying *Karen* shook the entries, too chipper for this moment. "Congratulations," she said, holding out a bowl. "That concludes your Experience. Did you put your name in? I heard you were very concerned about this, but it looks to me that your odds are pretty good."

Harriet stared at her. Her hands flexed at her sides. "Where is he?"

She blinked. "If you experienced any issues with your simulation —" The woman's voice prattled on. Harriet blinked and shook her head slightly, her vision slowing coming into focus.

"I need to talk to that guy, Ted. He, or whoever he really is, has a lot of explaining to do." She waved the woman off. Her eyes scanned the nearby booths, banners, and attendees, each face just wrong enough to deepen the panic.

"Oh. Okay. I was told people have different Experiences. Here's a drink of cold water." She handed Harriet a complementary bottle of ice water and took off the cap. "Maybe sit here for a moment. Mr. Hopper will be right back."

"What did you say?" Harriet took a sip. The cool water refreshed her and perked her up.

But the woman was off in search for him. "I'll check for him. I'll be back in a sec!" she called back to Harriet.

Her fingers dipped into the bowl to look at the entries. She didn't care whether she won or not at this point. She wasn't sure she would trust any vacation this company provided after the debacle she had just encountered. But the Experience lingered with her. The reflection, forced or otherwise, of the life choices she had made, the possibilities that were unfolding in front of her even now. She withdrew a card: *Miles Hopper—CEO, EXR Labs.*

Sweet holy moly. Confirmation.

She pawed through the cards... Hopper, Hopper... they were all his. Was this another one of the prank-level situations she had already gone through? Not only was the vacation a ruse, it was rigged in *his* favor. But where was he? What if she were truly stuck like in an infinite variety of Experiences, the overlaps where her life and Miles's intertwined, but never actually connected? Like some penitent ghost send to haunt her until she made some decision the universe would be happier with.

And then she saw him. Polo shirt, gray curls, hands tucked into his front pockets, walking toward the exhibit with a mission, but sheepish and a bit guilty-looking.

"You." She took another swig of water. "We have to talk."

"Yes. We do. We have a standard set of questions we ask each participant. Are you ready to answer these?" He adjusted his collar like it didn't belong to him. "It's part of what you signed off on. The free Experience in exchange for feedback."

"Bring on the questions. Have I got some information," she said. "But first . . ." She capped the water bottle. "I have some questions for *you*."

"Alright, given the circumstances, I think that's fair." He ushered her to an unused booth table nearby.

"Like, who are you, actually?" She folded her arms tightly. "Because I know you're not anyone named Ted."

Karen the intern walked by and handed Miles the tablet with the outtake papers uploaded. Overhearing Harriet, she scoffed, "Him? Ted? Of course not. Ted got the day off. That's why I'm here. I never get to do the conventions."

"I needed a shirt," the man-formerly-known-as-Ted, otherwise-known-as-Miles-Hopper offered. "It's been a long day."

"So tell me, then." She tapped her foot, her face shifting from anger to disappointment to utter frustration as he stalled.

"He's Miles Hopper. The CEO, ma'am."

Harriet groaned at her "ma'am" comment. "I realized that, but I just need him to say it."

"Wow, lady. Maybe you need to relax a little."

"It's okay, Karen. Please bring some of this back to the truck? I'll finish the questionnaire myself."

"Whatever you say, boss." She scooped up the rest of the items from the display table and set them into the crate, one by one.

"So, hi! I'm Miles Hopper."

"I know who you are." Her voice clipped and cracked on the way out. "You put this here. All of it."

He nodded. "I did."

"Why?"

Miles stepped closer. "Because of the simulations. Harriet, I was having a personal crisis, and I wanted to test my technology on some decisions I was going to make. The social emotional aspects of a person's life as the test. But it wasn't about fixing things. It was about seeing them more clearly."

"For something that was supposed to add clarity, I absolutely just feel bewildered and confused. How does any of this relate to me?"

"It was uncanny how many instances you showed up in my life. It was picked up by the algorithm right away. I cross-referenced your publicly know data and such. And it just made a very clear pattern I am surprised I never saw before. And I couldn't live with not showing you this."

She clenched the card tighter. "You built a memory theater. For me. Using my memories, without asking me."

"I built it for myself and tested it on me first. But I placed it here for you."

He didn't speak. Just waited.

Her hands fell to her sides. The silence between them had a shape now. Full of everything they didn't say.

"So," she said, her voice dry, "I am nowhere near being ready to fully talk about this. To take your little questionnaire. But I'm sure you see I am in desperate need of some rest after all that. Besides, you have a lot of say in what happens in your company, I mean, you took this thing to an insurance convention. That doesn't make any sense."

"The algorithm said the probability was very high you would try it. It was confirmation enough for me to invest time and money into this."

"Time and money. After all that, do I at least get the vacation?"

He shrugged. "I won it. Technically." He pointed to the card sitting next to the bowl.

"Ah, come on, that's bogus. I pulled that out. All those cards have your name on them. The vacation sweepstakes wasn't real, was it?" She raised a brow. Sitting in this convention hall was no way to debrief all the life events she had just experienced. "Fine. Whatever. I'm pretty sure I don't want any type of vacation crafted by your company. But it's going to take me at least a week to process all those memories I just watched. It seems like if you want those answers, you may want to give me that time to relax and think about them."

"That makes sense. I still think I won, though."

"Huh, so, hypothetically, and if the CEO of his own company winning his own sweepstakes isn't a complete legal debacle, and somehow, if you are declared the winner of this sweepstakes, are you going alone?"

"Only if you say no."

"That's a little bold."

"So I have a shot?"

She stared at him. Neither moved a muscle. "To be clear, if I were to go on this vacation, I would expect to answer your questions and then do whatever else I want. By myself."

"Understood. That can be arranged."

"What about coconut drinks with umbrellas?"

"Guaranteed."

"And a doctor's appointment?"

He paused and chuckled, nodded slowly. "Already scheduled."

"I don't know. This feels like a lot. Like maybe I should think about it a little bit." She looked at her watch. Less than forty minutes had passed. "Oh crap! I was supposed to go to that session!"

"Where are you going? The debrief isn't done! We want to make sure you're safe, Harriet!"

"I'll think about it!" she shouted as she rushed out to the main hall of the conference center.

Chapter Forty-Three

Miles caught up to her near the hallway's edge, just before the overflow booths turned into pop-up coffee carts. She hadn't looked back once. "Wait!" he shouted, his voice filled with concern and confusion.

She stopped at a wall kiosk of information and ran her finger down to find the room she was looking for. "Positivity . . . Positivity . . ."

Miles placed his hand against the wall and looked sideways at her. "Were you in track in high school?"

"There it is," she said and switched to a map on her phone.

"After all that?" he asked, breathless and disbelieving. "That's what you're worried about?"

"Uh-huh." She scanned the map. "Maybe there's still time."

"If you don't remember, you were trying to avoid going to this session. And now . . . you're trying to attend. Harriet, you are so confusing. Stay. Let's talk more about what you saw, what you went through. I don't know if you're being yourself right now."

Harriet whirled on him, her voice low but fierce. "Uh, yeah. Your memory circus may have rewired my emotional center, but it's not paying my rent."

He threw up his hands. "You can change your life."

"Sure. But I also have to buy groceries, pay for my mystery channel subscription, and I've got a boss who thinks I'm still somewhat reliable, although not the life of the party."

"You want a job?" he asked, half-serious, half-desperate. "I may have an opening for someone good at promoting products."

Harriet crossed her arms. "Not this thing. No way. It's buggy as hell."

"No. Not that. Working with our sponsors. Running their events." Miles rubbed the back of his neck. "You were good at it. Think of the Experience as a sort of job tryout."

"Are you kidding me?"

"Not really. Would you say you were happy and comfortable doing that kind of work?"

"Yeah, but that wasn't real."

He exhaled sharply. "It was never meant to be perfect. It was meant to be . . . honest."

She laughed once, sharply. "You think that was honesty? You fed me a whole lineup of could-have-beens without context or prep. That's not clarity. That's chaos in a zip file."

He stepped forward. "We're arguing already."

"What do you mean . . . already?" Harriet stepped back and looked him over. "Do you really think you and I are going to be a thing?"

"Don't you think it's worth a taking a chance?" Miles folded his arms and stared to the left. "Can you tell me that didn't strike an emotional chord with you?"

"It's a lot, okay?" Her voice cracked slightly and she looked away, blinking hard. "You pop back into my life wearing a corporate polo like we're just catching up over coffee, and meanwhile, I've been reliving my most private moments on a 360-degree loop. Just . . . give me an hour. A full hour. To think about what the hell this even is."

He nodded. No pushback. No well-placed comeback. Just a quiet, almost humbled understanding. "Take your time. But don't take forever. Remember we only live one day at a time out here, but we can never get those days back."

At that moment, Adriana popped into his headset. "Hey, Miles? We've got a problem," she said.

"Harriet, I'll be right over here. Please hang around a few minutes?"

"Fine. But remember, I only have this day to live once," she said, slightly mocking as he turned to his phone. She looked up and grunted as reality came tumbling toward her and shoved her in the gut. "And . . . oh my gawd. It's my boss!"

Miles ducked into an alcove to chat with Adriana. "Yes. Yes . . . I'm taking care of it right now," she overheard while she looked for another place to hide. Then she stopped, straightened her lanyard, and brushed off the front of her shirt. What made her want to hide from this man, this job, this whole part of her life she had accepted?

Her boss, Chad, approached, red-faced and breathing like a drunken pufferfish. His arms pumping as he searched the booths, brows pitched in righteous HR fury.

Harriet dipped her head over a water fountain, pretending to drink as she thought through her options. Her last hour within The Experience or so had been strangely forever, but this jolt back into reality made her remember instantly what she needed to do. This was no time to hide. Hiding did no good for the office morale, no good for clients trying to access their insurance claims, no good for her own fragile soul. She reached for her lanyard, peeled it from around her neck, and looked it over like a parking ticket she was ready to contest as the meter guy passed them out like Halloween candy.

"Harriet Last!" Chad announced with the false niceties one would use for meeting one's future in-laws or to get someone to help you move to a new apartment. "I see you are making the most of your time. I hope you have something to share with our team during the next meeting."

"Hi, Chad," she said. The hesitation in her wavering voice not living up to her new resolutions caused her to pause. She knew now what she had to say. What she had to do. "About that session . . . I didn't go."

He pulled out a flyer. "That's alright, Harriet. We all make mistakes sometimes."

She wondered how someone so young could sound so much like her father, guilting her into better behavior when she was a child.

"There's another session at three. Let's see to it that you make it to that one, and we will just forget all about this little mistake of yours?" He grinned, reaching out to pat her on the back.

Harriet flinched. She pulled back and looked squarely in his face.

"Chad, what I am trying to say is . . . that I've had a change of heart. And I no longer feel that I can promote True Blue Insurance's mission or to complete my work in good faith."

Chad's jaw dropped. "You're walking off the floor during peak claims season?"

"I'm resigning." Harriet blew her breath out, hard and final. The weight of that statement was replaced by the heady lightness of the unknown.

Chad shoved his clawlike finger at her, his face twisting into a frenzy, "You're going to regret this. Try finding a job with benefits in this economy. You'll be crawling back for this job. And you might not get it!" He looked at his watch and rushed off in the other direction.

Harriet's shoulders dropped. An overwhelming need to sit down overtook her as her knees shook slightly. She jumped when all of a sudden, Lilli appeared from behind a cardboard standee of a smiling family and an *INSURE-A-FRIEND!* QR code.

"You quitting?" she asked, eyes twinkling. "Yeah. I heard it. I was looking for that death box thingie you took a picture of."

Harriet nodded. "Yeah. Finally."

Lilli grinned. "Good. You deserve better. But I'll miss our little break-room talks." She hugged Harriet—a quick, no-theatrics hug, a solid squeeze of a coworker who knew what had been endured. It meant something.

Harriet stepped back. "I have so much to tell you."

"Like what? Quitting isn't news enough? Harriet, if it's about Sal this morning, forget about it. He's old news. He can lick the bottom of my shoe as far as I'm concerned." Lilli raised a brow, glancing just over Harriet's shoulder. "Wait a sec . . . that guy over by the pens. Is that who I think it is?"

Harriet followed her glance. Miles, awkward in his borrowed company polo, stood near a tower of branded tote bags, pretending to read a promo flyer. "The guy in the red shirt?"

"Yes. What's he doing at this insurance gig?" Lilli pulled up a picture from a financial newsletter she read to prove how professional she was. "Look at this." She showed a photo of Miles holding an award for some innovation in medicine.

"Yeah," Harriet said. "That's him."

"Wait. You know this guy?"

His posture screamed that he was trying to look casual. Then he hung up and walked back to Harriet.

Lilli leaned closer. "I thought he looked familiar. Wait—wasn't he in that tech spotlight article last year? Something about neuro-responsive software and . . . avocado toast vending machines?"

"Unfortunately, I couldn't tell you." Harriet rolled her eyes but looked at the article Lilli showed her. "That looks like it was his cofounder. Miles was the one who actually designed the software, I guess."

"Well," Lilli said, gearing up her business smile as he approached, "he still has the vibe. Like he hasn't slept in three years but can explain cloud computing in his sleep."

Harriet smirked. "That tracks."

Lilli grinned. "Go talk to him. Or don't. But definitely don't ghost him." She winked. "Engineers take that personally."

"Ghost him? I hardly know him . . . sort of."

"Hi!" Miles said cheerfully. "I'm Miles and you are?"

"Lilli Monterrey. Underwriting."

"Pleased to meet you. Do you know Harriet?"

"Yeah, she's a good friend."

"I bet she is. Harriet, I've got to go soon . . . catching a plane. But I do want to follow up on that Experience. Do you have a few minutes?"

"Oh, I've got a session to attend." Lilli smirked. "Well. Good luck. Let's get lunch Saturday? I want to hear all about what you'll do next. And don't take any weird jobs unless they come with dental."

Harriet laughed, lighter now. "Copy that."

The Experience was being taken from the space on a long, flat roller cart. Miles said, "But we're not finished yet."

As Harriet turned back toward Miles, her shoulders lowered just slightly. Her voice was a little less guarded.

"So," she said, "pottery classes?"

"Hypothetical ones?" He smiled, softer now. Not a pitchman. Not a genius. Just Miles. "Definitely."

They stood in the artificial lighting of the expo hall, surrounded by vendors, free samples, and abandoned tote bags. Maybe the start of something unfinished. Something real.

Chapter Forty-Four

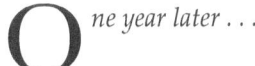 *ne year later . . .*

HARRIET LAST:

Eventually made it to Hawaii, renting a small condo walking distance from the beach.

Got sunburned on the first day, complained about sand in her snacks, and declared it all "deeply overrated."

She also ordered three coconut drinks with umbrellas.

One was for Miles. One was for her.

One was for enduring the Experience.

MILES HOPPER:

Attended all his doctor appointments.

Made an pottery app sim instead of signing up for pottery lessons.

Also bought Josie a thank-you mug that read, *I survived pottery class and all I got was this lousy cardiac episode.* Even though the foot-making pottery student had never actually existed. Miles had it glazed with blood-red slip and sold it on Etsy for thirty-four dollars.

Vowed to make his personal decisions from this time forward, in person.

THE EXPERIENCE APP:

Was pulled from the insurance convention circuit, and all exhibits after Harriet's detailed, profanity-laced review went mildly viral. The highlight quote: *It's like a haunted escape room, but emotionally targeted and run by your ex.*

CHAD FROM TRUE BLUE INSURANCE:

Tried to guilt Harriet into coming back. She texted him a picture of her neatly manicured feet in the ocean sand with the caption: *Morale = restored.*

LILLI:

Did not attempt to move to Hawaii with Harriet, but did make her promise monthly check-ins.

She also dated someone new, broke up with them, and took up salsa again. She remained impressed with Miles, admitting his shoulders "held up surprisingly well."

IT TOOK SOME TIME, as real living does, but Harriet and Miles finally broke the pattern.

After a few weeks of joint pottery classes, a lot of late-night texts, and one failed attempt to build a bookshelf together, they realized they were no longer living in parallel lives.

They were on the same wavelength. For the first time ever.

They didn't rush. They didn't label it.

But when they boarded the plane to Hawaii—two seats, aisle and window, no middle—they shared one suitcase. Inside it: sunscreen, two books neither of them would finish, and a beat-up handbook about the rules of pickleball.

No one used the Experience App again.

But this time, neither of them needed to.

THE END

Chapter Forty-Five

O^{r is it?}

Chapter Forty-Six

Meanwhile, in London, Adriana picked up the phone. Startled, she whispered under her breath, "There's just absolutely no way. No. Way." She fumbled around with her screen. "Call Miles Hopper."

She waited several rings, tapping her fingers nervously along her desktop. Finally, the call connected.

"Miles, you're going to want to sit down for this."

"Hello, Dria. Haven't talked to you in a long time." He set down his drink to check his watch. It was a Wednesday. "How are you?"

"No time for that. We've got a problem."

He paused, thinking. "What could we possibly have a problem with? We sold the Experience to that therapy company. We've been doing well since then."

"It's Karen. The intern. She wanted to try the Experience before it shipped out for good and popped in there after her shift. She's stuck in there."

"Oh shit," he said, setting down a cocktail and wrapping his drenched swim trunks with a towel. "I'll get on a plane right away."

"Where are you going?" Harriet asked, looking up from her novel. She was lounging on a deck chair.

"To work. We're both going. I need your expertise on this one."

"Ha. An insurance problem?" She snorted. "I'm off the clock."

"No. An intern tried out the Experience." He looked her dead in the eye. "And she's trapped."

"Oh my gawd." Harriet jumped from her spot, and they ran from the poolside.

Miles told Dria, "We're on the way."

Author's Note

Some of the places and moments in this novel began as pieces of my own life. Streets I have walked, jobs I have held, and feelings from the growing pains we all share. But like any story worth telling, those seeds quickly grew into something entirely new.

I set out to write a rom-com. Light, fun, with a happy ending. But I am also a horror writer, drawn to big *what-if* questions that haunt the mind and the universe alike. So my *Sleepless in Seattle* turned out a bit more like *Sleepy Hollow*, and that is alright.

The characters you will meet are not portraits of real people, and the events they live through never happened. I borrowed details from memory the way a painter borrows colors. Mixing, reshaping, and blending them into something new. What remains is fiction meant to spark reflection and stir nostalgia.

Writing this book reminded me that the heart of a story lies not in whether it happened, but in what it makes us feel. I hope these pages offer moments that surprise you, comfort you, and stay with you.

Thank you for stepping into this imagined world with me. I hope you always find your way back to a satisfying reality.

— Kris

Kris Maze is a speculative fiction author who creates suspenseful, heartfelt stories with complex, twisty plotlines, and a smidge of romance. See more at KrisMaze.com.

She also writes darker fiction, psychological horror in a gothic style as **Krissy Knoxx**. When not writing or publishing, she's probably hiking and pondering plot twists and the quiet wisdom of Bob Ross.

Also by Kris Maze

Want to be one of the first to find out what happens next?

Join the Kris Maze Newsletter at KrisMaze.com to get the latest updates on new releases.

www.ingramcontent.com/pod-product-compliance
Lightning Source LLC
Chambersburg PA
CBHW052019240626
47153CB00006B/1877